INKED NOVELLA
COLLECTION

MEN OF INKED SERIES

CHELLE BLISS

USA TODAY BESTSELLING AUTHOR

THE GALLOS

THE BEGINNING

MEN OF INKED SERIES PREQUEL

USA TODAY BESTSELLING AUTHOR

CHELLE BLISS

1

MARIA

Sitting on the couch, I watched my husband, Salvatore, as he spoke to our eldest son, Anthony. The holidays always made me feel happy, but I longed for the days when the kids were young. The yelling, giggles, and kisses that came with youth had passed, leaving me with five grown children with no one to call their own.

As they grew, I wished they'd find that special someone and settle down, starting a family of their own and bringing a grandchild or two into our lives. But not my children—no, they lived as if they had all the time in the world, enjoying life on their terms and making no apologies.

Part of me envied them. They were young, unattached, and following their dreams. It's not that I was jealous of my children because I wasn't. There wasn't one moment in my life I would change, but I'd love to do it all again. Time passed so quickly that it was hard to savor the moments as they happened. I wanted to experience it again. Falling in love, having children, raising a family, and every moment in between happened in the blink of an eye. The years passed with greater speed each year, no matter how slow I tried to make it go.

As I looked down at the floor, Izzy was stretched out next to Anthony with her chin resting in her palms. She listened to Sal and Anth laughing and teasing each other, throwing in a crack or two herself. She was stunning with her long brown hair, big blue eyes, and high cheekbones. She was a knockout and single.

Izzy, my only daughter, was most like me. She was a free spirit who didn't take shit from anyone, most of all men. I raised her to be strong, independent, and fierce. I wasn't sure there was a man on the planet who could wrangle her and keep her attention. She was easily bored with the opposite sex or found them too demanding. Izzy did everything on her own terms. The quickest way to end a relationship with her was to lay down rules or have expectations.

Growing up with four older brothers made her rebel against any kind of restraints a man tried to place on her in adulthood. No one bossed her around, except for maybe Sal and me. She was a daddy's girl and never wanted to disappoint him. Even now at the age of twenty-two, she'd do everything in her power to make him happy. I loved her for everything she was, seeing so much of myself in her.

Today was New Year's Day, a day for new beginnings and fresh starts with new dreams for the upcoming year. If someone were to ask me what I wished for, I would answer for my children to find the one person who completes them, bringing them peace and love in the new year.

"Is it going to be the year the Cubs finally win the pennant, Pop?"

Anthony laughed as he spoke with Sal, seeming happier than he had in a while. By trade, he was a tattoo artist at Inked, a shop the kids owned together nearby. If you asked him, he'd say he was a musician. It was his true calling, his passion for as long as I could remember.

He hummed before he could talk, quickly learning to sing as soon as he was able to form words. I'd hear him in his crib, babbling to a beat until I'd grab him in the morning. He was content to lie there, signing to himself until I could drag myself from my bed. Music was his love, always had been. Preferring it to a real relationship, he told me that it was the one thing in life that never let him down. He had soured on women after high school, maintaining playboy behavior into his thirties.

Someone would capture his heart, but it would take that rare breed, a woman so spectacular that he'd fall in insta-love, and fall hard. I prayed she wouldn't break his heart, turning him off to any possibility of a lasting relationship. His focus now, besides tattooing and music, was the groupies. I wasn't a fool. I heard him talk with his brothers about the women who threw themselves at him. Manwhore is a term I've heard Izzy use, and Anthony seemed to fit the bill. My baby needed someone to knock him on his ass and steal his breath. He'd find her if he wasn't too busy with the trash with whom he spent his nights.

"I'm so hungover," Mike groaned, throwing his arm over his face as he stretched out on the love seat.

"You never knew how to pace yourself, man," Joe replied,

leaning back, his foot resting on his knee as he kicked back on the couch.

"I watched how much I drank for the first few hours, but then it all turned into a blur. Fuck!" Mike spat, clutching his head.

"Want me to make you something to help with it?" Joe asked, grabbing Mike's foot.

"I don't pollute my body this way. I just need time to adjust, Joe."

Mike was my fighter—more prone to violence ever since the day Anthony punched him in the gut when he was three. From that day forward, Mike wanted to learn to protect himself and usually tested out the moves on his siblings. More shit had a red hue in our home, caused by the blood that was often lost during a fight. Having four boys hadn't allowed for peace and tranquility.

Mike had beefed up since high school. Working out during his free time, training for a championship bout, and piercing at Inked left him little time to fall in love and settle down.

He was a man driven with a purpose. He wanted a championship, proving that he was the biggest, baddest Gallo brother. He'd deny it, but I knew it was about him showing his superiority over the others. It was an internal drive, set at a young age, and combined with the unhealthy competition that developed between the siblings over the years.

Mike needed someone like his sister. One who could put him in his place and love him at the same time. It wasn't going to be easy, but a mother could dream.

Joe was in a league of his own. He was a no-nonsense guy, so much like his father in looks and attitude that he held a special place in my heart. I'd never admit to having a favorite child, but being so much like Sal, the love of my life, often got him brownie points. He was tough but kind. His heart was bigger than any of my other boys, but he didn't take bullshit from anyone. He was always quick to rescue someone in need, chip in when required, and loved his family with a protectiveness that made a mama proud.

The only thing about Joe I didn't like was his love of motorcycles. When he was a teenager, his friends started with dirt bikes, riding through the woods and doing things I never want to know. I probably would've had a heart attack if I had witnessed most of it, and I am thankful to this day that he survived in one piece.

He hung around with rowdy guys, preferring the company of the bikers at the Neon Cowboy above any other crowd. I worried that they'd lure him into the biker world, turning my son into a hellion and criminal. Joe assured me they were good guys and many of them repeat customers at Inked. Over the years, I learned to let go of my fear, seeing as my son stayed out of the world of the Hells Angels and other MCs in the area.

Although Mike was the fighter, Joe probably came home with torn clothes and bloodied fists more often than any of my sons. It was the protective nature engrained in him, unable to walk away when provoked or rescuing a damsel in distress. No matter how many times I told him violence wasn't the way, he'd assure me "it was my only option, Ma. I don't look for fights."

I was proud of the man he became—tough, independent, rugged, and caring. Even though he was a bruiser, he'd do anything to help a friend. If he loved you, he loved you intensely and with his entire being. Joe didn't give up on people, trying to

CHELLE BLISS

bring out their good sides and rescue them, even if it meant saving them from themselves.

He was so much like Sal. I could see the passion he felt toward his family at an early age. He chased away every boy who tried to kiss his sister. Lord help anyone who wanted to date her.

Although the four of them were a handful when it came to Izzy, Joe was the most overprotective. I never had to worry about something bad happening to Izzy. Every male in the city knew she was a Gallo and that touching her meant risking your life. Even today, I smiled when I see Joe get in the face of her boyfriends. I had to remind him that she was grown and could make her own decisions.

"Thomas called me this morning, Ma," Izzy said, pulling my attention away from Mike and Joe.

I smiled, thinking about my other son. Thomas wasn't with us today and made my heart ache with the loss. "Me too, baby."

"He sounded good." She smiled, pushing herself into a sitting position and pulling her knees against her chest.

"He did. I don't like not hearing from him every day. I don't know how I'm going to get through the next couple of years."

Thomas was the one who wasn't content with the family business and declared he had other plans. He was always my little rebel, not going with the program, and declaring himself boss. Oftentimes it led to his getting a punch to the gut, but he never wavered from his self-imposed authority above the others.

A few months ago, he finished his training at the Drug Enforcement Agency, DEA, and was prepping to work under-cover. Right before Christmas he was given his assignment, the details of which we weren't privy to, and he made it clear that contact would be minimal. He couldn't tell us for how long he'd be gone or where he'd be, just that he'd check in when he could.

I spoke with each of my children a couple times a week, stopping in to the shop sometimes just to see their beautiful faces. I wouldn't have that luxury with Thomas. Not knowing if he was okay would tear at my heart, slowing taking away a chunk until I'd be able to touch him again.

I always thought Thomas would be an actor. The classic looks of James Dean with blue eyes and a strong jawbone. He made the girls swoon at an early age, giving me hope that he'd settle down first and start a family.

Once again, I was wrong, although I'd never admit it. He'd kissed us goodbye, leaving home and dedicating his life to putting away the bad guys, making the world a better place. That was my son. He was always the enforcer, the one trying to keep everyone in line when even I had given up. To say I was proud of him for joining the DEA would be an understatement, but I was worried and mourned for my son who was still alive.

Seeing someone often and then having him disappear felt like a death. Even though my mind knew he was still walking the earth, my heart didn't understand it. I wanted him with me, sitting here today with the rest of the family, but my wish won't come true—not today at least.

"I'm sure he'll call as often as he can, Ma," Joe interrupted, standing from the couch and heading toward the kitchen. "Thomas always calls," he said over his shoulder as he disappeared.

9

Sal turned toward me, a small smile on his face. "Maria, he'll be fine. Stop worrying about the man."

"I know, sweetheart. It's my job as his mother to worry." My nose tingled as my eyes started to fill with water. Damn it. I promised myself that I wouldn't get choked up today, but talking about him was just too much. Wiping away my tears lingering at the corner of my eyes, I smiled at Sal, shrugging my shoulders.

"Aww, love. Don't cry," he said as he stood, crouching down next to me as he wrapped his arms around me. "Thomas is a strong man. He has a good head on his shoulders. He'll be fine."

I drew in a shaky breath, trying to stop the onslaught of tears that were ready to break loose. "I want to believe that, Sal." I rested my head on his shoulder, letting myself feel the protection and safety I always felt in his arms.

"I love you, Mar," he whispered in my ear, brushing his lips against my skin, causing a shiver to slide down my spine.

Even at our age, he still did it for me. I didn't see a man in his fifties, but the muscular, sexy man I met over thirty years ago.

He swept me off my feet during my senior year in high school. I hadn't caught his eye until he left for college and returned on Christmas break the following year. During that time, my chest filled out and my body took a more womanly form. We ran into each other at a party and spent the night dancing and laughing. From then on, we were inseparable. The Christmas break had flown by in a flash before he returned to college.

We didn't see each other again until summer rolled around and I was officially done with high school. I had a world of opportunities at my feet; living in Chicago in the early eighties, the world was my oyster. Spending time with Sal left me wanting more time with him. Unable to say goodbye in fall, I applied and was accepted to Notre Dame University, where he attended.

It wasn't like we had a fairy-tale romance. There were moments when our relationship was on the verge of collapse. His overprotective and jealous ways nearly had me running back to the city, looking for a reprieve. Every time I started to pull away, he sucked me back in. I saw that side of him in each of our boys, knowing now that it wasn't something he could control.

He wasn't the type of jealous that scared me, but he always reminded me that I was his. He was right, too. From the moment he put his lips on mine and wrapped me in his arms, I only had eyes for him. No other men existed for me. Sal Gallo had me hook, line, and sinker. Listening to him tell the story of us, people would think it was the other way around.

"Love you too, Sal," I whispered back, turning my face and kissing his cheek.

Pulling away, he smiled, the small wrinkles around his blue eyes growing more visible. His jet-black hair was combed back, showing off his masculine good looks. The man had grown better looking with age, as was often the case. He looked like a man of the world, rugged and sexy, ready to take on anything that came his way

"You two are making my head hurt more," Mike chimed in, peeking underneath his arm with a smile. "Aren't you too old for that type of behavior yet?"

Sal turned, stalking toward Mike and slapping him on the arm. "Son, when you find the right woman, age will never matter. She'll always be the one you fell in love with."

"What's the secret, Pop?" Anthony asked, turning his attention away from the television. "After one night with someone, I can't stand to be in the same room with them."

Sal laughed at Anthony, rolling his eyes as he often did when Anthony spoke about his groupies. "You haven't met the right one, Anthony. When you do, she's going to knock you on your ass...*hard.*"

"I can't wait to see that," I added, the small smile on my face growing into a giant grin.

"Doesn't it get old? Being with the same person for over thirty years?" Anthony asked, ignoring my statement.

"Never. I love your mother more each day. I never thought a love like that was possible. Do you know the best part of my day?" Sal asked, looking at our children, including Joe, who had returned to his spot on the couch.

"Waking up?" Mike asked, trying to hold in his laughter. "Being old and all."

"Smartass," Sal said, whacking Mike on the head again.

"Ouch! Damn, stop that." Mike held his head, rubbing his temples with his thumbs.

"Stop being a jagoff. The best part of my day is when your mother and I crawl in bed and—"

"Don't you dare say it!" Izzy yelled, covering her ears and squeezing her eyes shut.

Sal laughed, tossing his head back as he held his stomach. The sound of his laughter, even after all these years, made my heart leap. "As I was saying, the best part of my day is when your mother crawls in bed with me and curls into my body. When she rests her head against my chest and I dig my fingers in her hair, I feel at peace."

"Way too much information, Pop," Joe stated, shaking his head and covering his eyes with one hand.

"When you find that—the one person who makes your day complete—that's the one you hold on to. Life can never be boring when you find your soul mate, like I found my Maria." He walked toward me, bent over, and placed a kiss on my lips.

The man still made my insides mushy. Butterflies would fill my stomach when he walked in a room. That's not to say we didn't have our fights, but they always ended the same—making love until everything was forgiven.

"So not happening for me. I hate anyone sleeping in my bed. I want to smack them if they even think about holding me. Makes my skin crawl." Izzy collapsed onto her back as she stared up at the ceiling, resting her hands across her stomach. "Never happening," she whispered.

"I'm with Izzy on this." Joe kicked his feet up on the coffee table, placing his hands behind his head. "I've never been one to want to hold someone. I like my space when I sleep. I get too hot to have someone else throwing off heat at me."

"Pfft," Sal stated, shaking his head. "You just wait. Shit is going to hit you like a ton of bricks. Find the one you want to hold at night, the person you *have* to touch, even in your sleep, and they're the one you can't live without."

My husband sounded like the world's biggest romantic. An outsider would never believe the soft side of my husband. He was much like Joe, steely exterior with a go-fuck-yourself atti-tude. But when it came to me, he was like putty in my hands. I liked to believe it was my softness and love that changed him, but I think that side of him was always buried inside, waiting for the right woman to make it blossom.

"Ma, what's for dessert?" Anthony asked, altering the course of the conversation. The boy had an insatiable appetite. How he stayed so thin without spending time in the gym was beyond me. He wasn't as big as his brothers; his body was lean and toned, and he was built more like my side of the family.

"Cassata cake." I pushed myself up from my chair, knowing that everyone would want a piece.

"I'll help, Ma," Izzy said, climbing to her feet and following me into the kitchen.

2

MARIA

As I reached in the fridge to pull out the cake, Izzy asked, "Do you think I'll find someone like Pop was talking about?"

I smiled with my face still hidden by the door. That was my hard-ass daughter, waiting until I was partially distracted and she was out of earshot of her brothers to ask a question like that.

"Yeah, baby girl. You'll find him someday." I picked up the cake, leaving the door open as I set it on the counter.

Izzy closed it, leaning against the fridge as she stared straight ahead, biting her lip. "I don't believe the fairy tales you told me as a child, Ma. I don't think I want someone to come charging into my life and changing who I am. I like myself. A lot. Too much to give myself freely to some man."

I chuckled, remembering thinking the same thing when I was just a few years younger than her. "The trick is to find someone who doesn't change you, but makes you better." I reached in the drawer, rifling through it for the cake server. Cassata cake could be tricky to serve, and I didn't like when it fell and turned into a pile of mush.

"Better how?"

Setting the knife and server on the counter, I turned to face her. "The person who makes you want to be better. They won't change who you are, but they'll bring out the good in you. Your father did that for me. Izzy, listen, I was scared when I met your father. I fell in love with him so fast it made me dizzy. He became my universe. Everything revolved around him, and it terrified me. You have to get beyond the fear to let in the love and allow the true Isabella Gallo to shine through."

"Are you sure you don't fucking work for Hallmark, Ma? I mean, Jesus, that was a bunch of lovely drivel, but I don't think I'm built for that kind of life. I don't think any of us have that ability like you and Pop. We're just too strong-willed." She pushed off the fridge and started to pull the plates out of the cabinet.

I touched her arm, stopping her. "Are you saying I'm weak, Isabella?"

She shook her head, her eyes dropping to the floor. "No, Ma. That's not what I meant."

"It sounded an awful lot like pity to me. When you fall in love someday, you'll have a different opinion." I touched her chin, bringing her eyes to mine. "It takes a strong woman to love a strong man. Strong women like us don't do well with a man who is less than us. You're going to find one who makes you want to run for the hills. It's in your nature to fight back, but if he's strong enough, he won't let you."

Izzy laughed, tilting her head as she looked at me. "We'll see, Ma. I haven't found one who has knocked my socks off. Do men ever grow up?"

Her question made me smile. It was valid and as old as time. "Eventually, baby girl. You're young, and the men your age are too much like children. Enjoy your youth and theirs. It takes many years before they grow up. Case in point," I said, tipping my head toward the living room and the loud group of *men* talking. "Most of them haven't grown up, but their time is coming." I dropped my hand, reaching for the knife to cut the cake.

"Maybe I'm just surrounded by *them* so much that they taint my view of men." She leaned on the counter next to me, crossing her arms over her chest.

"Your brothers aren't very different than most men. They're stronger and more protective than others, but at their core they're all the same."

"Yeah," she whispered, releasing a deep sigh. "Doesn't matter. I'm having too much fun anyway."

"How's it going with Rob?" I asked, wondering why she hadn't mentioned him lately. Rob, Mike's trainer, was a cocky son of a bitch, and I didn't care for him too much. He wasn't right for Izzy. He didn't have the highest opinion of women, from what I could tell the few times I met him. He was a macho asshole and not the sexy type either.

"We're over."

"Why?" I asked, pretending to be sad.

"He made some dickhead comment, so I kneed him in the balls. It was a dirty way to end it, but swift." She snickered, wrinkling her nose and covering her mouth.

"That's my girl," I said, bumping her with my hip. She was exactly how I wanted her to be. Her brothers taught her the skills to protect herself, although sometimes she used them for other means, but in the end they were always necessary. Izzy was girly when she wanted to be and strong whenever possible. She was the rock of the family, the person who bound us together. "Go tell the boys that dessert is ready, please."

She cupped her hands in front of her mouth and yelled, "Dessert!"

"Jesus. I could've done that, Izzy." I balanced four plates in my hands, trying not to drop the china that was given to me as a wedding present. "Grab a couple since you're in the helpful mood."

She sighed, taking the rest of the cassata cake that was on the counter and following me into the dining room. The boys had beaten us and were already in their seats, waiting to be served.

"Lazy bastards," Izzy muttered under her breath as I set a dish in front of Sal.

I smiled, making eyes at him. "Here you go, sweetheart."

As he winked at me, one side of his mouth rose as a grin played on his lips. "Thanks, love," he whispered, rubbing his chin between his fingers and licking his lips. He was giving me the look I loved, the one that said I was getting lucky as soon as the kids left.

3

SAL

God knows I love my children, but right now, I wanted to wish them well and send them on their way. Right before they arrived, I had Maria pinned against the kitchen counter, kissing her neck as I ran my hand along her inner thigh. Just as I was about to pull out my cock and bury it deep inside her, the doorbell rang.

I swear to shit that kids are born with the ability to cock block. Ever since they were little, they'd walk in at the most inopportune time, putting an end to a very promising evening. Izzy was the worst. Maybe it was her being a female or needier than the others, but it seemed like every time I got Maria naked while still awake, Izzy would knock on the door. There's nothing that'll make your boner disappear along with your naked wife than a little girl crying over a nightmare.

I spent more nights sleeping in my bed with aching balls as my little girl slept in my wife's arms curled against her side.

Even with that, Izzy was always my favorite. She's the one who wrapped her arms around my neck every day, giving me small kisses and calling me "Daddy." Her being so much like Maria didn't hurt either. Thomas, Joe, Mike, and Anthony were more like me, but Izzy—Izzy was an exact replica of my wife.

"Daddy, do you want coffee?" Izzy asked as I dug my fork into the cake.

Even to this day, hearing her call me that made my heart melt. Her voice could turn a shit day into something magical. "Sure, baby girl. If you're getting yourself one." I smiled as I brought the fork to my mouth.

"What about me?" Mike asked as Izzy headed toward the kitchen.

"Get your own," she spat over her shoulder as she walked out of the room.

"Asshole," Mike mumbled, stabbing the cake.

Maria touched my hand, rubbing my wedding ring with her thumb. Her touch, no matter how innocent, made my pants feel a little bit tighter. Turning my wrist, I checked the time, calculating the minutes until the kids left and I could finish what I started earlier.

Locking eyes with Maria, I watched as she put a sliver of cake on her tongue, pulling the fork out slowly. She licked her lips, moaning quietly as a small smile spread across her face. I sucked in a breath, closing my eyes to break the contact.

As Izzy set a coffee cup in front of me, I opened my eyes and sighed. "So, do you kids have plans tonight?" If they did, they'd be gone sooner rather than later.

"Yeah," Joe said, wiping the whipped frosting from his lips.

"We're all headed to Karma tonight to hang out with some friends."

"Didn't you go out last night?" Maria asked, looking down the table.

"Yeah, Ma, but it's ladies' night at the club," Anthony replied, shoveling a strawberry that had escaped from his cake in his mouth.

"It's my favorite night of the week at Karma," Mike said, rubbing his hands together and smiling.

Izzy placed a cup in front of Maria, pouring each of us coffee before she set the carafe on the table. "I get to drink for free, so I'm not missing that shit for the world."

I coughed, choking on a piece of cake. The thought of Izzy in a club filled with horny men made my stomach turn. "You're going to watch out for her, aren't you?" I asked, looking down the length of the table at each of my sons.

"Yes, Pop." Joe nodded, scraping the plate clean with his fork.

"We always do," Mike assured me, turning to look at Izzy. "If anyone gives her shit, we'll deal with them."

"That's the problem." Izzy rolled her eyes, crossing her arms over her chest. "They never let me have any fun. I swear to God if you douchebags do what you did last time, I'm going to lose my shit." She glared at Mike.

He shrugged, wiping his lips before placing his napkin on the table. "Yeah, I'm scared of that."

"I'm not a child," she hissed, uncrossing her arms before gripping the armrests on the chair.

"We know, or we wouldn't be so watchful," Joe replied, smiling at Izzy. "Too many assholes out there."

"That's for me to decide. You can't keep treating me like I'm fifteen anymore. I'm a woman, and it's for me to decide who I talk to or not."

"Sometimes it's our job to decide that, Izzy. We know everyone at the club. Some men aren't worthy of you, babe," Anthony stated, rubbing his eyes as he yawned.

"What did they do last time?" Maria asked, her thumb still stroking the skin of my hand.

"Mike kept coming over and pretending to be my boyfriend. He chased off every guy who tried to talk to me. It was so embarrassing, Ma." She placed her face in her hands as she shook her head. "The men ran away from me. Word spread to leave me alone," she mumbled into her palms.

"Clever," I replied, proud of my sons for their quick thinking.

"Oh, honey. They just love you." Maria reached over, grabbing Izzy's forearm and giving it a quick squeeze.

Izzy dropped her hands, turning to face Maria with a frown. "I wish they'd love me a little less."

"It's almost six. Aren't you guys going to be late?" I asked, hoping they'd be running out the door at any minute.

"Nah, Pop, no one even shows up until after ten."

"Oh," I said, my voice betraying my unhappiness. "Good." I cleared my throat, trying to change my voice. "You won't be late then."

"We have plenty of time," Anthony said, licking the whipped cream off the back of his fork. "I could go for a nap, actually. I'm so damn full." He rubbed his stomach, yawning as he kicked back.

"You better go home and get a little rest, dear," Maria said quickly, her foot sliding underneath the bottom of my pants leg. Her soft toes slid across my skin, making the need I felt for her feel worse than it did the moment the doorbell rang.

"I can just sleep on the couch here."

"No," Maria and I said in unison, turning to look at each other with a smile.

"Do you want us to go?" Joe asked, eyeing us both with a suspicious look.

"No, sweetheart. We just don't want to keep you kids from a fun night." Maria smiled, and I wondered if the kids bought her load of crap.

"I think they want us to go," Mike chimed in, pushing back from the table with his plate in his hand. "Maybe we should take a hint."

"What hint?" Anthony asked, scratching his forehead.

"They've been giving each other goo-goo eyes for hours now."

"Seriously?" Izzy asked with her mouth gaping open, looking between Maria and me.

Maria's cheeks turned a bright shade of pink as she covered her smile. "No, we love having you kids here. We were *not* making goo-goo eyes."

"Shit you not," Joe blurted out, standing and picking his plate up. "Let's head out and give the lovebirds some time alone."

"Really?" Izzy asked again, shaking her head. "Even after thirty years, you two want us to go so you can have...sex?" She made a face when she said sex, her body visibly heaving forward.

Maria laughed, the pink from her cheeks spreading across her face. "I love your dad."

"Aren't you two too old to have sex?" she asked as she too stood, pushing away from the table. "No. Don't answer that. I don't want to know. There are some things your children don't want to know."

I smiled at Maria, winking as she looked at me under her eyelashes. "Victory," I whispered, blowing her a kiss.

"I think we've scarred Izzy for life."

"She'll get over it, love."

Their muffled voices, mixed with the clanking of dishes, filled the house. I knew within minutes we'd have peace and quiet and be totally alone.

Joe walked back in the dining room and looked at us both with a smile. "We're out."

"Thanks," I said, smiling at my son. He knew. Men always understood the unspoken truth about sex. Sometimes it was a necessity, the feeling of needing someone gnawing at you from the inside with only one way to make it go away.

He nodded, turning his head back toward the kitchen. "Let's go!" he yelled, walking to Maria and giving her a kiss on the cheek. "Pop," he said, holding out his hand to me. "Have some fun tonight, old man."

"You got it, son." I couldn't help but laugh. My poor wife probably wanted to crawl under the table, which gave me a thought—I wanted her under the table, taking my cock deep between her beautiful lips.

The kids left in a hurry. I assumed the thought of me having sex with their mother drove them out fast. "They're finally gone," I said, pulling her hand to my lips.

"Real smooth, Sal." She laughed, pulling her hand from my grip as she stood.

"Come here, love." I held out my hand to her, pushing back from the table a few inches.

Sliding her hand in mine, I pulled her into my lap, wrapping my arm around her and gripping her thigh with my other hand. Running my nose along her jaw, I could still smell the cake on her lips. I sank my teeth into her neck, stroking her skin with my tongue as she whimpered.

I fucking wanted her more than I had in a long time. Maybe having to wait and being unable to finish what we started this afternoon had amplified it. I would've never expected the want I felt for her to grow over the years, but it fucking did.

Gripping her thigh roughly, I nibbled on her neck, finding the one spot that had her quivering in my arms. Her body twitched as she gripped my arms, digging her nails into my flesh. I moaned, pushing her legs apart before sliding my hand in between.

My hard-on poked her in the ass, begging to be freed. I moaned as I ran my fingers along the side of her lace panties, feeling her wetness soaking through the thin material. Capturing her lips, I kissed her with passion, intertwining our tongues as I slipped my fingers under the lace.

Her legs fell open, inviting my touch, as she moaned into my mouth. I groaned in response, her ass pushing against my cock as she opened to me further.

"Fuck," I murmured against her mouth, thrusting my fingers

inside her. She shuddered, her lips leaving mine as her head fell back. With her neck exposed, I kissed a trail across her skin, working my finger inside her pussy. Stroking her G-spot, I circled her clit with my thumb, feeling her pussy milking my fingers.

Maria loved to be finger-fucked. It was the quickest way to get her off. Her body had always been responsive to my touch, even more so as we aged. I turned her in my lap and she moved easily, knowing how I wanted her positioned. Her back to my front, her legs spread with her head on my shoulder, I dipped two fingers back inside her, using my palm to stroke her clit.

I bit her shoulder, digging my teeth into the tender muscle at the base of her neck as I continued to assault her pussy, bringing her closer to coming apart in my arms. Palming her breast, I held her in place, toying with her nipples through her dress.

"Oh, Sal," she moaned, spreading her legs wider in my lap.

"I fucking love your cunt," I whispered against her neck, pulling up with my fingers as I pushed against her G-spot and rubbed my palm harder against her clit.

Her thighs began to quake, and her head fell back on my shoulder as her eyes fluttered closed. My dick strained against my jeans, pushing against her ass as it throbbed for relief. Just as I felt her pussy contracting around my fingers, I dug my teeth deeper into her neck, moving my palm away from her skin and denying her the orgasm she so desperately sought.

"Not yet," I growled, withdrawing my fingers from her body as her bottom followed my hand, trying to get my fingers back inside her.

"Fuck," she muttered, lifting her head from my shoulder and squeezing her legs together.

Bringing my fingers to my lips, I licked them clean, tasting her on my tongue. "God, you taste so fuckin' good, love." I moaned, drawing them from my mouth. "I need to taste more."

"Oh." Maria turned, crushing her lips against mine, moaning as her tongue entered my mouth.

Grabbing her arms, I lifted her ass to the table. Moving the plates, I cleared a spot for her to lie back. "Lie down," I demanded, helping her recline on the dining room table.

Spreading her legs, I stared down at my wife. Her face was flushed, covered with a thin sheen of sweat, and absolutely stunning. Pushing up her dress, I reached for her panties, pulling them down her legs and tossing them to the floor. Reaching behind her knees, I pulled her down the table, letting her feet dangle and bringing her ass to the edge. I smiled at the sight of my wife spread-eagled and waiting.

Sitting back in my seat, I took a moment to look at her lying there with her dress hoisted up, legs open, and her pussy glistening. "Fucking beautiful," I muttered, resting my hands on each leg as I pushed her legs open wider.

"Sal," she whimpered, wiggling her ass against the table as she begged to be taken.

I pushed two fingers inside her, filling her as I latched on to her clit, flicking it with my tongue. Feeling her body shake with my touch, I thrust my fingers in deeper and sucked a little harder, bringing her back to the edge. Her legs clamped around my head, holding my face against her pussy, not letting me escape and leave her hanging.

"Don't stop. Oh my God. Yes!" she yelled, digging her fingers in my hair, pushing my face against her body. "Yes!"

Adding a third finger, I stretched her wide, sucking her clit deeper in my mouth as I caressed it with my tongue.

Her body seized as her head lifted from the table, her breath stuttering before she held it inside. There was nothing like watching a woman come as you ate her, tasting her orgasm against your lips.

Moaning, I chased her up the table as she tried to pull away while she rode the orgasm. Shaking and moaning, she wrapped her legs around my head, giving up on getting away. As her legs relaxed, her head fell back against the table while she sucked in a breath, her chest heaving as she tried to get air.

She rested her hand against her throat, swallowing hard as she grew limp in my arms. Withdrawing my fingers, I stood from the chair and undid my pants. Her eyes looked down her body, zeroing in on my crotch as I pulled out my throbbing cock. "It's my turn now, love."

"Oh God," she moaned, bringing her finger to her lip and biting down on it.

"I plan to make you say that a couple more times before I'm done with you." I smiled, sliding the tip against her wetness.

As I pushed my dick inside, her pussy was tight, still contracting from coming. I gripped her hips, pulling her body down to meet my thrusts as I grunted, chasing the release I so badly sought. Tonight I wouldn't last long; the teasing and waiting had had me on edge all day.

I pumped into her, feeling my balls tighten as my cock hardened inside her pussy. "Fuck," I hissed, gripping her thighs tighter as I held her in place. "Maria," I moaned, thrusting a couple more times before emptying myself inside her.

She locked her ankles around my ass, holding my body against hers as my body shook from pleasure. Tiny aftershocks overcame me, causing my body to collapse against her.

The top of her breast peeked out through her dress as I peppered it with small kisses, tasting the sweat on her skin. She moaned, digging her heels into my ass as she kept my dick inside her. Looking up, I trailed kisses up her chest, up her neck before capturing her lips. "I love you," I mumbled against her mouth as our breathing stayed heavy, both still trying to get enough air in our lungs. I opened my eyes with my lips still attached to hers.

"I love you too, sweetheart." She wrapped her arms around my neck, tangling her fingers in my hair. "Thanks for chasing the kids away."

"I'd do it again in a heartbeat." I laughed, giving her one last kiss before pushing off the table and pulling out. "That's the best dessert you could ever give me."

"Much easier than baking a cake too," she said, a small smile spreading across her face, still flushed from her orgasm.

I laughed as I helped her sit up, wrapping my arms around her body. She rested her head against my chest, returning the hug. "I thank God every day that you didn't let me get away."

"I couldn't," I declared with my face buried in her hair. "I was too in love with you not to spend eternity with you, Mar."

Whenever she told the story of how we met, she always made it seem like she fell first, but to be truthful, I knew I loved her the moment I laid eyes on her. It was like the world melted away, leaving only her and me.

Her senior year in high school was like torture. We couldn't see each other often, only when I had a break and could go back to Chicago for a few days. There weren't cell phones and Skype, just phone calls that were monitored by her parents and letters we wrote. Things were simpler then. Couples had time to miss each other, unlike today, constantly connected through technology.

I enjoyed the chase, trying to keep her as mine. She tried to run, pushing against what was inevitable from the moment we met. The way she blushed, pretending to be shy, she captured my attention. I couldn't think about anyone else, wanting only Maria and setting myself on a path to make it happen.

She was set to attend college close to home under the watchful eye of her parents. After some convincing and reassuring her family, she changed her mind and applied at Notre Dame. It was a Catholic college and got the nod from her parents, who were religious and figured she'd be safe. She was too, just not from me.

Before she joined me in Indiana, we'd only kissed, making it to second base. I never pushed her, happy with the small touches and kisses. I loved her, wanting to spend the rest of my life with her, and I would wait until she was ready.

Maria was innocent when I started dating her. Looking back at our beginning, I was selfish. I couldn't stand by and watch her date other men, playing the field like most college-age women. No, I made her mine and held on tight, not giving her any wiggle room.

My senior year at ND, I popped the question, making sure I had her entirely. I couldn't bear the thought of leaving her in

Indiana for a job in Chicago, choosing to stay and to find a lower-paying job just to be close to her.

As senior year ended, we found out she was pregnant. The wedding was already set and would take place before she started to show. By the time the family found out she was carrying my child, we were husband and wife, and there was nothing that could be said. Her parents were pissed but held their tongues, knowing we were in love.

From that day forward, I swore to love her, and I've spent my life making her happy.

4

MARIA

L ying in his arms, I listened to his snores as I thought about my life. I was truly blessed. I had five healthy children who grew up to be amazing adults. I still had the love of a good man, and there was nothing I wanted for. My life was made, filled with love and family.

I wanted our kids to experience a life filled with as much love as we had, finding happiness and peace. I feared it wouldn't happen anytime soon, most of them too content partying and womanizing to settle down. Kids today were different than when I was young. Things were simpler then.

I didn't worry about Isabella. She'd find her Prince Charming as soon as the right man entered her life. She was too much like me to give up on love. Even if she claimed her independence, wanting no man to weigh her down, she'd cave if *the one* walked into her life. I worried most about my boys, especially Anthony.

The rock-star lifestyle didn't lend itself to relationships. One-night stands, yes, but not companionship and love. Maybe he'd surprise me, settling down with a good woman first, but the likelihood of that happening was almost impossible. He loved the playboy lifestyle, living life by the seat of his pants as he jumped from one bed to another.

Maybe our children just hadn't found their match because of the love that Sal and I shared. We were deeply in love, openly showing our feelings for each other in front of the children. They grew up knowing how we felt for each other, and maybe that hindered their ability to settle. I looked at the ceiling, saying a prayer for my children before curling against Sal's body and drifting asleep.

I don't know if it was how he took me on the dining room table, but I dreamed of Sal in his youth. The way he touched me, commanding my body as he stole my heart.

In our youth, he was a wild man. In the dictionary, I swear there was a picture of him next to the word crazy. A stranger would have thought he was a good Italian Catholic man, attending college and working hard. It was the furthest thing from the truth. He did attend college and was hard-working, but he was also a die-hard partier, loved to drag race, and had a voracious sexual appetite.

I lost my virginity to him in college. Waiting for me to graduate, he was a gentleman and didn't force me into anything. Our first time wasn't in the back of a car or some seedy hotel room. That wasn't Sal's style. No, he whisked me away on a weekend trip, taking me to New York City and booking a room at the Waldorf Astoria. When we arrived, the room was filled with flowers, rose petals thrown about, and champagne chilling on the nightstand.

My mouth dropped open when we walked in the room. Soft music played as we sipped champagne and danced in front of the windows, watching the lights of NYC twinkle in the distance. It was one of the most romantic moments in my life. That night he made love to me, taking it slow and being tender. I cried when it was over, overcome with emotion.

After our first time, I wanted more. My appetite matched his as I tried to make up for lost time. We did it wherever we could —in his car, in a dance club, and in the dorms. The hunger I felt for him never died.

The man hadn't stopped romancing me, even now he'd come home with flowers or cook me a beautiful, candlelit dinner. When the kids were growing up, date night was a necessity. Needing to escape the five screaming kids, we'd go to dinner and sometimes a hotel just for some private time.

My life has been perfect. There wasn't one thing I'd change looking back on the years.

I dreamed of New York, the night in the hotel feeling so real I thought I was living it again. The feel of his lips on my skin and the way he touched my body had my skin tingling.

My eyes flew open, breaking the wonderful memory that my sleep brought me, as I heard his voice.

"You okay, Marie?" he asked, stroking my arm with his fingertips.

Turning to face him, I smiled and covered my mouth with the back of my hand as I yawned. "I'm perfect, sweetheart. I was having such a nice dream."

He kissed my forehead, lingering on my skin. "What was it about?"

I reached up, rubbing his cheek with my hand. "It was about you. Us. The first time we were together."

"Our first date?" he asked, a smile spreading across his face.

"No," I replied, feeling my cheeks heat at the memory.

"Oh," he whispered, his smile turning into a sly grin. "New York?"

"Yes," I admitted, closing my eyes as I tried to picture the room.

"I was slick, huh?" He laughed, kissing a path down my face, sucking my earlobe into his mouth.

"You were that, Sal." I giggled as his scruff tickled my skin.

"It had to be romantic, Mar. I wanted to knock your knickers off."

"You did that and more." I opened my eyes, looking up at my amazing husband, the man to whom I'd given everything and received more in return.

"I wanted you to be mine forever. I didn't want to leave any doubt in your mind that your heart belonged to me," he whispered against my ear, sending small shivers across my skin.

"I always knew. That's why it scared the shit out of me. You were too much for a girl like me."

"A girl like you?" he asked, one eyebrow moving toward his hairline.

"An innocent." I smiled, knowing it was a crock of complete shit.

"Mar, I was there. I know you weren't an innocent. You may

have been a virgin, but innocent? Not a fucking' chance." He laughed, running his lips down my neck, sucking my skin lightly.

"I was too," I argued.

"Were not," he reiterated. "You weren't easy, but I didn't corrupt you."

"Sal," I whispered as my eyes fluttered closed, feeling his tongue against my flesh.

"Yes?" he murmured against my neck.

"Once you touched me, I knew I could never get enough of you," I confessed, tipping my head back to give him greater access.

"Mar, I *knew* you'd never get enough once I touched you. I just needed to convince your mind what your heart already knew. I marked you, making you mine, and I've never regretted a moment of our life."

"Sal?" I asked, my voice breathy and full of want.

"Yes?"

"Mark me again and take me back to that night in NYC."

He laughed, his body shaking against mine as he continued the trail down my flesh with his mouth. "There's nothing I'd rather do this morning than make love to the woman of my dreams."

"Mmm," I mumbled as he captured my nipple in his mouth, sucking lightly as he nibbled with his teeth.

Sal made love to me, taking his time and touching me the way he did the first time so many years ago. I relished it, soaking in every moment and locking it away to look back on with the fondness with which I remembered our first night together. After we both collapsed, exhausted and realizing we weren't as young as were in NYC, we drifted back to sleep with our limbs tangled together.

An annoying ringing sound woke me. Taking a minute to realize what the noise was, I reached for the phone, checking the caller ID. Inked. One of the kids had interrupted a peaceful slumber.

"Who is it?" Sal asked as he rolled away from me with the sheets tangled around his waist.

"The kids," I replied, tapping ON to answer the call.

"Who else?" he muttered, throwing his arm over his face as he tried to block out the sunlight that streamed into the room.

"Hello." I tried to make my voice sound chipper, not like I'd just woken up.

"Ma?" Mike asked, his voice laced with concern.

"Yeah." I moved the phone, muffling my yawn with my hand against the receiver.

"Were you sleeping?"

"No, Michael."

"Are you sick?"

"No." Fuck, the kids knew our pattern. Typically when they called this late in the day, I was already buzzing from my multiple cups of coffee.

"You sound weird."

"I'm fine, baby. What's up?" I asked, trying to change the subject.

"Um, okay. We were wondering if you could stop by the shop today. I finished decorating the piercing room, and Izzy wants your opinion."

"Sure, Michael. I'll be there in a couple hours." I turned,

looking at the clock and staring at it as it showed one in the afternoon.

"She'll be here in a couple hours!" Mike yelled before speaking to me again. "Okay, Ma. Bring Pop if you want to." Static filled my ear, and I could hear muffled voices. "Izzy wants to know what time?"

"Tell her I'll be there around three, and I'll see if your father wants to come too." I moved the phone above my head, yawning and trying to hide it.

"I don't know, Izzy. She said three. You fucking talk to her," Mike barked, his voice sounding distant.

"Ma, are you okay?" Izzy asked.

"I'm fine, Izzy. I'll be there at three." I closed my eyes, knowing she was going to start asking questions.

"Are you still in bed? You sound like you were sleeping."

"Baby girl, your father and I fell back to sleep. Everything is fine. I'll be there in two hours."

"You were sleeping? What the hell, Ma? It's afternoon."

"We were exhausted and fell back to sleep. It happens sometimes."

"I think they're sick, Mike. Maybe you should go check on them," Izzy said to Mike as the muffled voices in the shop were barely audible.

"No!" I yelled, sitting up in bed. "Izzy, do not come here. Jesus."

"I'm worried about you two."

"We had sex and fell back to sleep."

"Fuck, Ma. I didn't need to know that. Oh my God. My ears," she hissed, a loud clank causing me to jerk the phone away from my ear. "They were having sex," she said in the background.

"Ma?" Mike asked, returning to the phone.

"Yeah?" I puffed out air, waiting to hear his smartass remark.

"Way to go. See you at three."

Before I could respond, the line clicked dead.

"Freak her out?" Sal asked, knowing how much Izzy hated hearing about our sex life.

"Yep," I replied curtly, breaking out into laughter.

"Kids," he mumbled, stretching as he yawned.

"It's nice to drive them crazy for a change," I said, still laughing as I thought about Izzy dropping the phone in horror.

"What time is it?" Sal asked, turning on his side and resting his hand on my leg.

"One."

"Mm, just enough time for a quickie." He smiled up at me, sliding his hand between my legs.

"Sal," I warned, spreading my legs as I welcomed his touch.

"Let them wonder why we're late, Mar." His fingers raked through my wetness, my body still ready from earlier.

"You're bad," I whispered, lying back down.

"I'm going to show you just how bad I really am," he promised, kissing my hip as he slipped his fingers inside.

Fuck. We were going to be really late. Sal wasn't into quickies. It was against his nature. Inked and the kids would have to wait. It was adult time now, spending the day naked in bed with my husband, reliving our youth.

5

SAL

Strolling into Inked, the kids' tattoo shop, we were about thirty minutes late. To my shock, Izzy wasn't prowling at the entrance waiting for us.

"Finally," Izzy moaned, standing from her chair as I let Maria walk in front of me when we entered the work area.

"Sorry," Maria said, holding up her hands to stop Izzy from continuing. "We were busy."

"Hey, Pop," Joe said, walking over to shake my hand and give his mother a kiss.

"Hey, son," I replied, looking around the shop. They'd done a ton of work. It looked nothing like it had when they purchased the store last year. Every time I visited, something would be changed, and I was truly in awe of their hard work. "It's looking damn good in here."

"Thanks. Just when we think we're done, Izzy has to change

something. She's so damn picky." Joe rolled his eyes, taking a deep breath.

"She's a Gallo. Nothing is ever perfect."

"Fuck, I know it," he hissed, raking his fingers through his hair as he walked back to his station.

"So what was so important for me to see?" Maria asked, walking over to the wall and checking out some new artwork that had been hung. "These are stunning," she said, touching the glass.

"Thanks, Ma. I just hung them up the other day," Joe replied, sitting in his chair as he cleaned off his workspace.

"You made these?" she asked, staring at them in amazement.

"Yeah." He smiled, puffing out his chest as he took pride in his work.

"You're so talented, Joseph." She turned, smiling at him.

His face turned pink, showing a moment of embarrassment. Joe wasn't one to take a compliment. "Thanks, Ma."

"I'm so proud of each of you. The shop looks amazing." I beamed with pride, watching their faces light up. No matter how old they were, they still wanted our approval.

"Thanks, Daddy." Izzy gave me a peck on the cheek before grabbing Maria's hand. "I wanted you to see how I changed the piercing room, Ma. Come see," she said, pulling Maria toward the back of the shop.

"Does it matter, Izzy? Why someone would want another hole in their body, I'll never understand." Maria shook her head as she sighed.

"It's decoration, Ma, and makes a statement. It's about beauty, just like a tattoo," Izzy answered.

41

"A necklace is a hell of a lot easier and less painful than a piercing. Kids these days. Thank God you kids haven't scarred your bodies in that way." She looked around the room, watching their reactions.

Each one of them looked away, staring at the floor or in the opposite direction. They didn't have to admit it, but they all had a piercing. I hadn't known firsthand, but their reactions confirmed it.

"All of you?" Maria asked as she turned to look at each of them. "Damn. How do I not know these things?" She put her face in her hands, shaking her head.

"It wasn't important," Anthony replied, looking at Maria when no one else would.

"I think it's important to know that my children added holes to their bodies. Jesus," she hissed, moving toward Michael. "Did you do them all?"

He shook his head, still staring at the floor as he whistled. "Nope," he replied, not giving any more detail.

She sighed, shaking her head. "Nothing I can do now." She shrugged. "Show me the room, Izzy."

"I'm sorry, Ma," Izzy stated, leaning over and kissing Maria on the cheek. "Don't be mad."

"I'm not. You're all grown and can make your own decisions. Just don't hide anything from me again. Got it?" she asked.

"Yes," they each answered, nodding their heads as they looked at Maria.

"Good. Now let's see it." Izzy smiled, grabbing Maria's hand and taking her in the back room.

"How's business?" I asked, sitting down in Joe's customer chair.

"Busy. We're booked the entire evening. People are still hungover from New Year's," Joe answered, kicking back in his chair and placing his hands behind his head.

"I knew the shop would be successful. Is there anything I can help with?" They never asked for anything. Whether it was painting, picking out the location, or setting up a business, they handled everything and never asked for help.

"Nah, Pop. We got everything handled," Anthony replied with a giant smile on his face.

"I'm always here if you ever need anything or just want advice."

"We know. How about we take you and Ma to lunch? Have you eaten?" Joe asked, rubbing his stomach. "I'm starving."

"Sure, son. I worked up quite an appetite this morning."

"Jesus," Izzy groaned as she walked back in the room right as I made the statement. "I love you two, really, I do. But there are some things that aren't meant to be shared."

I laughed, knowing she was probably right, but it was too much fun watching her freak out. "Okay, baby girl. You're right."

"Did someone say lunch?" Maria asked, resting her hand on Izzy's shoulder and smiling at me.

"Yeah, Ma. We want to take you and Pop to lunch." Anthony stood from his chair, tossing garbage that was on his station in the trash. "Up for it?"

"I'm famished," she responded, walking toward me.

I slid my arm around her, tucking her under my arm. "How was the room, love?"

"It's beautiful. Way nicer than I'd expect for a room that inflicts so much pain."

"It's not painful, Ma," Mike stated, shaking his head as he locked up the register. "Some find it a turn-on actually."

Maria's body jerked as she turned toward Anthony. "You've got to be kidding me."

"Nope," Mike replied with a small smile.

"I finally understand when Izzy says it's too much information. I don't want to know anymore. Take me to lunch."

"Anything you want, my love." I smiled at her, holding her by the shoulder as we walked toward the door. "We'll wait for you outside while you lock up," I said, pushing opening the door and walking outside with Maria.

"I'm proud of them, Sal. They've done so well, you know?"

I stopped, moving her body in front of mine. Holding her face in my hands, I kissed her lips, inhaling her scent. "I do. They're great kids. You've blessed my life more than I can ever express, Maria. I'm eternally grateful for everything you've done for our family. My family."

"I couldn't have done it without such an amazing husband," she whispered, rubbing her nose against mine.

"I can't wait to get you home." I kissed her again, taking my time as I held the back of her neck, pulling her body against mine.

"You're insatiable," she murmured against my lips.

"Only for you."

I slid my hands down her back, groping her ass and grinding my cock against her. "This is only for you."

"Sal," she moaned, her body stiffening as the door opened behind us.

"Can't leave you two alone for five minutes," Anthony said, walking past us with a small smile on his face.

"How do you think you were all born?" I asked, releasing Maria from my grasp and holding her hand.

"I like to believe it was like the Immaculate Conception," Izzy stated, standing behind us as we walked into the parking lot.

"Someday you'll have someone you can't keep your hands off of, baby girl," Maria said, squeezing my hand as we approached the car.

"Shh," I whispered. "I don't want to hear that." I wrinkled my nose, unable to think of my daughter as anything but a little girl.

"Enough talking about love and all that mushy shit," Anthony said, opening the car doors for everyone to pile in. "One car?" he asked, turning to face me as I was about to open our car door for Maria.

"Where are we going?" I asked, opening the passenger door for my lovely wife.

"Let's hit the diner down the street. They have amazing burgers," Joe said, climbing in the passenger seat of Anthony's SUV.

"We'll meet you kids there. I want to be alone with your mother, and then we can head home from there."

"Okay, Pop," Anthony replied, jogging around to the driver's side as the rest of the gang piled into the vehicle.

I closed Maria's door, strolling to my side and climbing in.

Starting the car, I placed my hand on the back of her seat, looking back before pulling out.

"We could've gone with the kids, Sal."

I shook my head, looking at my beautiful wife. "Not as long as I have a hard-on. I don't know what has gotten into me, Mar, but I feel like I did when I was twenty-five." I pulled out of my parking spot, following behind Anthony as we left the parking lot.

"They say we only get better when we age." Maria smiled, touching my cheek with her soft fingers.

"I can't wait to see what the next thirty years holds, love," I said, bringing her hand to my lips, kissing each finger tenderly as I drove.

"Me either, Sal. There's no one else I'd rather spend it with."

I don't know what I did to deserve such a blessed life. To have the love of a good woman, amazing children who have grown up to be spectacular adults, and health on our side—it was more than I could've ever dreamed for when I was young. I was a proud father and husband, the best thing in the world.

I had a feeling the best was yet to come.

If you want to find out more about Joe, Izzy, Mike, Thomas, and Anthony, you can find the hot addictive Gallo alphas, in the rest of the Men of Inked series. Each book in the Men of Inked series is a standalone. Find out more by tapping on the titles below.

Throttle Me (Book 1 - Joe)

Hook Me (Book 2 - Mike)
Resist Me (Book 3 - Izzy)
Uncover Me (Book 4 - Thomas)
Without Me (Book 5 - Anthony)
Honor Me (Book 6 - City & Suzy)
Worship Me (Book 7 Izzy & James)

RESISTING

MEN OF INK2ED SERIES NOVELLA

USA TODAY BESTSELLING AUTHOR

CHELLE BLISS

1

IZZY

I'm a simple woman. I grew up in a house with four brothers and loving parents who have remained married even after more than thirty years together. They showered us with love and affection. I'm the youngest of their children.

I have four very annoying older brothers. They're overprotective, and even though I'm an adult, that's never changed. They chased every man I ever liked (fuck the L-word) away as they screamed bloody murder and ran for their lives. Some would call the Gallo men alphas, but not me. I call them pains in my ass.

They helped mold me into the woman I am today. I don't take shit from anyone. I know how to throw an amazing right hook, just the right angle to knee a guy in the balls so he'll never have children, and how to keep my mouth shut.

A couple years ago, we opened a tattoo shop together. We simply named it Inked. Our family has money, but we were raised to not sit on our asses like spoiled brats. We get up each day and go to work. It's our goal to stand on our own two feet. So far, we've been successful. Even though we fight like cats and dogs, we love each other fiercely and are very careful whom we let into our little Gallo Family Club.

Thomas, my eldest brother and an undercover DEA agent, is the only one who doesn't work in the shop. He's a silent partner, and we pray that, one day, he'll get sick of his undercover work and settle down. He's been working inside the Sun Devils MC for some time. Moving up the ranks, he's made his mark and is on the verge of bringing the entire club to its knees.

Joe is one badass motherfucker. He's kinda my favorite, but I'll never tell him that. Shit, I'm not stupid. He's an amazing artist and tattooist, and will be an amazing father. A while back, he rescued a little hot blond named Suzy. She's sweet as pie and used to be innocent. His badass biker ways ruined her, but naturally, I rubbed off on her, too. Some of his friends call him City because he was born in Chicago. The name fits him, but he'll always still be my Joey.

Mike is our shop's piercer, and he's built like a brick shithouse. He trained for years to be an MMA fighter. He was moving up the ranks and making a name for himself. That was until he literally knocked the woman of his dreams on her ass. He traded in his fighting days to help the love of his life, Mia, with her medical clinic. I'd almost say that he lost his balls somewhere along the way, but that would just be my jaded, fucked-up perception of love talking.

Anthony. What can I say about him? He's my partner in crime most of the time. He and I are the single ones out of the group. Thomas doesn't count, because we never know anything about his life. Anthony wants to be a rock god. He wants ladies falling at his feet, professing their love, and freely offering their pussies to him with no strings attached. It makes me laugh, because honestly, he's already arrived if those are his criteria. He's stunning. One day, someone is going to steal him from me and I'll end up being a lonely ol' biddy.

Then there's me—youngest child who still uses the word *daddy*. I'm not talking about some sick fuckin' fetish shit either. I melt into a puddle of goo when my father's around. I've always been a daddy's girl. I don't think that'll ever change.

I live by no one's rules—well, maybe my daddy's at times—and I try to cram as much fun as I possibly can in my one shot at this life. I don't make apologies for my behavior. I shoot straight and tell it like it is. I never want to be tied down. Fuck convention. I don't need a husband to complete me a la Tom Cruise in *Jerry Maguire*.

Men are only good for a few things. One—they're handy when you have a flat tire or some other thing that requires heavy lifting. Two—their cocks are beautiful. Three—did I mention cock? Four—fucking. Wait... that's still cock-related.

I take it back. They're only good for two things in life: lifting heavy shit and fucking. Walks of shame are for pansy asses. I proudly leave them hanging, walking out the door, and I make no apologies for it. I'm not looking for a prince charming or knight in shining armor. I want to be fucked and then left the hell alone.

That is where my life was headed. I was blissfully happy and unencumbered. Life was grand—one big fucking party and I was the guest of honor.

Ever have a man walk into your life and alter your entire universe?

I'm not talking about the small shit. I'm talking about the "big fuckin' bang." You're minding your own business, enjoying yourself, and then *WHAM*. Everything you think is right suddenly spins on its axis and bitch-slaps you in the face.

The party came to a screeching halt the night of my brother's wedding.

He changed everything. He fucked it all up.

World altered. Party over.

James Caldo became something bigger.

I couldn't resist him.

2

IZZY

"Everyone's ass better be at my house tomorrow at two," Joe said as he finished cleaning his station.

"Yeah, yeah." Anthony kicked back and sipped a beer.

"Don't give me that shit. Be there on time."

"Is Suzy cooking?" Mike emptied the trashcan, not turning around to look at Joe as he waited for an answer.

"Fuck no," Joe said, breaking out into laughter.

We all knew that Suzy couldn't cook. God love her, and Lord knows she'd tried, but it wasn't in her DNA.

"Thank fuck," I huffed out, walking to the backroom to grab a cold one.

"Dude, someday you have to teach her to cook," Mike said, shaking his head.

"Fuck that. She doesn't need to learn how to cook. It's not why I love her."

"We all fucking know that," Anthony said, rolling his eyes as he rolled the beer bottle between his hands.

"Shut your fucking mouth. You're talking about my fiancée."

"Uh huh," Anthony muttered, wiping the drops of beer from his mouth.

Moments like this I loved. Sitting around, shooting the shit, and just laughing made me happy. I loved my brothers and their women, but I liked having them all to myself.

"I couldn't give a shit about Thanksgiving dinner, Joe. I'm waiting for the bachelorette party," I said, smiling as I walked toward my station. Then I kicked my feet up, leaned back, and took a sip.

"Izzy," Joe warned, glaring at me from his chair.

"Oh, shove it, mister. It's a girls' night and we're going to have fun. Don't tell me you boys are just going to sit around and watch sports all night. I know what the fuck happens at bachelor parties. What's good for the goose is good for the gander."

"What the fuck does that shit even mean?" Mike snorted.

"Dumb fuck," I mumbled against the rim of my Corona.

"What the hell did you just say?" His voice boomed as he turned to stare at me.

I gave him an innocent smile. "Love you."

"Dude, I can't believe you're getting married in a week. What the fuck? I never thought you'd be the first to be tied down," Anthony said, getting up from his chair. "I'm grabbing a beer. Anyone else want one while I'm up?"

I picked up my phone to scroll through my Facebook newsfeed. "Nope," I said.

To my delight, there was a message from Flash. We grew up

together and I think I've known him forever. We used to play doctor when we were alone. It was the first time I ever saw a penis. As we grew up, the quick peeks turned into touching— then fucking when we hit high school.

Flash and I had an understanding. Neither of us wanted to be tied down, and we weren't exclusive. He was my booty call when I had an itch that needed to be scratched. He moved away a couple of years ago, and since then, every time he was in town, I would get the call offering a quick fuck and an even quicker goodbye. It was a match made in heaven.

Flash: Whatcha doin' baby?

He was the only person in the world I let call me baby. It was patronizing and I fucking hated it. Typically, it would earn a man a punch to his junk, but when Flash said it, I let it slide.

Me: Getting ready to head home. U?

"Izzy, are you listening to me?" Joe asked, casting a shadow on me as his big body blocked out the light.

I shook my head as I looked up at him. "What?"

"Do not have naked men at the bachelorette party."

"What's a little peen between friends?" I asked, laughing in his face.

"You know I love you, Izzy. I never judge you, but do not have *peen* at my soon-to-be wife's party." He put his hands on his hips and tapped his foot.

"Pfft," I said, standing up. "You having pussy at yours?" I asked.

"No."

"Fucking liar!" I shouted, hitting him in the chest with my finger.

He looked down, watching me as I poked him. "I mean it, sister. I don't want any nasty-ass stripper touching my woman."

I kept poking him. "Do you hear yourself?"

"I ain't fuckin' deaf and neither are you. I never ask for much, but this is non-negotiable. I believe Suzy told you she didn't want one."

"Suzy doesn't know how to have fun." I waved him off as I tossed the empty bottle in the trash.

"Suzy does. She just prefers my dick. She doesn't need some greasy male dancer touching her."

"Joe," I said, sliding my arm around his waist, "the stripper is only there for the other girls, not for Suzy."

"Bullshit," he mumbled, kissing the top of my head. "Please, Iz. For me."

I puffed out a breath, moving the hair that had fallen in my eyes. "Fine, Joe. As long as you're happy," I lied.

There was no way in hell I'd throw a bachelorette party for my soon-to-be sister-in-law and not have a stripper. If the boys got to see snatch, then fuck yeah, we were seeing peen.

"Thanks, baby girl," he said, squeezing me tight.

"Any time." I looked up and smiled. Releasing him, I stuck out my tongue at Anthony as I sat.

He winked, knowing I was full of shit, and started talking with Mike about the big Thanksgiving football matchups. I tuned out, picking up my phone as I waited for us to close the shop.

Flash: *Interested in a little company tonight?*

I tapped my phone as I thought about his offer. Did I want to see Flash? I didn't have to be up early the next day, but then again, I never had to be up early. I hadn't had sex since the last time he'd dropped by, and that was over a month ago. I could use a good fuck.

Me: Hell yeah. Get your sexy ass to my place. Meet ya there?

Flash: On my way. Be there in 30.

I stood, shoving the phone in my pocket. "I gotta go, boys."

"Where the hell you runnin' off to?" Mike asked, stretching out and looking comfortable.

"None of your business. I got shit to do," I said as I grabbed my purse out of the backroom.

"Two o'clock tomorrow, Izzy," Joe said as I reached for the door handle.

"Got it!" I yelled over my shoulder, leaving my brothers behind, and headed home.

"Yo!" Flash bellowed as I heard the door slam shut.

"Back here," I replied, before spitting out my toothpaste.

He walked into the room and said, "Get your sweet ass over here and gimme a kiss, baby."

I turned toward him, glaring as I wiped the leftover paste from my lips. "You must have me confused with someone else." I winked at him and laughed.

He smiled, leaning against the doorframe with his arms crossed. "I know exactly who I'm talking to." Then he closed his eyes and puckered his lips.

I threw the washcloth at him, hitting him square in the face.

His eyes flew open as the cloth fell to the floor. "What the fuck was that for?"

"You're not the boss of me, Flash," I said, putting my hands on my hips as I stared at him.

His eyes softened as he pushed off the doorframe. "I've missed you," he whispered, trying to wrap his arms around me.

"Flash," I warned, pushing him away. "I'm not your girlfriend."

"A guy can dream, can't he?" He brushed his lips against my temples, finally gaining a firm grasp around my body.

He felt nice. I'd never admit it, but I did like Flash. I loved him, but no way in hell was I *in* love with him.

"Might as well shoot for the stars." I giggled, snuggling my face into his chest and inhaling. My nose tickled. His normal smell was missing and seemed to have been replaced by something offensive and stinky as fuck. "Flash, you smell like shit," I said, pushing him away.

He lifted his arms, sniffing his pit as he wrinkled his nose. "Fuck," he muttered, pulling off his shirt. "Let me grab a shower and I'm yours." He kicked off his shoes and unzipped his pants. Bending over, he pushed down the jeans and tossed them to the side.

"You're mighty comfy here, aren't you?" I asked, taking my turn to lean in the doorway and stare at him. He was rough around the edges but beautiful. His smile was killer, but he wasn't the boy I'd had a crush on when I was a kid.

As he reached in the shower, turning on the water, he turned to me and smiled. "I can fuck you smelling like shit." His back stiffened as he stood straight, cracking his knuckles.

"As long as I get some pussy, I don't give a fuck what I smell like."

"Get your dirty ass in the shower," I groaned, ready to rip my hair out but itching to touch him.

He laughed, climbing in the shower. Flash was always cute, but as he'd aged, he'd turned into a ruggedly handsome man. Less and less of his skin was visible, replaced by tattoos that decorated his body like a storyboard—most of the work I'd done over the years. He'd been my best test subject when I was learning my craft. Stupid fucker, if you ask me. I wouldn't let some newbie put ink that soap couldn't wash off on my body. He was tall, a couple of inches taller than I was, and lean. He wasn't overly muscular or bulky, but he fit between my thighs like a glove.

"You starin', baby?" he asked, his voice muffled by the water.

I blinked, pulling my eyes away. "Fuck no. Hurry your ass up," I said, stomping out of the bathroom.

I pulled back the blankets as I waited for Flash. His whistling filled the room, along with the plops of water that cascaded off his body, hitting the shower floor. I stripped off my clothes, fell on the bed, sprawled out, and stared at the ceiling.

I used to get so excited when he said that he was dropping by for a little while. Not so much anymore. I kept telling myself, "It'll pass," but it never did. He'd grown more loving and tender, and both of those freaked me the hell out. It ain't my bag.

Years ago, I'd be jumping up and down on the bed, waiting for the big, bad Sam, a.k.a. Flash, to come toss my apples. Now, it was—

"Ready or not, here I come!" he yelled from the bathroom, interrupting my thoughts.

"Yippee," I muttered, rolling my eyes as I leaned up on my elbows.

He strode into the room stark naked and dripping wet. "You look edible." He stopped at the foot of my bed and stared down at me. "I think you need to come, Izzy. You're wound tight tonight. Let me help you out." He grabbed my feet and yanked my body to the edge of the bed.

"Up for the challenge?" I asked, raising an eyebrow as I placed the bottom of my feet on his chest.

"Babe, really?" he asked, holding my ankles.

"You think you're that good at eating pussy?" I laughed, trying not to hurt his male ego.

"I munch like no other."

I knew the man tried to be sexy, but ew. He wasn't. "Show me whatcha got. If you're a good boy, I'll give ya some pussy."

He rubbed his hands together before placing my foot on his shoulder. "I'm going to eat it like it's my last fucking meal."

I melted into the bed, feeling his hot breath on me as he inhaled.

"Better than fresh-baked apple pie."

"Less talking, more eating, Flash." I threw my arm over my face, blocking out all light as he placed his mouth on me.

Moaning, he sucked my clit into his mouth, making my eyes roll back into my head.

"Fuck," I hissed, drawing in a sharp breath.

He mumbled, the vibration penetrating my skin, as he drew

me deeper into his mouth. Sinking into the bed, I reached down and grabbed his head.

"Right there, Flash," I pleaded, grinding my pussy against his face.

He gripped my thighs, pulling me closer as his tongue traced tiny circles around my clit.

Shivers raked my body. He knew exactly how I liked it. Many years of fooling around had given him that advantage over other men. His fingers slid through my wetness, causing my body to clench in anticipation.

"You missed me, baby," he murmured against my pussy, his hot breath lashing my clit like a whip.

"Flash," I warned, pushing myself against his face. "Shut up and eat."

"Mmm hmmm," he mumbled, closing his lips around my clit, sucking gently.

Needing something more, I touched my nipples, rolling them between my fingers. Waves of pleasure came over me as I stared at him. Moaning and writhing underneath his touch, I closed my eyes and rode the crest, waiting for it to come crashing down and wash away the stress.

The warmth of his mouth, the flicks of his tongue, the pressure of his sucking, and my fingers on my breasts had me screaming within minutes.

"Fuck," I mumbled, my body growing limp as I sagged into the mattress.

"Damn," Flash groaned, licking his lips as he pushed himself up. Resting on his heels, he stroked his shaft and stared. "Baby, I can't wait to tap that pussy. I've missed you and being deep inside you."

I giggled, grabbing my sides as I rolled over. "Oh my God. When did you turn so wishy-washy?" I asked, gasping for air.

"Fuck you, Izzy. I know you fucking love me," he said as he started to lean over me.

"Wait," I said, putting my feet against his chest, pushing him away. "We're friends, Sam. Nothing more." I needed him to understand this. He and I would never be any more than what we were right now—fuck buddies.

We didn't go for drinks like girlfriends to talk about our lives. He never took me to dinner, unless you count the shithole bar in town as a restaurant, or McDonald's. We didn't hold hands, walk along the beach, or snuggle. We fucked and he left. Plain. Simple. No feelings involved.

"I know, Izzy." He swallowed hard, his Adam's apple bobbing, as he looked down at me. "I meant as a friend. I've known you my entire life."

"Just as long as we're clear, Flash." I slid my feet down his chest, rubbing against his hard length before I opened my legs to him. The look on his face was closer to a little boy losing a puppy dog than one about to fuck my brains out. "Come here and kiss me already," I said, holding out my arms to him.

A small smile spread across his face as he leaned over me, placing his arms under my body. "I thought you'd never ask," he said with a chuckle.

I'd known Flash long enough to know that there was something more he wanted to say, but he always held back. I loved him. Don't get me wrong. We'd gone to kindergarten together, but I wasn't in love with him. I never would be, either.

I grabbed his face as he hovered over me. "Hey," I whispered, "I'm happy you're here."

His eyes lit up as he rested his forehead against mine. "Thanks, Izzy. It's just so hard at times."

"What is, babe?" I asked, moving my arms around his shoulders.

"Being part of the Sun Devils MC. I feel so lonely."

"Get yourself an ol' lady," I replied.

He rolled his eyes, pushing himself up on his elbows. "They're bullshit."

"Come on. I'm sure there's someone you're sweet on, Flash."

"She's not—"

"Babe, listen to me. Everyone needs someone. You need to fill that void."

He sprawled out on the mattress, putting his hands behind his head. "It's not that simple, Izzy."

Resting my head in my hand, I placed the other on his chest. "I know. You have a big heart, and any girl would be lucky to have you, Sam."

He didn't like anyone calling him that anymore, but I was always the exception to the rule. I only used it to help drive home the point. He needed to finally comprehend that he and I would never be a "we."

"Not the one I want, though," he mumbled, blowing out a breath.

My heart hurt for him, but I just couldn't give myself to him in that way. "I'm sorry. You know I love you, but not in that way.

You'll always be one of my best friends. You need to forget about me and find someone who's going to love you the way you deserve to be loved."

"Yeah, maybe." He closed his eyes as he laid his hand on top of mine and stroked my skin. "No woman will ever measure up to you, though, Isabella."

"I know I'm pretty fanfuckingtastic, but I'm not the one. She'll fall into your lap when you least expect it," I said as I nuzzled my face against his chest.

"What about you?" he asked, kissing the top of my head.

"What about me?" I looked at him.

"When are you going to find someone to love?"

"Aw, baby. I have my family. I don't need anyone else."

"We all do, Iz. When are you going to stop lying to yourself?"

I winked at him, laying my head back down against his skin as I twirled his dark chest hair in my fingers. "I have as much love as I can handle. I don't want to be tied down. I'm happy with my life. The last thing I am is lonely."

"Liar." He laughed, pulling me flush against his side. "Can we just sleep like this tonight?"

"Snuggle?" I asked, wanting to run out of the room.

"I just want to feel close to someone tonight. Please, Iz. I'm so comfortable like this. I don't want to sleep on the couch."

I bit my lip, feeling shitty about always doing that to him. Having him sleep in my bed always felt too intimate for me to handle. "Fine," I said, hoping I wouldn't regret it later. "Don't get used to it."

"Thanks," he whispered, burrowing his nose in my hair. "Night."

"Night," I mumbled as I closed my eyes.

An overwhelming sense of guilt came over me as I lay in his arms. Flash loved me, and had voiced it many times over the years. I'd always set him straight. Tonight felt different, though. It was as if I'd had a knife and jammed it in his heart. I felt like such a cunt for telling him I wouldn't love him—not in that way, at least.

We'd sworn that it wouldn't be any more than a physical friendship. He'd promised me years ago that he wouldn't fall in love with me. Sam had given me that amazing smile while speaking the words I'd wanted to hear but meaning none of them. I felt the end near for us, because I couldn't handle having to kill his heart and hurt him every time we were together.

Hurting someone, no matter the reason, sucks—especially when they're a friend. Someone who has been by your side and had your back since you were a little girl is an important person. He meant the world to me, but I could never settle down and spend my life with Flash.

I needed to let him down easy, and that wasn't my strong suit. I always spoke my mind, and sometimes I came off as brash or unkind.

I curled into his side, letting my old friend drift to sleep while I mulled over my future without Flash weaving himself in and out of my life through the months. I needed to move on. More importantly, he needed to move on and find himself someone to love.

As long as it wasn't me.

3

IZZY

"Morning, beautiful," Flash whispered in my ear as I hugged my pillow, facing away from him.

"Morning," I said, groaning as I stretched.

I wasn't a morning person. I'd slept like shit with Flash in my bed. He'd been a hog and snored no matter how much I'd elbowed him to move. The noise just kept coming. I'd thought about pinching his nose, but I'd also thought that'd earn me an elbow to the face by accident. So I'd covered my head with my pillow, faced away from him, and prayed for him to shut the fuck up.

"Sleep well?" he asked, stroking my arm lightly as goose bumps broke out across my skin.

"Ugh," I whined, turning toward him. "No."

"I slept like a fuckin' rock." He smiled, brushing the hair out of my eyes.

"Yeah, I know," I mumbled.

His slow blinks and sappy smile made my stomach turn. He wasn't staring at me like a piece of meat or a hit-it-and-quit-it kind of thing. His face screamed that he loved me, and it freaked me the fuck out.

"So, what do you want to do today?" he asked, his eyes searching my face.

I bit the inside of my lip. "It's Thanksgiving, Flash. I'm going to spend the day with my family."

"Fuck," he muttered as he stared at the ceiling.

"What?" I asked, pulling the sheet over my breasts as I sat up and rested against the headboard.

"I forgot it's Thanksgiving."

"I'm sure your parents are expecting you."

"No, they're out of town. I'll just do what I came here for and head back to the clubhouse."

Fucking great. I don't want him to be alone on a holiday. No one deserves that. "I'm sure Joe wouldn't mind if you came to dinner. He cooks for an army, just like my ma."

"You wouldn't care?" he asked, looking over at me with puppy-dog eyes.

"No. You know everybody, and my mom has always liked you."

"Your mom is the best damn cook. That's one of the reasons I liked you as a kid. Your mom fed everybody."

"You liked me because I let you feel me up in eighth grade." I laughed, hitting him in the face with my pillow.

"Yeah, that too." He grabbed me by the arms, pulling me down on top of him.

"Flash," I warned.

"I know, Izzy. I'm just a cock to you."

I hit his shoulder hard, making my palm sting. "Fucker, you're a friend, but your cock is mighty fine."

"My cock could use some attention."

"So could my pussy."

"Listen, you greedy little cunt. I ate you so fucking good last night and what did I get?"

"You just said what you got. You got to eat my pussy."

"Izzy," he said, grabbing my shoulder. "My balls are gonna burst. You gotta help a guy out here."

I crawled on top of him, straddling him, and felt his dick already hard underneath me. "Flash, what do I get if I let you?"

"Woman," he said as he swatted my ass. "You'll get to come on my 'mighty fine cock,' as you called it."

"I want two," I demanded, grinding myself against him.

He shivered as a small moan escaped his lips. "Anything you want."

I looked at the ceiling, resting my index finger against my lips as I moved my hips. "Well, my house could use a good cleaning," I teased.

"You'll get what I give you," he growled.

"Oh, I like big, bad biker Flash." I laughed, leaning back and pushing the tip of his cock farther into my wetness.

He tossed me through the air, and I landed on the bed and bounced. I snorted as I laughed. He grabbed the condom off the nightstand and moved his body between my legs.

"I'll show you big, bad biker Flash."

"Shit better be good."

"You talk too fucking much," he said as he rolled the condom down his shaft. "I always do you good, Izzy. No one does it better."

On a consistent basis, he was the best, but I'd had better one-night stands. There's something about the explosion of passion that happens when two strangers get together and there's an undeniable attraction. Clothes get torn, bodies get bruised, and everyone walks away with exactly what they wanted to begin with—a quick fuck, no strings attached.

"Gimme those lips," he said, leaning over me as he stuck the tip of his cock inside me.

"No," I whispered, turning my head.

He stopped all movement. "No?"

"Your breath." I laughed, but it was more than that. It felt too personal, and the last thing I wanted was anything that involved feelings.

"Gotcha," he replied as he jammed his dick inside me, causing me to cry out in pleasure.

"Jesus," I mumbled, pushing my head into my pillow and arching my back to give him better access.

"So fuckin' good," he whispered, rocking back and forth.

I sighed, letting myself get lost in the pleasure and blocking everything out. As his thrusts grew more punishing, I dug my fingers into his skin, trying to ground myself.

Closing my eyes, I listened to our moans as he moved. The sound of our bodies connecting filled the room, mingled with our breathing. He drove me closer to the edge. Each thrust hit my clit, bringing the orgasm just within reach.

Within minutes, I was flying off a cliff. A kaleidoscope of colors filled my vision as the orgasm that tore through me stole the air from my lungs. Flash had that ability. That's one reason why I always welcomed him into my bed.

"Oh God, yes!" I screamed, meeting his thrusts as the orgasm waned. I wanted more, needed more. I wasn't done, and neither was he.

He stared down at me, his eyes blazing as he gritted his teeth, chasing his own release. Picking up the pace, he grabbed my ass and tilted my hips, causing him to slide in farther.

"Right there!" I screeched, kicking my feet against the bed.

"Fuck," he hissed, his momentum quickening to an impressive speed.

Moments later, his movement stuttered as he groaned though his release. Sweat dripped from his chin, landing on my breast and sliding down to rest in between my tits.

The very last thrust he gave me sent me over the edge. The second orgasm was just as intense as the first and left me a puddle of jelly.

We lay there panting, sweaty, and exhausted. Trying to gulp air as if we were fish searching for water as we flopped in a new atmosphere. I wanted to fall back asleep. My eyes felt heavy as the tiredness I felt went bone deep.

Just as my breathing slowed and my mind started to turn off, my phone beeped.

"Fuck," I muttered, reaching out and feeling around my nightstand. Cracking one eye, I brought the phone to my face, too tired to open both.

Joe: Be on time today.

I rolled my eyes, tossing the phone to the floor. Yawning, I moving away from Flash and snuggled with my pillow. I had hours until I needed to be there for dinner. It was a holiday, for shit's sake, and I needed rest after having listened to Flash snore all night.

Comfortable and sated sleep took me quickly. Everything faded away.

"Izzy," a voice said inside my dream, but I ignored it. "Izzy," the voice repeated.

"What?" I mumbled, annoyed to have my darkness interrupted.

"Izzy," Flash said, shaking my shoulders. "What time do we have to be at your brother's?"

"Two," I muttered, placing the pillow over my head.

"It's one thirty, babe."

I jumped from the bed, my heart racing at the thought of being late. "Fuck. Why did you let me sleep so long?" I grabbed my jeans off the dresser, slipping them on and quickly fastening them. Then I turned to see Flash staring at me. "Get your ass up. We gotta go."

"Is someone scared of her brother?" He smiled, stretching out across my bed.

"No. I just don't want to hear bullshit about being late."

"Pussy." He laughed, climbing off the bed.

"If you ever want my pussy again, you'll move your ass." I threw his dirty clothes at him before he could react. They hit him square in the chest and fell to his feet.

"What the fuck, dude?" he asked, holding out his hands.

"Put something on. You can't go like that," I said, waving my hands up and down.

"My clothes are outside."

I crossed my arms over my chest, highly irritated at this point. "Flash, move it. Stop fucking around. Get your shit and get ready. I'm leaving in ten with or without you."

"Fine," he said, pulling on his jeans before stomping out the door as I walked into my closet to grab a cami.

It was bad enough that I was bringing Flash with me. Joe hated him. Fuck, all my brothers hated him. Hopefully, with it being a holiday, they could put aside their bullshit and welcome him inside. I could hope, but I knew the reality. I'd be playing interference the entire day to stop fists from flying.

Exactly ten minutes later, I grabbed my keys off the counter and threw on my heels. Then I stood by the front door, about to walk out, when Flash rounded the corner looking as good as biker Flash could. His outfit wasn't fancy, but it would do. Time to get the clusterfuck over with.

4

IZZY

Thank goodness Anthony showed up when we did. I wouldn't have to hear Joe's mouth about being the last one to dinner.

"Hey, Anth."

Anthony hugged me, moving in closer to my ear and whispering, "Why the fuck did you bring him?"

I looked at Flash, giving him a smile before responding to Anthony. "He didn't have anywhere else to go." I batted my eyelashes at him as he backed away and gave Flash a once-over.

"Joe is going to shit a motherfucking brick." Anthony winked and grinned.

"Just thought I'd keep the day interesting."

"Hey, man," Flash said as he walked up to Anthony with his hand outstretched.

"Long time no see, Sam." Anthony grasped his hand, shaking it for longer than normal.

"Yeah." Flash flinched from the handshake. Then he flexed his hands as Anthony released him. "It's Flash now."

I rolled my eyes and shook my head. *This shit should go over real well with my family.* Anthony looked at me, and I shrugged before pinching my nose.

"Stay behind me," I said, looking at Flash and pointing at the ground.

"Why?"

"'Cause Joe won't punch me when he sees you, but by all means," I said, motioning in front of me with my hand. "Go ahead in front if you want a fist in the face as a greeting."

Flash grimaced and sighed. "I don't know why your brother doesn't fuckin' like me."

"Maybe 'cause you've been fucking his little sister for years."

Flash mumbled something under his breath, moving to stand behind me as we approached the door. As Anthony knocked, I fidgeted with my hands, praying that the day didn't turn into a clusterfuck.

"Fucker hated me before that," Flash snarled behind me.

Anthony's fists didn't relent as he pounded on the door.

"Why don't you just open it?"

"This isn't Ma's and I don't just walk in without being told it's okay," he said, landing another blow.

"Pussy," I whispered, moving around Anthony and walking inside.

Flash laughed, following behind me as Anthony grumbled.

"Smells damn good in here." I inhaled deeply.

"Hey, sis," Joe said, walking over to hug me.

"I brought someone. I hope you don't mind." I smiled, looking up into his eyes. I knew I was laying it on thick, but I was just trying to cushion the blow.

"Who?" Joe asked, looking over my shoulder. "Really?" he growled in my ear, grabbing my shoulder.

"Come on, Joey. He didn't have anywhere else to be. He was in town and I told him he could spend the day with us. I know you made enough food for an entire army." I batted my eyelashes at Joe.

"He's here now." Joe shook his head, staring down at me. "Next time ask, Izzy."

"Okay," I whispered against his chest, giving him a squeeze before ducking under his arms.

Joe held out his hand to Flash as Anthony walked by and grimaced. "Nice to see you again, Sam," Joe bit out through gritted teeth.

"I go by Flash now."

I cringed at his response. I always knew Flash wasn't the most intelligent man, but to reply to my brother in that way was just plain idiotic—or he had a death wish.

"Whatever," Joe said, rolling his eyes. "Welcome to my home." He pulled Flash closer. "If you hurt my sister, I'll fucking bury you. Got me?"

"Easy now, City. I wouldn't dream of it. We're just friends." He stood toe to toe with Joe, gripping his shoulder.

I swear to fuck that all I could see was a train wreck. I thought I was standing in the middle of a Looney Tunes cartoon. There had to be a big kaboom coming at any second. Joe and Flash wouldn't be parting on a happy note, but hopefully they could keep their hands to themselves for Thanksgiving.

"I don't care who the fuck you think you are or what MC you're in. You're still Sam to me and I can still whip your ass. Just so we're clear." Joe glared at him.

Suzy's arms slid around Joe as she looked at Flash. "Everything okay, baby?" she asked.

"Just perfect, sugar. This is Sam, Izzy's friend."

She released him, holding out her hand to Flash. "Hi, Sam. I'm Suzy. Nice to meet you," she said, smiling.

"It's my pleasure, Suzy." He pulled her hand to his lips and gently kissed it. "You have a beautiful home."

"Thank you, Sam."

Joe growled. Honest to motherfucking god, the man growled. I knew that my brother was a caveman, but this was beyond the realm of normal behavior. Flash looked at Joe, his lips turning up in a half-smirk before he turned back to Suzy.

"Joe's a very lucky man. I hope you don't mind me crashing the party." Sam looked to Joe with a shit-eating grin before he looked at Suzy.

Yep—death wish.

"Not at all. Come on in and make yourself at home," Suzy said with a smile before stepping aside and wrapping her arms around my big brother.

"Let's go say hi to my parents, dumbass," I said to Flash, grabbing his shirt and pulling him toward the living room.

"Why the fuck am I a dumbass?" he asked, looking at me with a furrowed brow.

I stopped, turning to face him. "Starting shit with my brother," I whispered, glaring at him.

"Dude, I gotta stand up to the guy. I can't be a doormat. Show no weakness."

"You're a fucking moron." I laughed. "Ma," I said, entering the room.

"Happy Thanksgiving, baby girl." She wrapped her arms around me.

I have the best fucking mother in the world. She had to be the best to raise us as children and come out without a scratch. We didn't make shit easy for her.

"Happy Thanksgiving, Ma." I kissed her cheek before releasing her. "I brought Sam with me." I turned to him and smirked. "He would've been all alone today."

"Aww, Sam, it's so good to see you. How have you been?" she asked as she moved toward him with open arms.

This was pure Mama Gallo. She welcomes everyone and doesn't hold a grudge. I, on the other hand, hold on to shit for too long and always wonder what angle the person is working when they are being nice.

"Mrs. G, looking amazing as always." He hugged her, lifting her off the ground.

She giggled as her face turned pink. "Oh, Sam. Put this old woman down."

"You're not old, Mrs. G. You never will be. You haven't aged a bit since I saw you last."

Flash may be a dumbass and a douche some of the time, but he knew how to talk to the ladies. He'd fine-tuned that skill since we were teenagers. I was immune to his charm.

My pop rose to his feet, moving toward Flash with his arm extended as he offered his hand. "Sam, good to see you, kid. How the hell have you been?" Pop asked, smacking Flash on the shoulder with his free hand.

I turned to look at my brothers. Snarls and glares were the Gallo boys' preferred mug of choice today. I knew deep down that this would be the longest fucking holiday of my life.

There wasn't a cock in the world worth this much bullshit at a family holiday. I just wanted to laugh and bust a few balls. I didn't want to play referee.

"Yo, Joe, is dinner almost ready?" I yelled, plopping down on the couch in an open spot. If everyone had their mouths full, they couldn't be spouting nonsense.

Suzy came flying out of the kitchen, adjusting her sundress as she walked. Her face was flushed and her lips looked swollen. "Food's ready. Go sit down while Joe and I bring everything to the table, please." She turned around and ran into the kitchen.

Flash held out his hand, helping me from the couch.

I smiled at him. "Thanks," I whispered, climbing off the couch.

"Any time, babe. Only thing better than tasting you is Thanksgiving dinner." He licked his lips as a small grin played on the corner of his mouth.

"Jesus. Not smooth, man. You need to work on your lines if that's the best you have," I said to him as we followed behind everyone else to the dining room table.

"What the fuck is wrong with my lines?"

"Totally not sexy. Does that shit work on the club girls?"

"I don't need lines with those ladies."

"Lucky for you then or you wouldn't be getting any pussy. *Ever.*"

"WHY THE FUCK WERE YOU GONE SO LONG?" FLASH ASKED AS we walked into the kitchen. His face was red and he was on edge.

Suzy, Mia, my ma, and I had been upstairs in the war room. It's what we referred to the room as, anyway. It was filled with information about Suzy's wedding. Everything was planned down to the last details. She's anal that way. She's a total over-achiever who has never done anything by the seat of her pants. She has plans for her plans. There's no room for error.

Suzy and Joe were getting married in a week. I had been elected to be in charge of the bachelorette party and nothing else. Thank Christ. I didn't want to be responsible for any fuck-ups. I am not a planner. I've winged shit my entire life.

"We were talking and got a little carried away."

Flash ran his fingers through his hair, making it a bigger mess than it'd already been. "I felt like you threw me to a pack of wolves."

I looked around the room, taking in the sight of my brothers and Pop sitting around the living room. I knew they could be ruthless, but they were harmless.

I ruffled his hair. "Stop being a drama queen."

"Izzy, why do they hate me so much?"

"They don't," I said, sitting next to him at the kitchen table.

"Bullshit," he murmured. "Joey wants to cut my fuckin' throat."

"Nah." I shook my head as I bit my lip. "He just wants you to know where you stand."

"What's his issue?"

"Where would I even begin?" I laughed. "Joe is protective of everyone in this family, especially me. You're in an MC, and for that reason alone, he'd hate you being around me. He knows you fuck me, and that makes him want to rip your cock off and shove it down your throat."

Flash's face paled and his Adam's apple bobbed as he swallowed roughly. "You know I'd protect you, Izzy. You may not be mine, but I'd never let anything happen to you."

"I know, Flash, but Joe doesn't. Let's have dessert and we'll be out of here in a couple of hours. Aren't you happy you came to Thanksgiving Gallo style?"

"Hell yeah." He burped, rubbing his stomach. "The food alone was worth all the trouble."

Suzy walked into the kitchen, giving me a devilish smile as she looked between Flash and me. "Hey, guys. Ready for dessert?"

I nodded my head, smirking at her. "Yeah. I have to get Flash home soon."

"Aww, really? I wanted to play cards or something." Suzy pouted and stomped to the counter to grab the pumpkin pie.

"We can stay," Flash interrupted before I could reply.

I glared at him, not really in the mood to play cards with the family. "Fine. We'll stay."

His smile grew wide as Suzy yipped and jumped up and down. "Heck yeah! I'm so excited!"

As she walked out of the room, I kept my eyes glued to Flash. This was going to be a very long evening.

"What time do you have to head back?" I asked him, hoping it was sooner than later.

"I'll leave whenever we get back to your place. I just have to be back tonight. I don't have a curfew, Izzy." He laughed, standing and walking to the counter to grab the other pie.

I put my head on the table, lightly smashing it against the surface. I hated bringing anyone with me to family dinners, even Flash. I always felt a sense of being restricted or tied down. They were two things I never wanted to feel.

I avoided relationships like the plague. I never begrudged anyone happiness, but togetherness wasn't for me.

5

IZZY

Tears stung the back of my eyes as I stood in the bridal suite at the church and stared at Suzy. She looked amazing. I'd worried this day wouldn't come, especially after the bachelorette party.

I'd kind of fucked up. She'd said no to male strippers, but shit... I never listen. Joe had flipped when he'd caught the scent of the guy as it lingered on her skin that night. Their entire relationship had almost exploded into a million tiny pieces, but their love was too strong. Plus, Joe had decided to take the stick out of his ass and apologize to her for acting like a complete caveman asshole.

I'd marked that shit down on my calendar because it wasn't likely to ever happen again. Gallo men aren't quick to take the blame for shit. They grunt, smile, and move on.

"She looks stunning, doesn't she?" Mia asked, nudging me in the shoulder.

I slowly nodded, unable to take my eyes off her. "She does." I turned to Mia with a small smile. "When am I going to see you in a wedding dress?"

"Oh," she said, her cheeks turning pink. "I'm just waiting for Mike to ask me."

"Haven't you two talked about marriage?"

"He's mentioned it a time or two, but I'm not pushing it on him." She shook her head and sighed.

"I need another sister-in-law. You're like my sister already, but I need it official and on paper." I smiled, happy that there were finally some females inside the family circle after years of dealing with the boys.

She laughed, tossing her head back, and held her stomach. "You're more demanding than my mom," she said, wiping the corner of her eyes.

"Hell yeah. I've gone too many years surrounded by testosterone. I need vadge in this family."

Mia and I stood side by side and stared at Suzy as she fussed with her dress and checked her makeup before moving closer to the mirror.

"You look beautiful, Suzy," I said, walking toward her.

The dress had a form-fitting bodice with a thick ribbon and a flower around the waist. The V-shaped neckline plunged just far enough to show off her chest. The bottom was comprised of loose tulle that kissed the floor and shifted when she walked. Suzy always looked amazing, but today she glowed.

"I'm so nervous. Why am I so nervous?" she asked, turning toward me and taking a deep breath.

I grabbed her hands, wanting to avoid messing up her dress. "You're going to be fine. Everything is ready. Don't stress."

"What if he changes his mind?" Her eyes grew wide as she said the words.

I shook my head, my mouth set in a firm line. "You can't be serious. My brother is so in love with you. Why would you even think that?"

"I don't know. I feel panicked."

I touched her forehead, thinking she had to be sick. "No fever," I said as I removed my hand. "Calm the fuck down, Suzy. Joe loves you. I've never seen him so sure about anything or anyone in his life."

She blew out a breath, touching her stomach and smoothing the fabric. "I know," she said, looking down at the floor.

"Are you sure, though?" I asked.

"I love him," she stated firmly.

"Is it enough?" I asked, cocking my eyebrow.

"Izzy, you're such a Debbie Downer on love," she said, laughing. "I can't wait until you find 'the one.'"

I doubled over in a fit of giggles. "You must clearly be ill. I don't want 'the one,'" I said, making air quotes. "I'm perfectly happy being single. The last thing I want is a ball and chain to tie my ass down."

"Uh huh," she said, looking in the mirror again.

"Izzy, when are you going to stop lying to yourself?" Mia interrupted.

"You two bitches need to slow your roll. I'm not the dating type, let alone the marrying kind."

"It's time." Ma clapped her hands as she sang the words.

"Someone do my veil. I'm too nervous!" Suzy shrieked, shaking her hands.

"I got it," I said, stepping in front of her and reaching behind to take the thin material. Then I placed it over her face, smoothing it to not block her vision. "Good?" I asked before moving away.

"Yes," she replied. "It's now or never."

"Suzy, you two were meant for each other. I may not want it for myself, but I have no doubt there's no one else out there for my brother."

"You're right, Izzy. Let's do this crap."

I chuckled, trying to cover my mouth. "You don't always talk like a Gallo, but you're one at heart."

She giggled nervously, moving toward the door. I grabbed her short train, not wanting it to get stuck on anything. When Suzy's father saw her, his face lit up like a Christmas tree.

"There's my girl," he cooed, holding out his arms.

"Hey, Dad." She wrapped her arms around him, trying to avoid touching his tuxedo with her face.

He backed away and stared at her. "You look beautiful, Suzette," he said, holding her shoulders and taking her in.

"Thanks," she said, linking her arm with his.

The music from inside the church filled the corridor where we stood. Nerves filled my belly as it flipped inside my body. I couldn't imagine how Suzy felt. Some would say that I love to be the center of attention, but having hundreds of pairs of eyes staring at you as you try to walk in a pair of five-inch heels and not fall on your face has to be daunting.

As I started down the aisle and smiled, I knew that no one

was really looking at me. Their eyes were trained on the back of the room, waiting for a peek at the bride.

Joe nodded at me as I moved into the pew and then turned to watch Suzy. He glowed. When Suzy came into view, his face lit up, his eyes grew wide, and a giant smile spread across his face.

I never thought he'd fall so head over heels for anyone like he did for Suzy. I would've never put the two of them together and thought, *Fuck yeah, that'll work*, but for some odd reason, it had. Her innocence had captured his attention, but we all knew she was a freak underneath that put-together-teacher exterior.

Joe looked handsome in his tuxedo. His hair was freshly cut and styled, his face cleanly shaven. Sun-kissed skin made his blue eyes stand out. All of my brothers looked killer today. Rarely did they all dress up, but weddings were the exception. Joe was the first out of the five of us to be married, and we knew it would be a while before another wedding would take place.

Mike and Mia had met months ago and were the next in line. That would only happen if my brother could get his head out of his ass and pop the question. Anthony and I were the two hold-outs on relationships of any sort. We were the free birds of the group.

I turned, taking in the sight of Suzy as she glided down the aisle. I could see the smile on her face even through her veil as she locked eyes with Joe. They were in a trance, staring at each other as she made her way toward the altar.

When Suzy stopped at the altar, the priest said, "Who gives this bride away today?"

"I do," her father answered, releasing her hand and lifting her veil. Then he placed a chaste kiss on her cheek before stepping back.

Suzy and Joe mouthed some words to each other, which looked like "I love you," as they held hands. After, they made their way to the center of the altar and stood with the priest.

I sat back, watching the beginning of their happily ever after. I wiggled my nose, stopping the tickling sensation from the tears that threatened to fall.

Even someone such as myself, someone against the entire institution of marriage, could grow misty-eyed at a wedding. I couldn't have been happier to have Suzy officially become a member of the Gallo family. It only took twenty-something years for me to finally have a sister.

Today would be a new beginning. The Gallo family would be forever changed.

6

IZZY

Standing in the reception line had to be the most mind-numbing experience of my entire life. Greeting people I didn't know, welcoming them, and thanking them for coming to my brother's wedding—totally fucking exhausting.

Then there were the people who liked to pinch my cheeks like I was still a five-year-old girl. It took everything I had not to slap their hands away and keep a smile glued to my face. By the time the line waned and I was able to hit the bar, my face hurt from my fake smile and my feet were screaming for relief.

I kicked off my shoes, pushing them under the bar and held my hand up to the bartender.

He sauntered over with a giant smile on his face. "What can I get you, darlin'?"

I leaned against the bar, putting my face in my hands, and stared him down. After the hour of awesomeness that was the receiving line, I wanted a drink and nothing more. I didn't feel like flirting or small talk.

"Jack, straight up," I said without cracking a smile.

"Single or double?"

"Double, please."

As he walked away to pour my drink, I turned and took in the room of people. The wedding was massive. Between Suzy and my ma, I think they had all of Tampa Bay crammed in the room.

"God, I need a drink," Mia said as she walked toward me.

"As bored as I am?" I asked as I leaned back, taking the pressure off my feet.

"At least you know all those people," she replied, motioning toward the bartender.

"The fuck I do. I know maybe half, and even then, I'm sketchy on their names."

"There's a small army here," she said. "Martini, please. Make it dirty with two olives."

"Someone looking to get a little buzzed, like me?"

"Just need to take the edge off," Mia replied. "Weddings make me itchy."

"Like you're allergic?"

"No, Izzy." She shook her head and laughed.

"Well, what the fuck? Clue a sister in."

We turned toward the bar, picking up our drinks and clinking them together.

"I feel I'll always be a bridesmaid and never a bride."

"You have Mike." I sipped the Jack, letting it slide down my throat in one quick swallow.

Mia sipped her martini and winced before her lips puckered.

"I could be an old hag before he finds just the right way to ask me to marry him."

"Fuck tradition. Ask him already."

"He'd die," she said, bringing the glass to her lips and looking at me over the rim.

I held up my hand, snapping my fingers for a refill. "He'll get over it. Make a deadline, then. If he doesn't ask by a certain date, then you ask him."

"Maybe," she replied, setting her drink on the bar. "I wouldn't walk away if he doesn't ask. I love him too much."

"He loves you too, Mia. It's really sickening how often I have to hear about you." I laughed, tapping my fingernails against the wooden surface as I waited for my drink. "I love you, of course, but Jesus. The man talks about nothing else except for you and the clinic."

She hit my shoulder, causing me to laugh. "Would you rather him talk about Rob and working out all the time?"

Rob was my brother's trainer before he quit fighting. Rob and I had had a "thing" for a short time. It'd ended badly. Mostly for him, though, since my knee had found its way to his balls and he'd ended up on the floor.

"Well, lesson one is don't refer to women as bitches."

"I'm sure he learned his lesson," she said, and laughed. "I've heard more than once about your wicked, bony-ass knee. I think he still has a thing for you, Izzy."

I turned, holding my glass near my lips. "Ain't no way in hell am I ever dating him. Never. Ever. He's a total asshole."

Mia's laughter turned into a fit of giggles as she held on to the bar to maintain her balance. Tears streamed down her face and her dark eyes twinkled in the lighting. "I know he is. Total douche, but he has a soft side."

"Mia, stop trying to get me to hook up with Rob." I sipped the Jack Daniel's, the feeling of the first shot already making its way through my system. My legs felt a little wobbly and my core warmed. "I don't want a boyfriend and I certainly don't want him."

"Someday, Izzy, you're going to meet that guy. One who makes your belly flip and toes curl. The electricity between you two will be undeniable. You just haven't met the right one."

"He's like a unicorn, Mia. Totally fictional bullshit."

She shook her head, finishing the last sip of her martini. "He's not. You just haven't found him yet. I feel those things when I'm with Michael."

"You're obviously mentally impaired," I chortled.

"I can't wait to see the day someone has you all in a fluster. You're going to be totally fucked."

"Mia, babe, there ain't no man tough enough to handle all this," I said, motioning down my body.

"Uh huh," she clucked, her shoulders shaking from laughter. "I can't wait to see the damn day."

"It's dinnertime, ladies," my ma sang as she walked through the bar area. "It's time to take your seats."

"I could use a little food and a damn chair," I said, wondering how I'd make it to the table with my feet feeling like someone was rubbing hot coals on them.

"Me too," Mia said, following behind me.

We both walked gingerly toward the table that was placed on the dance floor and facing the entire room. I felt almost like a zoo animal as I sat down and looked around the large ballroom.

I ate my food and chatted with Mia throughout the dinner. Joe and Suzy were interrupted so many times with clinking glasses that I didn't have any idea if they were able to consume half their meal. It was cute, and at some point, I thought Joe would tell them to use their fucking forks to eat, but he didn't.

Suzy did that to him. She chilled him out at times when he was ready to burst. I knew he wanted the day to be special, and did everything in his power to make sure it was perfect. Even held his tongue when I know he had to be biting it so hard that he drew blood.

"I'm hitting the bar again after dinner," I told Mia, hoping she'd join me.

"I'm in," she replied. "Until Michael drags me on the dance floor."

"I wish you luck with that." I laughed, placing the last bit of pasta in my mouth.

I didn't get up immediately. My mother would have given me the stink eye if I'd looked too eager to run to the bar. I sat there staring at the crowd, smiling, and making small talk with the others at the table. Sipping my wine, I counted the minutes until I could stand again on my aching feet and drink myself into oblivion.

Weddings, even my brother's, were bullshit. There was no fucking way in hell I'd be standing on the dance floor later, knocking over girls to get a bouquet of flowers. I wasn't looking for some symbolic nonsense that I'd be the next one walking down the aisle and giving up my freedom. Fuck tradition.

7

IZZY

After downing countless drinks and chatting up Mia and all the long-lost family members who'd shown their asses at the wedding, I turned to see a very red-faced Suzy enter the ballroom. Joe stood by her side, but he looked calm—besides the small smirk on his face.

"Hey, sister," I said as I walked toward her. "I'm so excited to be able to say that and it be true. I've always wanted a sister." I wrapped my arms around her, squeezing her a little too tight.

"Can't breathe," she whispered.

"Man up," I said, releasing her.

"I'll be back, ladies. I'm going to grab a drink at the bar with my boys," Joe said before he kissed her cheek and left us alone.

"Where's your sister?" I asked, looking around the crowd.

Suzy had a sister, but they weren't close. The Gallos were closer to her, and more of a family than hers would ever be. I felt bad for her, but it made me love her more.

"Don't know and don't give a shit either." She shrugged and looked at the floor.

"You know you've turned into a badass with a potty mouth, Suz."

She smiled, shaking her head. "City. It's all his fault."

"I'd like to think I played a part in it, too." I laughed.

"You're always getting me in trouble, Izzy."

"Me?" I asked, holding my hand to my chest.

"Always."

A man cleared his throat next to us and we both turned in his direction. "Excuse me, ladies. I don't mean to interrupt."

"Well then don't," I slurred, looking the stranger up and down. Handsome, well built, great hair, and totally doable. Maybe I shouldn't have been such a bitch, but then again, Jack was talking after I'd consumed more than necessary.

"Don't be rude, Izzy," Suzy said, turning to face him. "How can I help you?"

"I'm a friend of Thomas's, and he asked me to drop off a gift on his behalf." The man held out an envelope and waited for her to take it.

I took this moment to study him further. His muscles bulged underneath his suit as he held out his hands. His eyes were green, but I couldn't tell the shade. His jaw line was sharp and strong.

"Is he okay?" I asked. I hadn't seen my brother in so long, and information wasn't freely flowing lately. He worked undercover for the DEA and was in deep with an MC in Florida. I wanted him home, safe and sound.

"He is, and he's very sorry he couldn't make it," he said, looking down at me.

"Don't mind her," Suzy said to him, her eyes moving from me to him. "Thomas is her brother."

"Ah, you're *that* Izzy," he said, his lips turning up into a smile. "I've heard a lot about you."

What the fuck did that mean? I snarled, not entirely liking the shit-eating grin on his face. "And you are?" I asked, holding out my hand for him to take.

"James." He slid his hand along my palm and stilled. "James Caldo."

"Never heard of you, Jimmy," I said, trying to knock him down a peg. I didn't like that he had heard of me, with his *"that Izzy"* comment, and I'd never even heard his name.

He brought my hand to his lips and placed a kiss just below my knuckles. "Perfect."

His lips scorched my skin. An overwhelming sense of want came over me. I felt the urge to jump into his arms and kiss his very full lips. My toes curled painfully in my shoes as I stared at his mouth against my skin. As he removed his lips from my hand and brought his eyes back to mine, I wiped all evidence of want from my face.

Suzy coughed, ruining my fantasy and bringing me back to reality. "Thanks, James. I'll give this to Joseph for you. Why don't you stay and enjoy the wedding?" She smiled at the man.

"What?" I asked, turning toward her. Suzy played dirty. Her angel act was just that—an act.

"We have plenty of food, and I'm sure the Gallos would love to talk with you about their Thomas," Suzy said, grinning like an idiot.

I gave her the look of death. What in the fuck was wrong with her?

"You can keep James company tonight, Izzy. You didn't bring a date."

She did not just say that. If it weren't her wedding, I swear to shit I would've smacked her. I could feel my cheeks turning red as his eyes flickered to mine.

"I'd love to stay. Thank you. Izzy, would you like a drink?" he asked, still holding my hand in his.

"Only because Suzy would want me to be a gracious host," I said, looking at her out of the corner of my eye.

"I don't want to put you out or anything. I'm a *big* boy and can handle myself. I just thought you could use a drink to unwind a bit. You feel a little tense, and that mouth of yours could get you into trouble."

Obviously, he was full of himself. Trust me when I say I can smell a cocky bastard from a mile away. I grew up with enough of them to sniff them out across a room.

"I don't need a babysitter, Jimmy, but I'll take the drink."

"It's James," he said, squeezing my hand.

"You two kids play nice," Suzy said before she waved and walked away.

"Bitch," I mumbled under my breath as I turned back toward the bar.

"Excuse me?" he asked, gripping my arm as he pulled me backward.

I stopped and faced him. "Are you going to release me anytime soon?"

"Highly unlikely." He smirked.

"Jimmy, listen. I don't know what your deal is or who the fuck you think you are, but no one touches me without permission."

With that, he released me, but not before squeezing my arm. "You'll be begging for my touch."

I glared at him, floored by his cockiness. "Obviously you know nothing about me then." I left him in the dust.

I leaned against the bar, feeling him behind me as I motioned to the bartender. At this point in the evening, I no longer had to verbalize my order. He knew it.

"Like what you see?" I asked as I kept my eyes forward.

"Your brother didn't do you justice."

Resting my back against the bar, I asked, "What exactly do you think of me?"

He smiled, stepping closer as he invaded my personal space. He brushed the hair from my cheek, running his fingertip down my face. "You're prettier in person. You arc tough as nails, just like your brother said, but I can see the real Izzy underneath."

I snarled, feeling all kinds of bitchy. "There's no hidden me underneath. This is who I am. I make no apologies for my bitchiness or candid comments."

"Oh, little girl, you're so much more than a smart mouth." He leaned in, hovering his mouth just above mine.

I held my breath, silently debating if I wanted him to kiss me. I had to be crazy. There was nothing about this man I liked, besides his face. His words were infuriating, his attitude was obnoxious, and the fact that he thought he had me pegged made me want to slap his face when he spoke.

His eyes searched mine as I stood there not breathing and just keeping myself upright against the bar.

"You're an asshole, Jimmy."

He didn't back away. Instead, he held his ground, pressing against my body. "It's James," he murmured.

I swallowed hard, my stomach flipping inside my body like I'd just gone down the giant hill on a roller-coaster. "Still an asshole," I whispered, my tongue darting out to caress my lips and almost touch his.

"Doll, I never claimed to be nice." His lips were turned up into a grin so large that it almost kissed his eyes.

"Can we drink now?" I asked, wanting to move our bodies apart. The heat coming off him was penetrating my dress and causing my body to break out into a sweat. The pop and sizzle I felt inside was more than just the alcohol. James, the asshole, did naughty things to my body, and I needed distance between us.

"Don't you think you've had enough?" he asked without moving out of my personal space.

I placed my hands against his chest and pushed. He didn't budge or falter as I pushed again.

He tipped his head back and laughed. "Is that all you got?"

"Fucker. First off, I have more, but I don't want to cause a scene at my brother's wedding. Second, I haven't had enough. You aren't my father and you don't get to tell me when to stop drinking. Last time I checked my driver's license, I was old enough to make that choice for myself." I crossed my arms over my chest, trying to put some space between his torso and mine.

"Let's get one thing straight, Isabella." His hot breath tickled the nape of my neck as he put his mouth against my ear and spoke. "I will have you in my bed tonight."

I rolled my eyes and pursed my lips, trying to hide exactly how excited that statement had made me. I didn't want to date the man, but shit, I wanted to fuck him.

"You're quite sure of yourself, *Jimmy*." I emphasized his name, knowing it would drive him crazy.

"There are things I'm very sure of."

"Like what?" I spat.

"From the moment I saw you, I knew I wanted to be inside you. When I touched you, I felt something, and I know you felt it, too. There's something between us. I think I need to fuck you out of my system."

"Is that the best line you have?" I hissed, feeling his lips against my ear. I groaned, closing my eyes to let the feel of his mouth on my skin soak into my bones.

"I don't need lines, Izzy," he growled, with his teeth caging the flesh of my ear.

My toes curled inside my heels; I felt him all over my body. No one had ever affected me in this way.

"I'm down for a challenge."

"Doll, there's no challenge with a willing participant."

I pulled back, feeling his mouth slip from my skin, and looked him in the eye. "I was referring to your ability to keep up with me."

Again, he laughed and held his stomach. "Izzy, Izzy. Baby, if you can walk right in the morning without still feeling me inside you, I'd be shocked. I have no doubt I can keep up with you. You'll never be the same after I've fucked you."

"You better buy me a drink, then. I'll go easier on you." I smiled, turning my back to him and facing the bartender. Then I snapped my fingers, pointing in front of me as he smiled and grabbed the bottle of Jack.

Over my shoulder, James called out, "Make it two." He placed one hand on the bar to my right and stood to the left of me. His forearm pressed against my back, holding me in place and leaving me no escape. "What shall we drink to?" he asked.

"My brother," I replied. Thomas was our link. The connection that James and I shared. "What did he say about me?" I asked.

James smiled, turning his head to face me. "That you're his favorite sister."

"Jackass, I'm his only sister."

"I know." He laughed. "He told me you're hard to please."

I shook my head. "I'm not. I'm just picky and I don't settle."

"Can't fault you there. He's proud of you."

"For what?" I asked, looking at him, stunned.

"He's proud of the strong woman you've grown into, and I'd have to agree with the little bit of you I've experienced."

"Ha," I said. "I learned everything I know from my four brothers."

The bartender placed our shots on the bar and started to walk away.

"Hey, can we get two more?" I asked before he could get too far.

He nodded and grabbed the bottle, making two more drinks.

I lifted my glass, waiting for James to pick his up before I spoke. "To Thomas." I tipped my drink, clinking the glass with his before downing the liquid.

I watched over the rim as James swallowed it and didn't wince. His features were so strong and manly. I mean, what the fuck was that? I'd never thought of any one as manly. *Maybe I shouldn't have another drink.*

"Tell me who you really are," James said as he placed his empty glass on the bar.

"What you see is what you get," I said before I licked the Jack off my lips.

"I know there's the Izzy everyone sees and the real woman underneath."

"James, what you see is what you get."

"Are you always so hard?" he asked, brushing his thumb against my hand as it rested on the bar.

"I don't know. Are you always so damn nosy?"

"I think you haven't found the right man to tame your sass."

I turned to glare at him. "Hold up. I need a man, is that what you're saying?"

"No," he said, shaking his head. "I think your tongue is so sharp because you haven't found the man who makes you whole. Someone who crawls inside you so deep that you finally figure out who you are, what you were always meant to be."

"What the fuck?" I asked, scrunching my eyebrows in confusion.

"It's for another day, doll. Sometimes, we just need someone to bring out our true nature."

"Either I've clearly had too much to drink or you're talking out of your ass. I'm going to go with option two."

He cupped my face in his hand, rubbing the spot just behind my ear with his fingertips. "Sometimes, we don't know who we really are until we find the perfect partner to bring it out."

"Jimmy, I think we were talking about one night. You and me fucking each other's brains out and then walking away. Now, you're talking crazy if you think I need you in my life to complete me. I'm certainly not Renée Zellweger and you're no Tom Cruise. I don't need any man to complete me. I'm quite happy with my life."

"Fine. Tell me who you are." His stare pinned me in place.

Swallowing, I didn't take my eyes off him as I thought about my reply. I'd never had to explain myself to anyone. "Who are you, James?"

He shook his head, a small smile on his face, as he laughed softly. "I'm a protector."

I cut him off. "Do you think I need protecting?"

"I don't know," he replied.

"I have four older brothers who have made it their life's mission to make sure I'm protected. It's the last thing I need in my life."

"Can I finish?" he asked, taking a deep breath and tilting his head.

"Yes," I said, gulping hard and searching for some moisture in my now parched mouth.

"As I was saying, I'm a natural protector. That's why I joined the agency. I'm loyal to the core. I know what I want in life, and I never give up until I get it. There's nothing better than a good chase. Once I have my mind set on something, I'll stop at nothing to get what I want."

"Am I your goal?" I asked, smirking and feeling a little playful.

"What if I said yes?" James asked, moving his face closer to mine.

"I'd say you better have a new game plan."

"Are you a secret lesbian?" he teased, the corner of his mouth twitching.

"No! Fuck!" I hissed. "I mean, more power to anyone who loves vadge, but I'm all about cock, baby."

He closed his eyes, his breath skidding across my face as he blew the air out of his lungs. "If you talk about cock one more time, I'm taking you upstairs and fucking you until you can't scream anymore."

"That sounds creepy."

His chest shook as a laugh fell from his lips. "You have to be the most difficult female I have ever met."

"Maybe I'm more woman than you can handle," I purred, running my hand down his chest. Underneath my fingertips, I could feel his muscles flexing. I splayed my palm against his shirt, letting my hand rest against his rock-hard pec.

"Doll, I'm more man than you've ever had. That I can guarantee."

The air between us crackled. Like it did in the movies. Sparks were probably visible to any guest milling around the bar area.

"Izzy," Mia said, interrupting my moment with James.

I blinked slowly, looking over his shoulder and smiling at her. "Hey, Mia."

"Who do we have here?" she asked, a grin on her face.

"Mia, this is Jimmy, Thomas's friend."

His eyes flashed before he turned to face her. "Mia, it's nice to meet you. I'm James." He held out his hand, waiting for her touch.

"James, I'm Mike's girl." She slid her hand into his palm, shaking it slowly.

"I'd say you're more than a girl." He pulled her hand to his mouth and placed a soft kiss on the top.

She laughed, her cheeks turning red. Did he have this effect on all women? "You know what I mean," she said, batting her eyelashes.

Thank Christ Mike wasn't here to see Mia blushing and flirting with Jimmy boy.

"Mike's a very lucky man," James replied, releasing her hand.

I sighed, rolling my eyes before glaring at Mia. "Where's Mike, anyway?" I asked, feeling a bit jealous of his flirting.

I was bothered that he was flirting with her, but why? I shouldn't have been. I didn't like him. I wanted to use him. That was all. I wanted to have my way with him for one night and walk away unscathed. Jealousy wasn't an emotion I was used to experiencing, and I sure as hell didn't know how to deal with it.

"He's dancing with his ma," she replied, winking at me and mouthing, "Wow," as James turned to look at me before returning his attention to her.

"Would you like a drink, Mia?"

She smiled, nodding. "Always."

James motioned to the bartender as I walked to stand next to Mia.

"He's sexy as fuck," Mia whispered in my ear.

"He's an asshole, though."

"Nah, he couldn't be. He seems to be a perfect gentleman."

"Maybe you shouldn't have another if you think he's not a total prick."

"You're just too damn hard on men, Iz."

"He's cocky, Mia. He makes Mike and Joe seem like teddy bears."

"I like him," she said, her eyes raking over him.

"Hey, slutty Aphrodite, you're taken."

"I can look, *putana*. I'm not dead. I can tell you like him."

My mouth dropped open. "What?" I whispered. "I do not."

She smiled, nodding at me. "You do."

"All right, ladies," James said as he held out two glasses of Jack.

"To love," Mia said. "And passion."

"For fuck's sake," I blurted, bringing the cup to my mouth.

"I'll drink to that," James said, holding me in place with his stare.

I didn't respond as I slammed back the drink, letting it slide down my throat. Instead, I started to picture sex with James. There was a simmering tension between us. An animal attraction that was undeniable. I wanted to slap him and fuck him at the same time. I wanted to let loose and show him what Izzy Gallo really had.

"Thanks for the drink, James. I'm going to find Mike. You two have a fun night," Mia said, winking and smiling as she waved and walked away.

"Traitor," I mumbled, turning to face James.

"You want to fuck me?" James asked, taking the drink from my hand.

"What?" I asked, wondering if he would be so bold.

"You in or you out?" he growled with his hand on my hip, gripping it roughly with his fingers.

"I don't even know you," I replied, as his hold on me felt like a branding iron under my dress.

"What do you want to know?" he asked, still touching my body.

"You could be a bad man." That sounded stupid and childish, but I was trying to not seem too eager to jump in the sack with him.

"Would your brother send me here if I were a total asshole?"

He had me there. "No," I admitted.

"Do you know everything about every man you sleep with?" he asked, running his free hand down my arm.

"No."

"Do you want to fuck me?"

I bit my lip, blinking slowly and processing my thoughts. Did I want to? Fuck yes, I did. Was it a good idea? Hell no, it wasn't a good idea. But then again, mistakes sometimes leave the biggest mark in one's life.

"Maybe," I squeaked out.

He released my hip, moving his hand to the small of my back. "Ready?" he asked, cocking an eyebrow.

"Now?"

"Are you scared, little girl?" he teased.

"Of you?" There wasn't a man on this planet who scared me. The fear I felt was from within. It was pointed directly at me. A man wasn't the issue. James was, and the way my body reacted to him had me on high alert.

"Yeah," he said, the side of his mouth turning up into a grin I wanted to smack off his face.

This was where I should've called a time-out. The words I should've spoken didn't come out of my mouth.

"James, I have four older brothers. You hardly scare me."

"But they want to protect you and love you. While I, on the other hand, want to bury my dick so far inside you that I ruin you for eternity."

"You say such beautiful things." I'd be lying if I didn't admit to myself that he made my pussy clench with his words.

"You in or you out?"

"The real question, Jimmy, is am I going to let you in?" I turned back toward the bar and signaled for another drink.

Let the games begin.

8

JAMES

What the fuck was wrong with me? This wasn't how I normally treated a woman I'd just met. There was something different about Izzy, though. I'd felt like I knew her the moment we met. Thomas had filled my head with stories about his little sister and made her bigger than life. Seeing her in person only drove the point home that she was different than other women.

If he'd heard how I was talking to her, he'd have my nuts in a vise, making sure I'd never be able to get another hard-on in my life. I needed to slow my shit down.

"I'm a patient man, and you'll be in my bed before the night is through."

She laughed, her head falling back as her teeth shone in the light. "I can't leave yet," she said, grabbing her drink and swirling the contents inside. "I have to do all the bridesmaid bullshit."

"I can tell by your comment that you believe in true love."

"Fuck love. Don't get me wrong. I'm thrilled for Joe and Suzy, but the shit isn't for me. Don't say it," she warned, her eyes turning into small slits as she glared at me.

"What? That you just haven't met the right man?" I stood next to her at the bar and leaned my arm against the wooden surface as I faced her.

"Yes. It's not about that. Love makes shit messy," she explained before bringing the glass to her lips.

"Can I get a beer?" I asked the bartender as he walked by, and his eyes flickered to us.

His eyes raked over Izzy, and I saw the hunger burning inside them. I felt an overwhelming urge to rip them from his skull just so he couldn't eye-fuck her again.

He looked to me and snarled as he reached in the cooler, popped the top of a Yuengling, and placed it in front of me. Grabbing the cool bottle, I let my fingers slide over the wetness. Then I wished I could squelch the internal burning I felt for Izzy.

"You sound like a woman who came from a broken home. Thomas speaks very highly of your parents and the love they feel for each other. What turned you off love?" Bringing the bottle to my lips, I watched her as she swallowed hard and played with the glass in her hand.

"It's not love that I have an issue with. It's the battle that ensues because of it."

After pulling the beer from my mouth, I shook my head, trying to make sense of her statement. "What battle?"

"The one every girl I've ever known has gone through. They

have to decide how much of themselves they're willing to lose to be with the man they love."

"That's bullshit."

"There isn't a female I know who didn't change after being in 'love,'" she said, making air quotes and rolling her eyes.

"Maybe they brought out the real woman who was always lurking at the surface and too scared to show."

"You can have your opinion, James, but I know what I see."

"Ladies and gentlemen," a man called through the microphone. "If we could have the bride and groom on the dance floor and all the single ladies and gentlemen join them."

"You going?" I asked with a cocked eyebrow.

"It's stupid," she said before taking a sip of Jack.

"You're such a party pooper. Get your fine ass to the dance floor."

"Or what?"

I smiled, shaking my head slowly. "Let's place a bet."

"Whatcha got in mind, Jimmy?" Izzy cooed, rubbing the lapels on my suit jacket with her fingers.

"If I catch the garter, then we ditch this place and head to my room. No questions asked and no lip from you." I'd knock every motherfucker on the dance floor over to get the garter and have Izzy underneath me within an hour.

"Okay, and if I catch the bouquet, then I don't have to go anywhere with you. You leave and I get to spend the rest of the night in peace." She tilted her head, waiting for me to accept that challenge.

"Fuck yeah. I'm game," I said. Then I gulped the last bit of beer as she downed her drink and placed it on the bar. Setting my hand on the small of her back, I guided her away from the bar.

She stood stiff next to me as we watched her brother use his teeth to remove the garter from underneath the dress of his new bride. The crowd cheered when he appeared from the dress victorious. Twirling the small scrap of material in his hands, he raised his arms in victory.

"You ready to lose?" I asked, looking down at Izzy.

"One thing I'm never good at is losing, Jimmy."

"Single gentlemen first. All others please clear the floor," the DJ said as everyone moved away, leaving about fifteen of us to jockey for the garter.

I looked around, sizing up the competition. I was the biggest besides Michael, Izzy's brother. I took my spot to the side, knowing I could move quickly in front of the crowd and snatch the material before it turned into a free-for-all.

As the DJ started the countdown, Joe turned his back, practicing his throw, and the men moved with his motion. I readied myself as my heart hammered in my chest louder than a drum at a Metallica concert. I kept my eyes locked to his hand as he moved, waiting to see it fly through the air.

As his hand jerked back, the material flew through the air only feet to my right. I moved quickly, stepping in front of everyone else, and snatched it easily. The wedding attendees cheered as I turned to Izzy with a sinful smile, and nothing but seeing her ass in the air, waiting for my dick filled my mind.

"Fucker," she mouthed at me as I walked toward her.

"It's all on you now. Better catch that bouquet," I said, running my index finger down her cheek.

She closed her eyes, swallowing hard before opening them. Inside her baby blues was a fire burning so hot that I could see her pupils dilate as she looked at me. She nodded before making her way toward the crowd of women now standing at the ready.

She whispered to Mia, and their eyes flickered to me. A giant smile spread across Mia's face as Izzy glared at me. Winking, Mia tipped her chin in my direction as her smile grew wider. I said a silent prayer as Suzy readied herself with her bouquet and turned her back on the crowd. Mia bent at the knees like an athlete waiting for the gunshot to sound.

Silently, I prayed that Mia could take Izzy down and make sure she didn't grab the flowers. I wouldn't want to lose a bet to Isabella Gallo, and certainly not one as important as this. I didn't need a bet to bed a woman, but I had a feeling Izzy needed to feel like the choice was out of her hands. She needed an out. Needed something to tell herself to make it all okay to spend the night with me.

I should have felt guilty about the bet, but I didn't. Not one fucking bit.

The countdown began, my heart matching the drum roll blaring through the speakers. "Come on, Mia," I whispered.

My palms grew sweaty as I formed my hands into a tight fist, trying to shake out some of the nervous energy. If Izzy caught the fucking bouquet, I'd have a very long night filled with fantasies and jacking off like a twelve-year-old boy.

As the flowers traveled through the air, Mia held out her arm, pushing Izzy backward. Mia jumped in the air, Izzy looking at Mia in horror. The flowers grazed Mia's fingers, sailing over her head to the woman standing behind her.

The redheaded beauty closed her hands around the flowers, jumped up and down, and squealed.

"Fuck," Izzy hissed, turning to me and glaring in my direction.

I smiled, shrugging as I held up the garter and twirled it in my fingers. "You're mine," I mouthed before licking my lips.

The hunger I felt inside when looking at her was unlike anything I'd ever felt before. I'd lusted after women in the past, but the want for her was so intense that I wasn't even sure one night with her would be enough to satisfy the craving.

She turned to Mia, saying a few things, with her hands flapping around. Clearly Izzy was angry, but all Mia did was shrug and smile. Then Izzy turned her back, quickly moving toward me.

"Mia totally fucked me," she said as she stood in front of me, looking up into my eyes.

My lips curved into a smile as I stuffed the garter in my jacket pocket. "I don't care how I get you, but tonight, I'm the only one fucking you, doll."

"Fine," she said, standing with her legs shoulder width apart and her arms crossed over her chest.

"I'll give you one out. Kiss me, and if you feel nothing, I'll let you out of the bet." It could all blow up in my face, but I couldn't be a total prick. I didn't want her to be an unwilling participant.

"Just one kiss?" she asked as her face softened.

"Yes," I said, holding her face in my hand and running my thumb across her bottom lip.

"I'll take you up on that offer, but I don't welsh on my bets."

"It's your only out. So use it if you need to or else we're going to my room. No more waiting."

"Come on," she said, grabbing my hand and pulling me toward the ballroom exit.

I laughed as I followed behind her, letting her lead me into the corridor.

"Over there," she said as she pointed down the hallway near the elevator bank.

"Anywhere you want, doll."

The crowd thinned as we walked to a small cutout near the bathrooms.

"Why don't we go outside for a moment? Grab some air," I said. I didn't want to kiss her outside the bathroom. There were too many wedding guests and it was not sexy at all.

"Are you pussying out?" she said as she stopped and turned to face me.

"Fuck no. I just don't feel like kissing you outside the bathroom. I've never been a pussy a day in my life."

"Fine, but fuck, these shoes are killing me," she said as she reached down and pulled one off her foot. When she removed the second one, she sighed, closing her eyes like she'd had a weight lifted off her shoulders. She shrank by at least three inches, making me feel even bigger than I was.

"Are *you* pussying out?" I asked, teasing her for taking a moment to enjoy the newfound freedom of being shoeless.

"You're fucking crazy. Just know that, once my lips touch yours, there's no turning back. Come on, Jimmy boy. Show me what you got," she said as she pushed open the exit door in the hallway.

We stepped outside, into the cool night air, into privacy. The back of the hotel was deserted as the parking lot light flickered above us.

"So now what?" she asked, turning to face me.

I looked down at her, taking in her body before staring into her eyes. I didn't respond as I stepped into her space and pulled her toward me. Holding her neck with one hand and her back with the other, I molded my body to hers. Pushing her against the brick façade, I hovered my lips above hers.

Her eyes were wide, the deep blue appearing black in the darkness. Her warm breath tickled my lips as her breathing grew harsh. I waited a moment, letting the anticipation build, knowing that the kiss would alter everything. There would be no turning back.

I crushed my lips to hers, feeling the warmth and softness, tasting the Jack as I ran my tongue along the seam of her closed mouth. A small moan from her filled my mouth, causing my dick to pulse. Pulling her closer to me, tipping her head back farther with the grip on her neck, I devoured her mouth.

Her hands found their way to my hair, trying to grab hold, but the cropped cut made it impossible. She dug her nails into my neck, kissing me back with such fervor that I knew I had her. Sliding my hand down her dress, I pulled the material between my fingers and hiked it up enough to touch the skin above her knee. Then she broke the kiss, backing away as she stared at me and tried to catch her breath.

Before she could respond or tell me to stop, I plunged my tongue into her mouth, stripping her ability to speak. Her hands found their way into my suit jacket, gripping my back and

CHELLE BLISS

kneading the muscles just above my ass. I ground myself against her, pinning her against the wall as I kissed her like a man possessed.

The ember of lust that had filled my body when I'd first touched her turned into an out-of-control wildfire. She shuddered as my fingers slid up her inner thigh, stopping just outside her panties. I rubbed my finger back and forth, touching the edge where the lace met her soft flesh. Her body grew soft in my arms as she moaned into my mouth.

Not waiting for approval, I pulled the material aside and dipped my fingers into her wetness. I slid my fingers up, circling her clit with my index and middle finger. A strangled moan escaped her lips as my touch grew more demanding. She pushed herself against my fingers, wanting more pressure from my touch.

Gliding my fingers down, I inserted a single finger inside her pussy. She was tight, slick, and ready. Her inner walls squeezed against my digit, sucking it farther inside. Moving my thumb to her clit, I finger-fucked her, bringing her to the brink of orgasm without breaking the kiss. She held on to my shoulder, digging her nails in so hard that I could feel the pinch through my suit jacket.

Just as her breathing grew more erratic and her pussy clamped down on my finger, I pulled out. She sucked in a breath as her eyes flew open.

"What the fuck?" she hissed as she glared at me.

"You want to come, doll?" I asked, sticking my finger in my mouth and groaning.

This was just as much of a fucking tease for me as it was for her. To taste her and feel her against me made my body blaze with need and want, and I wasn't sure one night could extinguish the flame.

"What kind of question is that?" she snapped.

"It's simple. If you want to come, you'll follow me to my room or I walk away and never look back."

She placed her hands against my chest, slightly pushing me away from her. Staring into my eyes, she stated firmly, "No strings attached."

"I didn't picture myself getting down on one knee and proposing." I instantly regretted the words. It wasn't that I wanted to propose, but I didn't want her to feel cheap and disposable. Then again, she'd set the stage for that type of statement. Izzy Gallo didn't want to be tied down and didn't want to have to explain shit to her brother. I liked my life and balls too much to tell him that I wanted her in my life.

"Music to my ears," she said, dropping her hand to my chest, sliding it down my abdomen and grabbing my dick. "Let's see if you're as good as you claim, Jimmy."

"Babe, I'm going to rock your world so fuckin' hard you're going to get down on one knee and propose to *me*."

She threw her head back and laughed. Her beauty was amplified when she smiled. With a small burst of giggles breaking free, she tried to speak. "You obviously think highly of yourself." She squeezed my hardness and bit her lip, stifling the laughter.

"I'm done talking," I said as I pulled her toward the door. "Time to put up or shut up, doll."

"I like a challenge," she replied as she touched the door handle.

Reaching in front of her, I placed my hand over hers. Pulling the door open, I waited for her to step inside. When she walked, she shook her hips, and the movement made it almost impossible to keep my hands to myself. I nestled my palm against the small of her back, helping her toward the bank of elevators.

"Last chance to chicken out," I teased in her ear.

"I may have a pussy, Jimmy, but I'm sure as hell *not* one."

"Usually, a mouth like that I'd say is crude, but hearing you talk dirty just makes me want to jam my cock inside to quiet you," I whispered, trying to avoid the attention of the people passing by us.

As soon as the elevator doors closed, I had her against the wall. I claimed her mouth, her tongue sweet from the Jack lingering on the surface as I devoured her. Caging her face in my hands, I stole her breath and replaced it with my own.

When we reached my floor, I broke the kiss. Her body was still as her eyes fluttered open, and her breathing was ragged. I grabbed her hand, pulling her toward my room, a little too eager to feel her skin.

The chemistry was off the charts. As soon as the door closed behind us, I pushed her against the door, capturing her lips. The need I felt to be inside her bordered on animalistic as our heavy breathing and panting filled the room. I grabbed the purse she had tucked under her arm and tossed it over my head, removing any distraction.

I dropped to my knees, looking up at her, and said, "I need to taste you."

She was a vision. She had on thigh-highs that connected to a garter belt and lace panties.

She didn't reply, but she did spread her legs. I cupped her ass, ripping the thin lace material from her body and bringing her forward before I swept my tongue against her skin. I could smell her arousal. I wanted to worship at her altar.

I lifted her with my hands, placing her legs over my shoulders as I feasted on her. I sucked like a starved man, licking every ridge and bump as she chanted, "Fuck yeah," and "Oh my God." I didn't relent when she came on my face, her legs almost a vise around my head. I dug in deeper, sucking harder as I brushed her asshole with my fingertip. Her body shuddered, the light touch against the sensitive spot sending her quickly over the edge for the second time.

I gave her a moment to catch her breath before I peeled her off me and stood. As soon as I did, her lips captured mine; the tiger inside her had been unleashed. Her tongue danced inside my mouth, intertwining with mine. She wrapped her legs around my waist, digging her pussy into my already hard and throbbing cock.

The wetness from her pussy soaked through my dress shirt, searing my flesh. I walked toward the bed, unzipping her dress and resting my palm against her back. I wanted to rip her dress off, take her fast and hard, but I knew I needed to take my time with her. This would be my only shot to have Izzy Gallo, and I wouldn't waste it. I wanted to spend all night inside her and hear her scream my name.

My first instinct kicked in as I pulled her dress down her shoulders. She released my hair, removing her arms from the small scraps of material that encased her. Holding her body with one arm, I slid my other hand up her side and cupped her breast.

Rolling her nipple between my fingers, I pulled her body closer and left no space between us. I toyed with the hoop piercing, gently tugging on her nipple to see her pain threshold.

Her breathing grew erratic as her body shuddered against mine. Biting her lip, I moaned into her mouth as I tried to keep myself upright. I had never kissed someone and felt weak-kneed, but with her, it was like my first kiss. World ending. Life altering. Completely fucked up.

She sucked the air from my lungs, capturing my moans as she rubbed her core against me. Unable to wait any longer, I reached between us and plunged my fingers back inside her. Her body sucked them in, pulsing around the length as I dragged them back out. Curling them up, I rubbed her G-spot with each lash of my digits.

Her fingers moved to my shoulders, digging into my flesh as I brought her close to coming. Claiming her mouth, stealing each other's air, and driving each other absolutely mad, I knew I was fucked.

That's the thing about sex. Touching someone for the first time is so intense that you feel like you'll never be the same. I felt that way with her in my arms and my fingers inside her. I knew I'd be changed forever. Izzy was my equal. Her wit, sass, and sexuality couldn't compare to any other woman I'd ever met. How could I go back to average when I'd had spectacular?

I removed my fingers, hearing her hiss at the loss of friction. I shrugged off my suit jacket; my body cooled, but not my need for her. I laid her down, her chest exposed and the bottom of the dress a mess as I pulled off my tie and started to open my shirt.

A small smile crept across her face as she fondled her tits.

Taking a deep breath, I tried to calm my insides as I watched her touch herself. Giving up on the slow-ass fucking buttons, I ripped my shirt open, and the buttons flew everywhere.

Fuck slow. I needed relief. I needed her.

The smile melted from her face as I stared down at her. She pulled at her nipples, her eyes raking over my chest. Moving forward, I unzipped my pants. I grabbed her ankles, yanking her to the edge of the bed. Unable to wait any longer, I pushed down my pants, letting my cock spring free.

Her eyes traveled down my body, landing on my dick. Then her eyes perked up and the corner of her mouth turned into a devilish smile.

"Impressive," she said as she cupped a breast in each hand and squeezed.

"Fuck," I hissed, realizing I didn't have a condom.

What a fucking idiot. I hadn't planned on taking her to bed, or else I would've been prepared. This hadn't been in the cards for this weekend, but I'd take the jackpot and ride the wave.

"I got it," she said as she rolled over and grabbed her purse off the floor, pulling a strip of condoms from inside.

Normally, the sight would disturb me, but not with her. "Planning on getting lucky?" I asked, staring down at her.

She laughed for a moment before her smile faded. "I'm not trashy, Jimmy. They're from the bachelorette party."

9

IZZY

I know how it looked. Like I was the type of girl who carried around a box of condoms because I never knew whom I'd be fucking from night to night. It was the furthest thing from the truth. Don't get me wrong. I'm not a prude, and I never put down any woman no matter how many partners they've had. Men can do it without being looked at with disdain, and I wanted to high-five every lady out there getting what she wants.

I had distanced myself from sleeping around. Men were a complication I didn't need or want. Flash was my standby. The one I called when I needed some cock and a quick goodbye. Lately, that in itself had turned into an issue and a fucking headache. I loved him, but as a best friend. We had passion and the sex was fantastic, but the spark wasn't there and neither were the feelings.

Flash was like my favorite teddy bear as a kid, but he ate

pussy like a pro. He was comfortable. Maybe a little too easy for me, and I'd grown complacent with just okay instead of fucking amazing. I knew I needed to make a change and kick Flash's ass to the curb, but I had to be gentle about it.

Looking up at James, I didn't see anything comfortable or easy about the man. He stared down at me with such passion and burning that I worried he'd burst into flames before my very eyes.

Sitting up, I tore one condom from the strip and threw the rest on the floor. I'd brought a bunch of them to the bachelorette party as party favors and to throw around at the girls. I'd wanted to make sure every cock was covered and that all the girls were safe. It was something I always preached.

"Must've been one hell of a party."

"Oh it was," I said before tearing open the package with my teeth.

I motioned with my finger for him to step closer, batting my eyelashes at him. I needed to taste him before I covered it. I moved, kneeling on the edge of the bed and waiting for his dick to come to eye level. The glimmer of shiny metal made my insides twist and my pussy convulse. There's something about a man with a piercing in his cock.

I grabbed his ass, bringing him closer to my face as I took in all his glory, feasting on him with my eyes. I opened wide, laying his hardness against my tongue and closing my lips around his length. The velvety firmness mixing with the saltiness made my mouth water. I swallowed around his dick, pulling it farther into my throat, and fought the urge to gag. It hit the back of my throat, cutting off my airway as my eyes watered.

Squeezing his ass, I sucked him deeper before pulling out and repeating the process. I looked up into his eyes, watching his head fall back in ecstasy. Digging my nails into his rock-hard muscles, I flicked the underside of the tip with my tongue. His body trembled beneath my fingertips and my body warmed. I felt powerful with him at my mercy.

The apadravya caressed my tongue and tapped my teeth as I worked his cock. Just as I felt him grow harder and his body shake uncontrollably, I released him, a popping noise filling the room.

His body jerked, his cock lurching forward as if it were searching for my mouth of its own volition. His teeth chattered as he sucked in air and glared at me.

I shrugged and smiled. "Sucks, doesn't it?" I said, and began to giggle.

He pushed me back before grabbing my feet and yanking me to the edge of the bed. I screamed from happiness—his strength had shocked me. I don't know why. The man was huge. He looked like a giant next to me, but I hadn't thought he could move me around like a fucking rag doll. Holding the condom up for him to take, I bit my lip. His cock was red and bulging as it bobbed in the air.

The shiny metal looked like it was ready to pop free on both sides. I couldn't wait any longer to feel it stroking my insides. He slid the rubber over his cock, paying careful attention to the piercing, while I took in the sight of him.

He had strong, broad shoulders covered in tattoos. I wanted to lean forward and get a better look, but I remained in place. If I hadn't known better or had seen a picture of him first, I would've bet money that he was airbrushed. He was too perfect, with all his rippling muscles, hard body, and flawless skin.

He caught me looking, and winked at me. My cheeks turned pink and heated. I don't know why. I was half dressed and had had his dick in my mouth and he'd tasted me. At this point, what was there to be embarrassed about?

He grabbed the bottom of my dress as I lifted my ass and let him remove it. It flew across the room, landing near the door, where we had begun. I held out my arm, looking to touch his skin, and he gripped my wrist and pulled me off the bed. Then I wrapped my legs around his body, trying not to fall to the floor, and instantly captured his lips.

He grunted, grinding his dick against my pussy as I clung to him. Reaching underneath my leg, he grabbed his dick, rubbing it back and forth twice before jamming it inside me.

I cried out, not having expected to feel so full and stretched. But then he stilled, letting my body adjust before he turned and pushed my back against the wall. The rough wallpaper scratched my skin with each thrust. I reached out, trying to grip the wall, and knocked over the lamp. The sound of glass shattering as it hit the floor didn't stop James.

The pictures on the walls rattled as he pounded into me. My tailbone felt like it was being beaten with a bat each time my body slammed up into the wall. With my back on fire, my ass in pain, and my head slamming against the wall, James pummeled me. Sweat trickled from the edge of his hairline, slowly running down his face.

Sweat and I didn't always get along. With him, I wanted to reach out and taste it. See if it had the same salty taste as his dick against my tongue. Just as I leaned forward, going for the wetness to alleviate the dryness inside my mouth, he placed his lips over mine.

Reaching between us, he flicked my clit with his fingers. It wasn't a gentle touch. There were no tentative feels to see if my body was sensitive. Each stroke felt like a slap against my pussy. My insides clamped down, the edge coming nearer as I sucked his tongue into my mouth.

His strokes became harsh and erratic, matching his breathing. I began to bounce off him, my body flying away from his from the forcefulness of his thighs. Slamming back down on his cock over and over again mingled with the flicks, sending me spiraling over the edge and screaming his name until my throat burned. My eyes rolled back in my head, my head slamming uncontrollably against the wall as my entire body went rigid.

He didn't let up his brutal assault on my pussy as I came down from an orgasm that left me dizzy. As he pummeled me over and over again, I gripped his shoulder, letting myself get lost in the moment.

He stilled, his abs clenching harder as he grunted and leaned his forehead against me. Then he sucked in a breath, his body shuddered, and he gulped for air.

"For fuck's sake," he muttered, swallowing again.

I rested my head against the wall, my entire body feeling like jelly. "Yeah," I said, not able to say anything else.

He held me there for a moment before carrying me to the bed and placing me on top of the mattress. He collapsed next to me, his chest heaving as he wiped his forehead.

"Tire you out already?" I asked as I turned to face him.

"Izzy," he said as he pushed the hair that had fallen behind my shoulder. "I'm just getting started, doll."

I rolled onto my back and stared at the ceiling. The room was spinning slightly from the amount of Jack I'd had at the reception. As I was lost in the passion and booze, he'd consumed my entire world and made everything else vanish.

My eyelids felt heavy as I lay there listening to his breathing slow. My mind was cluttered and I wanted to shut it off and drift off to sleep, but my body had other plans—and so did James. The bed dipped and sprang up as he climbed off the bed. A squeak from the shoddy mattress pulled me back to reality. I opened one eye, watching him walk over to the minibar and grab something inside.

"Want a drink?" he asked, dangling a bottle of Jack.

At this point in the night, there were two options. I could either stop drinking and fall asleep or have another and party to the point that, tomorrow, I wouldn't remember what had happened in this room.

"Yes," I said, sitting up on my elbows.

He twisted off the cap, plopped some ice cubes in a glass, and poured the amber liquid inside before handing it to me. I took shallow sips, not wanting to swallow it too quickly. The wetness on my tongue and burn down my throat helped breathe new life into me. We stared at each other, sipping our drinks stark naked. He leaned against the small bar area, while I sat on the bed with my shoulder back, giving him a full show.

Unable to take the silence, I sloshed back the rest of my drink, shaking the glass, causing the ice cubes to clink together.

A small grin spread across his face as he placed his cup on the bar and walked toward me.

"What?" I asked before I stared down into my empty glass.

"Gave me an idea," he said as he grabbed his tie off the floor. Then he removed the knot from the silk material. "Lie back."

"Why?"

"Jesus, just lie the fuck back," he growled, taking the glass from my hand and setting it on the nightstand.

The growl had been a little bit scary, but sexy as fuck. A shiver ran down my spine as I crawled up the bed backward before placing my head on the pillow.

"Give me your hands," he commanded, straddling my body.

I swallowed hard, my mouth feeling dry again as I held up my hands and offered myself to him.

"Hold them together. Clasp them."

"What are you going to do?" I asked out of pure curiosity.

"I'm tying you to the headboard, doll." He smiled, snapping the tie between his hands.

My natural reaction in this situation should have been "fuck no," but since I'd had more Jack than I could remember and James was hot as fuck, I said, "Okay," before clasping my hands together and holding them in front of him without a care.

James twisted the tie around my hands, securing it in a tight knot and drawing them over my head to the headboard. "You okay with this?" he asked, leaning over me with his dick in my face.

"Yes," I said, reaching forward with my lips to lick the tip of his cock.

He shuddered as he fastened the tie to the headboard before

grabbing a spare pillow and placing it under my head. "This should help your arms."

"It's not my arms I'm worried about." Really, I wasn't. I knew he wouldn't hurt me. Thomas would kill him, and then the rest of the Gallo men would be in line to revive him and kill him again.

He laughed, nudging my legs apart with his knees. "Wait. Something's missing," he said as he climbed off the bed. He walked to his suitcase, rifled through the contents, and returned with another tie. "For your eyes. Lift your head."

"I want to see," I said, pissed off that he wanted to take away my sight.

"It'll be better."

"I've been blindfolded before, Jimmy. I'm not a virgin."

"Did you like it?" he asked, studying my face.

"Y-yes," I stammered, hating myself the instant I said it.

"Good. Head up."

I sighed, lifting my head from the pillow and watching as he drew closer to me before darkness came.

"Comfortable?" he asked as he tied the knot around the back. "Can you see?"

"It's fine. I may fall asleep. Just warning you now," I lied with a smile.

"Impossible," he whispered against my lips, running his tongue along the seam.

I opened my mouth, trapping his tongue between my teeth. Sliding his hand down my torso, he cupped my pussy.

I smiled, still holding his tongue as his hand left my skin. Suddenly, shooting pain radiated from my core, spreading down my legs. The smack of his hand against my pussy sent shock waves through me.

Instantly, I released his tongue and shrieked, "Fuck!" as I tried to free my hands. I wanted to rub my pussy, hold it, and make the sting go away. "Asshole," I hissed.

"Doll, I'm in control. You can challenge me all you want, but I'll get my way."

I grumbled, twisting my body to change the sensation and pulsating heat between my legs. My breathing was fast from the shock of his assault. Laying his hands against my legs to hold them down, he waited for me to calm.

"Can you handle me, little girl?"

"Fuck you," I seethed. "I can handle anything you give." Being full of liquor didn't help with my ability to make rational statements or judgment calls.

I wanted to see his face. Being robbed of my vision made it impossible to read his emotions. The tone of his voice didn't betray his intentions. I hadn't expected him to smack my pussy, and without seeing his hand move, I couldn't prepare for it.

"Does it burn?" he whispered, the bed jostling as he moved.

I nodded, not able to speak without my voice trembling. The sound of something moving against the woodgrain of the nightstand made me turn to the side. I needed to be able to hear what was about to happen, especially if I couldn't see, but how I'd turned just blocked one of my ears.

I faced forward, waiting for the next sharp sting, when I heard the sound of ice against the glass. I cried out as the cold penetrated through the burn. He held the ice against me, letting tiny droplets of water drip between my legs.

The heat of the slap melted the ice, and the sting of the cold gave way to a feeling of relief. I ground my body against it, craving the coolness of the ice against me. Making tiny circles, he moved the hardness around my clit, making sure to keep it far enough away from the one place I wanted it most.

Goose bumps dotted my flesh as he slid the ice cube up the center of my body, stopping at my belly button, dipping it inside, and resting it there. Then I heard the sound of more ice before a second one touched my skin and both started the ascent toward my breasts.

My nipples were rock hard, throbbing with need, and the thought of the ice touching them had me on edge. I wanted warmth, the feel of his mouth sucking on my tit. My body shook as he circled my breasts, tightening the ring until it landed on the center. The ice instantly cooled my piercings, sending the bite deeper into my flesh.

"Your mouth," I snapped, craving the heat.

"You don't call the shots."

Water dripped down each breast, pooling in the center of my chest. My skin felt like it was on fire except for the spots he touched with the ice and the small stream running down my torso.

Suddenly, his warm tongue blazed a trail up my stomach, sucking the water that had collected on my skin. I lurched forward, trying to offer him my nipple, but he pushed me back down with his palm.

"Be still," he warned, holding me against the mattress.

I gulped, trying to find an ounce of wetness in my mouth, but came up empty. After licking a path to my left breast, he sucked it between his warm lips and drew it into his mouth. My other nipple was still being blasted by the cold, the opposite sensations causing my eyes to roll back in my head as I lay there immobile.

Once he released my left breast, he placed the ice back on my nipple and moved to my right. The sensation overwhelmed me. No longer could I tell if it was water or my own moisture dripping off my pussy.

Squirming, I needed to find something to stop the throbbing and intense need I felt. With the earth-shattering orgasm I'd had minutes ago, I hadn't thought he could have me so close to the edge that fast.

The ice, cupped in his hand, slid down my body to my core and rested against my clit. I sucked in air, the cold more than I could bear without wanting to claw his face off.

After letting the ice slip toward my center, he pushed it against my opening. As he moved his fingers inside me, the ice slid inside too, burning a path as it slid deeper. I hissed as his cold fingers pushed against the ice, filling me completely.

Water started to trickle out between his fingers as he worked them in and out. He adjusted, moving his body farther down mine and lashing at my clit with his hot tongue. I shook my head, ready to explode from the overload of hot and cold. When he added a third finger, a burn settled between my legs and he lapped at my core.

I pulled against my restraints, feeling the need to move, but it was no use. I was his prisoner as he devoured my body, sucking and finger-fucking me.

I began to chant softly, calling his name at first. As my orgasm neared and he curled his fingers inside me, I began to yell, "Yes!" and "Fuck!" over and over again. I couldn't stop pushing myself down on his hand, feeling his tongue slide across my clit. I felt my toes curl as my body grew rigid. Then I held my breath, riding out the wave of pleasure.

Behind the blindfold, my world filled with colors. Vibrant yellows, reds, and oranges danced inside my eyes as I finally gulped air.

I didn't move as he left the bed. My hands were still above my head, growing tinglier by the second. My chest heaved, the hot breath from my body skidding across the droplets of water. The rip and snap alerted me that he was putting on a condom.

He wasn't done with me yet.

Since I hadn't caught my breath, I couldn't speak before he was between my legs again, rubbing the head of his sheathed dick against my cold opening.

"So fuckin' amazing," he growled as he pushed inside.

I mumbled some bullshit even I didn't understand in my post-orgasm haze. He grabbed my legs, placing my knees over my shoulders as he rammed his dick to the hilt. His fingers pulled on my piercings, sending an aftershock from my tits to my pussy as I gripped him tight, milking his cock.

Linking my feet behind his head, I held his body to mine and pushed against his thrusts. The man was a beast. No other way to describe him. There wasn't a moment I felt in control of the situation, and for once, I liked it. Maybe it was the alcohol that had me going against everything I believed in and had allowed me to give up control so easily. I liked to think it was Jack and not James causing me to give in and become complacent.

What seemed like a lifetime passed before his rhythm slowed

and his body convulsed against me. His weight crushed me as he collapsed, drawing breath as if he couldn't get enough.

"Hands," I mumbled as I shook them, hoping to give them more blood. The prickly feeling wouldn't allow me to be comfortable.

He lifted off me, untying my hands before removing the blindfold. I blinked and squinted, the light blinding me. I closed my eyes, trying to stop the pain caused by the brightness.

"My eyes hurt," I whined.

He curled his arms around me, pulling my body tight against his. "Sleep, Izzy," he said into my ear.

The warmth and comfort of being in his arms sucked me in. Peace and sleep came to me as the darkness took me.

10

My stomach turned as I moved. It felt like someone was hammering a nail into my skull. *Tap. Tap. Boom. Tap. Tap. Boom.* I winced, trying to pry my eyes open from their sleepy state. The little construction worker inside my skull didn't relent as I looked around.

I swallowed, not recognizing the room before closing my eyes again. Where the fuck was I? Last night was a blur. I remembered the boring-ass reception line, dinner that had seemed to go on forever, and then drinks at the bar. Not just any drink, but my best friend Jack, sliding back and wrapping me up in his warmth.

I tried to smile when looking back on the evening, but everything hurt—even my cheeks. *What the fuck happened?* I slowly shook my head, trying to clear the fog that clouded my thoughts. My head fell to the side and I opened my eyes to get another look around the room.

I blinked twice, clearing the haze from my vision, and saw *him.* James. My stomach fell as I looked down his body and then to mine. We were naked, our clothes thrown around the room haphazardly. I'd fucked him. My pussy ached, the muscles in my arms burned, and my nipples throbbed at the memory of the night before.

I thought I'd dreamt being awoken from my sleep for another go, but nope, I hadn't. James was insatiable. Even while asleep, his dick was semi-hard, staring at me as a reminder of the multiple orgasms he'd brought me.

I stared at James, watching him sleep. He looked peaceful and kind and not like the man I'd met the night before. James had a sharp tongue, a commanding tone, and an air of authority about him. Everything that made me run for the hills and hide. My body liked him, though. Fuck, even my mind tried to tell me that he was a great guy.

I knew better than that. No man, especially one like James, would make me change my mind on love and relationships. He'd promised me a night with no strings attached, and that was exactly how I wanted it.

Saying goodbye was overrated. I didn't feel the need to chitchat and thank him for the amazing fuck. Once I had a good grip on the side of the bed, I slowly pulled myself up, praying that the room would stop spinning. Then I turned toward him, waiting to see how heavy a sleeper he was and if I could slink out unnoticed.

I climbed to my feet, holding my head as I collected my dress and panties from the floor. I had to pee like a motherfucker, but I couldn't risk him waking and finding me in his room.

After placing my panties in my purse, I opened my dress and stepped inside. I zipped it, keeping my eyes locked on him and holding my breath. Then I strapped on my heels, looked around the room one last time to make sure I hadn't left anything behind, and made my way toward the door. Before I turned the handle, I turned and stared at James.

He really was beautiful when he was sleeping. His rock-hard body covered in tattoos, his cock ready for more, and his beauty was enough to suck any girl in, but not me.

A wave of guilt overcame me, but I pushed it aside as I opened the door, trying to avoid waking him. As I entered the hallway, I exhaled and clicked the door closed. I swear, fucking hotels and their loud-ass doors pissed me off more than anything.

A man passed by, looking me up and down, and I felt like a tramp. Dressed in my gown from the night before, my hair a mess, and probably with makeup out of place, but fuck it. I straightened my back, standing tall as I walked to the elevator.

Pushing the elevator button, I glanced back toward his room, silently chanting, "Please don't come out," over and over again.

I couldn't calm my breath as my heart pounded inside my chest at the thought of him finding me in the hallway trying to sneak out.

When the doors opened, I ran to the back of the elevator and held the walls as if they were my lifeline. I'd made it inside without being discovered. I relaxed, almost sliding down the faux-wood walls, allowing the enormity of the situation to hit me.

I'd fucked my brother's friend. I'd fucked him more than once. I'd left without saying goodbye. Would he come after me?

Was he a man of his word? There was so much I didn't know about James.

I'd never been the type of girl to sneak out without so much as a goodbye. The night before started flashing before my eyes. Being tied to the bed, the feel of his fingers inside me, the way he'd fucked me, how he tasted—instantly, my body responded. I wanted more, but I closed my eyes and tried to cool off. There was no way in hell I'd allow myself to go there again.

I needed to forget James Caldo.

11

JAMES

My eyes flew open as I heard the click of the door closing. Reaching over, I felt the empty space that was still warm from her skin. Groaning, I rolled over and stared at the door. My first instinct was to run after her and drag her back to my room, but I fought it. It wasn't right. Izzy and I weren't meant to have more than a night together... at least not yet.

I'd have my time with her again. There was a connection that couldn't be denied, but she wasn't ready. She still had wildness to her. A rebellious attitude that felt the need to fight against the norm, and that included relationships. Izzy wanted to be the badass chick who didn't need anyone in her life, but that was the furthest thing from the truth.

Her tough shell seemed impenetrable, but I'd witnessed the small crack and peered inside. I could see the fire in her eyes, love in her heart, and the wild animal waging a battle inside. I needed to break down the walls, but timing was key. I couldn't chase after her. I was all about the chase, but not yet.

Her brother, Thomas, and I were tied together through work. We had a mission, and I couldn't do anything that may put his life in danger. Izzy would have to wait until the Sun Devils MC was removed from the equation and Thomas was free from the club.

Throwing my arm across my face, I could smell her on my skin. Inhaling deeply, memories of the night before flooded my mind. I'd never felt weak in the knees before *her*. The electricity in the air as we touched could've lit an entire house and possibly blown out a few light bulbs in the process.

If I said that it didn't sting a little that she didn't stick around to say goodbye, I'd be lying. Izzy was as affected by me as I was her, and she had to slink away before she would have to confront the feeling I invoked in her last night.

I knew I'd have her again. She couldn't escape the inevitable. The connection we felt was undeniable. I'd let her go… for now. I knew in the end she'd be mine.

A chase would ensue and I'd get exactly what I wanted—Izzy Gallo.

The end… or is it?

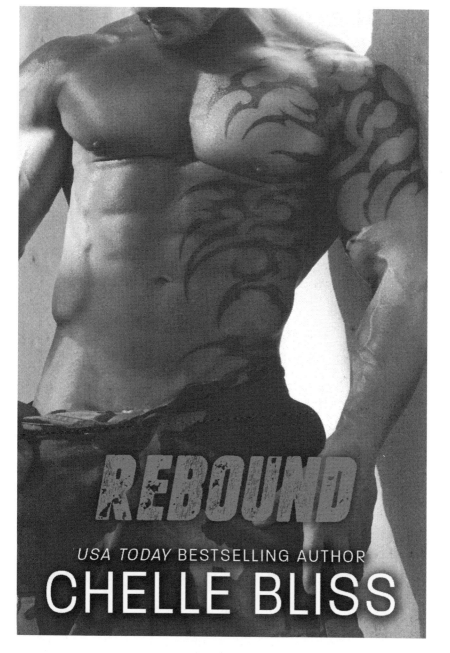

REBOUND

USA TODAY BESTSELLING AUTHOR
CHELLE BLISS

1

"Oh my God, Sam!" she cried out. "Yes!" I pounded into her. She was on all fours, fisting the sheets with her head tipped back.

"So fuckin' good," I bit out through gritted teeth. I held her by the waist, pulling her against my cock as I took the strokes deep. Her smooth skin was almost translucent under my hands. Perspiration started to collect on her flesh, glimmering in the candlelight. If my cock didn't feel so damn good inside her pussy, I would've licked a path up her spine, collecting the moisture.

"Harder," she begged.

I slowed my pace. Her short hair bounced with each thrust. I'd give her exactly what she asked for. I grabbed the strands in one hand, gathering them into a ponytail and gripping it tightly. Using it like reins, I pulled her back as I slammed into her.

"Oh!" she yelled as my dick rammed into her, leaving no

space between us. She tried to pull away, trying to crawl forward, but I didn't give her the chance. I smacked her ass with my free hand, landing it on the fleshy part of her thigh.

"Fuckkk," she hissed and her body froze.

I couldn't help but smile. Her pussy contracted, gripping my cock like a vise as the effect of the crack radiated across her skin. Without warning, I brought down my palm on the spot next to my previous strike. Again her pussy contracted as she cried out, curse words spilling from her mouth.

I held her hair tighter, pulled her back hard, and pummeled into her wetness. I couldn't keep my eyes off her body. The way her waist curved in just above her hips, creating an amazing hourglass figure, drove me crazy. Her hips were significantly larger than her waist, making the visual even more impressive.

I couldn't wipe the dumb-ass smile off my face. This isn't how I thought I'd spend the weekend in New Orleans. Instead of losing myself in a drunken stupor, I had met an amazing woman and was currently banging the hell out of her.

"You like this?" I growled, soothing her thigh after the blow.

"Yesss," she drawled, pushing her ass farther into the air as her shoulder melted into the mattress.

I hadn't felt this wanted in forever. The way she tore at my clothes and worshiped my body was astounding. I felt like a Greek god when she removed my shirt and fell to her knees, licking the ridges of my abdominal muscles. If I had any doubts about fucking her tonight, they melted away as soon as her tongue touched my flesh.

The orgasm I had been fighting since the second I slipped my dick inside her was begging to be unleashed. Unable to resist the urge, I released her hair and tipped her ass higher in the air. Needing to hit her at just the right angle to send her over the edge with me. Planting my feet on the mattress, I held on to the headboard, using my arms as well as my hips to batter her inside with my dick.

Her face was sideways, giving me a full view as her mouth fell open and her eyes squeezed shut. She sucked in a breath, holding it as I moved inside her. Each time she held the air in her lungs, I could feel her pussy bearing down on my cock, trying to shove it out. She was close and exactly where I wanted her. Adjusting my body, I grasped the headboard tighter, using my arms to pull myself forward. As her pussy contracted around my shaft, I dove in deeper, leaving no space untouched. My body hummed with pleasure. My entire being craved the orgasm. The weight of my balls and the tingling down my spine made it clear that I couldn't wait any longer.

"Oh God. Oh God," she mumbled as I slammed into her a couple more times.

Unable to hold out any longer, I gave in, letting the orgasm rip through my system. Everything in my body began to quake. As the ecstasy gripped me, my fingers began to slip, sliding down the headboard.

"Fuck," I roared, throwing my head back and pushing through the burning pain in my thighs.

With my body still trembling, I fell forward onto her back. Breathing heavily, I gulped for air, exhausted. She collapsed beneath my weight. There were no words for the way I felt after being with Fiona. Not just hanging out or fucking her but the entire experience.

"Wow," she whispered, peering up at me.

"Yeah," I replied, still lost for words. Is this where I'm supposed to say thank you? But then again, maybe she was saying "Wow" as in, "Wow, that sucked."

"You're quite the stud, Sam." She giggled and wiggled her ass against my semi-erect cock, still partially buried inside her.

The laughter burst from my lips before I could stop it. I don't think anyone had ever called me a stud while my dick was still in her. I'd admit that I was a good fuck. I took pride in it.

Getting a woman off was the ultimate turn-on. The men who didn't give a fuck and only cared about getting their rocks off always baffled me. Who the fuck would come back for seconds when you're a selfish lover?

I rolled over, taking her with me. "Fiona, it's not hard to be when you're involved." My fingertips traced circles down her arm as she nestled into my side. "You're so beautiful. God, I was turned on. I'd stay buried inside you all night if I could."

Her mouth formed an O as she blinked. "So you're a one-hit wonder?" she teased, quickly biting her lip as her body shook from laughter.

"Fuck no, I'm not! I'm not done with you yet, woman." I grabbed her shoulder, bringing her lips to mine. My breathing still hadn't returned to normal, but I wouldn't let something like that stop me.

"I was kidding," she mumbled against my lips, laughing.

"I wasn't," I replied, lifting my body above hers.

I kissed her jaw.

"Really," she said and exhaled.

Licking a trail down her neck, I stopped on her jugular and nestled my body between her legs.

"You don't have to, Sam," she mumbled as her back arched.

Sinking my teeth into her flesh, I tongued her skin between my teeth and ignored her. I watched her face as her cheeks grew pink and her mouth fell open. She wanted more, no matter what she said.

"I was kidding." Her eyes fluttered back and sealed shut.

I slid my tongue down her collarbone as I made a beeline for her nipple. It was still hard and ready. Capturing it in my mouth, I nipped it with my teeth.

"Fuck," she moaned. "It feels so damn good." Her back arched higher, pushing her breast into my mouth.

"Mmm," I mumbled against her nipple, letting the vibrations work with my mouth.

She trembled as her hands moved to my shoulders and dug in. The bite of her nails was divine, making my dick jump in reaction. Between the ways she reacted to me, the scent of her arousal, and the feel of her body, I knew I wanted more. I didn't know if I'd ever get my fill.

The need to taste her overtook my thoughts, sending me on a path down her body. Glancing up at her, I slid myself between her legs. God, she was so fucking beautiful. The paleness of her skin dancing in the light was a thing of grace. The roundness of her breasts hid her face, but the space between gave me just enough to gauge her reactions to my movements.

My mouth salivated with the scent of her arousal. Sweetness with a hint of my scent still clinging to her skin made my mouth water. I brushed my nose against her hair, taking a deep breath and getting my fill.

I stuck out my tongue, capturing her wetness on the tip. The taste was better than the smell as it spread through my mouth. A deep growl escaped my lips as I moved forward and licked her with the flat of my tongue. Using just enough to tease yet not enough to bring her sufficient pleasure to be satisfying.

"More," she demanded, thrusting herself toward my face.

Resting my hands on her thighs, I pushed down and out, holding her open and still. This was my show. She wouldn't control what happened, how hard, or where I licked. I wanted to touch her everywhere with my mouth.

I kept my licks light as she whimpered and struggled against my hands. There was no way I'd let her take charge. When she finally stopped moving, I drew her clit into my mouth and tongued it.

There was nothing more amazing than having the most sensitive spot on a woman's body inside my mouth. The feeling of power gave me a high. Staring up her body, I watched her respond to my touch. Even though I'd just fucked her like a champ, my dick grew stiff.

I was ready. Ready for more Fiona. Listening to her moan and scream my name in ecstasy was better than anything I'd ever heard. Maybe I was just drunk on pussy, overthinking everything that had happened. It felt right. Being with Fiona made me feel at peace.

There was no way in hell I'd fuck her again until I made her come against my tongue. My fingers itched to move, wanting to feel her pulse against them. I stroked her opening, feeling her legs spreading to my touch as an invitation.

Thrusting my fingers inside, I sucked her clit harder as she writhed against the mattress and bore down on my fingers. God, how I wished it were my dick inside her, feeling her from the inside, but it wasn't. My time would come. My cock's time was near.

This wasn't a sprint. I wanted a marathon. When I felt her begin to quake and her breathing grew uneven, I backed off and removed my mouth from her body

"Oh God," she moaned and pushed her pussy against my face. "Don't stop. Fuck," she hissed. She raised her head off the pillow and glared at me.

Before she had another chance to protest, I curled my fingers and brought my mouth down on her fast and hard. Her head dropped back onto the pillow as her fingers tangled in my hair. I wanted to laugh as she held my head against her pussy. I loved her greediness and knew the feeling of being denied an orgasm.

I made love to her pussy with my mouth. Luxuriating in her softness, engulfing her with the warmth of my lips. I was drunk on pussy. Drunk on her and intoxicated by her body, I relished every ounce of her wetness I swallowed.

"Yes!" she cried out, pushing my face against her almost to the point of suffocating me.

There are worse ways to go than being choked to death in the pussy of a lovely woman. When she cried out, her legs closed and trapped my head. I used my last bit of air to bring her through her orgasm without depriving her of the grand finish she deserved.

When her legs fell away and her body grew slack, I gasped for air. My brain felt light-headed as I tried to draw in breath but struggled. Watching her coming apart and feeling her body quake in my arms was worth the lack of oxygen.

I pushed myself up, still struggling to steady my breathing. "Whew," I snickered. "You almost killed me there," I huffed out, rubbing the sweat from my forehead. Sex sweat was the best kind. Fuck, it was cathartic.

She laughed, throwing her arms out to her sides. She swallowed hard and sighed. "If you would've stopped, I would've killed you."

As I crawled up her body, I laughed and shook my head. "You're an amazing woman, Fiona." It wasn't a lie. Less than twenty-four hours ago I didn't know she existed, but now I can't imagine going back to that lost soul. She was like an angel sent to bring me back to life.

"Stay with me tonight," she whispered as I hovered above her lips.

"I planned on it. I'm still not done with you." I smiled against her mouth before crushing my lips against hers.

I lost count of the number of times I made her come. Using my cock, tongue, and hands, I brought her more pleasure than any other woman in my life. Why did I care so much? I wanted her to remember me. I wanted her to want me. I didn't want to be a one-hit wonder. It was the only way I could think of to get an invitation back. This couldn't be the end for us. My future was before me, and I'd do anything to see how it turned out.

2

The Day Before...

New Orleans is a place to get lost. Blending into the endless sea of people as you wander the streets, drowning your sorrows in Hand Grenades and Hurricanes.

Sex is everywhere. Strippers shaking their asses in doorways and tourists flashing their tits to get beads from a stranger on a balcony. Scantily clad women stagger down the streets, clutching their drinks like they are a lifeline.

All I wanted to do was forget about women—actually one woman in particular. I chose New Orleans for a weekend of fun, hoping to feel alive again.

It was an epic fucking fail.

After drinking enough alcohol that I should've passed out or at least become sedated, I was coherent and pissed off. I was angrier than I had been before I sat down at the bar inside the Funky Pirate. The man sitting on stage singing his lungs out was talking about lost love. Another reminder of the girl I was trying to forget.

She wasn't just any girl.

No. No.

She was the one I had been pining for since my very first boner. I followed her around like a puppy dog my entire life. Sloppy Seconds could've been my nickname. No matter how hard I tried to forget her and move on, I always went back for more. Really I was a fucking idiot, but I could never say I didn't try. And try. And try. And try.

Izzy Gallo brought me to the brink, leading me around by the balls for years. I never wavered in my love for her, no matter how hard she tried to push me away. It's hard not to love a woman who had my heart doing backflips ever since she kissed me on the playground in middle school.

I can't blame her though. She never claimed to be mine. We were "friends with benefits," and she was never my girlfriend. I hoped for years that she'd change her mind. She never did. For the last ten years, I never opened my heart to anyone else, saving myself for her. It was all in vain.

James Caldo stole her heart. He's a prick, but she loves him. I bowed out graciously, giving up my imaginary claim to Izzy. He was in law enforcement like me, and I brought them back together through a series of unfortunate events. I owned my fuckup.

Sometimes I think I was too nice to Izzy. A pushover, some would say, although her brothers think I'm an asshole. I treated her with kid gloves, cherishing her as I put her on a pedestal my entire life. James strolled in and bossed her ass around, and she fell to her knees, pledging her love for him. Go figure. I had been doing it wrong for years. I'm done being the sweet guy, the one who chases a piece of ass. Izzy fucking wrecked me.

I had to push her out of my mind. Rid myself of everything Gallo and move the fuck on with my life. She made her choice, and it wasn't me. It was plain and simple. I wasn't the one. There wasn't a damn thing I could do about it short of killing her boyfriend and stealing the girl, but I didn't have the stomach for it.

"Hey, sweetie." The female bartender touched my hand, dragging me back to reality. "Did you want another?" she asked in a raspy voice.

"Pleaaase," I slurred, staring down at her hand where it was still connected with mine.

"Same?" Her fingers slid across my skin as she pulled them back.

Usually a move like that from a beautiful woman would have my dick taking notice, but tonight...nada. I looked up at her and couldn't even picture fucking her. Did Izzy ruin me that badly? "Yeah," I said with a smile. The answer could've been to my question about Izzy too. She did fucking ruin me.

I need to find me again. The man I am without Isabella Gallo. She'd never be mine. I'd never be hers.

There's no better place than New Orleans to find yourself again. When they say the world is your oyster, they must've been referencing this city. It's filled with life. The beauty and history are intoxicating. There's an undercurrent of something that I just can't put my finger on to describe it properly, but it's stirred something inside me.

"Is this seat taken?" a quiet voice asked as the bartender set my gin in front of me.

"No," I replied without even turning to look at her.

"Thanks," she said, setting her purse on the bar before she sat.

I took tiny sips, nursing the gin instead of giving in and downing it quickly. Gin wasn't made for slamming. It was like a woman. Put on this earth to be savored, tasted slowly, and enjoyed.

I rolled the glass in my hand, letting my fingertip glide against the smooth surface as I watched the amber liquid dance.

"Hard night?" the quiet voice asked from the stool next to me.

I sighed. I really wasn't in the mood for small talk, but I wasn't rude. Glancing out of the corner of my eye, I replied, "Tough year."

Fuck. Who was I kidding? It wasn't a year. It was my entire life. Wasted on Izzy.

"I know the feeling." Her body shifted, moving closer to me. "Want to talk about it?"

"Not really." I didn't feel like sharing my problems with a stranger and especially not with a woman. I wanted to forget and pretend that period in my life never happened.

"I didn't mean to intrude."

I looked at her for the first time, feeling like an asshole. "I'm sorry. That was a total dick move. I didn't mean to be rude."

"No. I understand." She had a slight smile on her face as she spoke. "I didn't mean to pry." She fidgeted with her hands as she diverted her eyes from mine, focusing on her fingers.

"Listen. Let me buy you a drink to make it up to you." I turned to face her. She looked very different than Izzy. Pale skin, blond hair, blue eyes, along with freckles scattered across her flesh like a connect the dots puzzle. Her hair was straight, ending at her jaw in a severe line.

"You don't have to do that." Her legs rubbed together as she shifted in her seat. "I was being nosy and I shouldn't have been."

"I insist. It's the least I can do after being a dick." Raising my hand, I waved over the bartender. "The lady would like a—"

Her eyes finally met mine. "Whiskey sour, please." A grin spread across her face. It was faint but visible.

I placed a ten on the bar as the bartender made the drink, but I kept my eyes on the woman to my side. "What's your name, doll?"

"Doll?" Her sparkling blue eyes shot up.

"You look like a doll. It's the first thing I could think of since I don't have your name."

"How do I look like a doll?" She grabbed the drink as the bartender set it down and gave it her full attention.

Oh boy. I could see she wasn't exactly happy about the nickname. I thought a moment before speaking, choosing my words very carefully. "Your skin is luminous. It glows even under these shitty lights. When I look at you, I think of a porcelain doll. God, that sounded like such a load of shit, but I meant it. You're stunning." My eyes dropped to her mouth and I stared, captivated by her red lips.

Pink flooded her cheeks as she played with the red straw in her mouth. Twirling it with her tongue. "My name is Fiona."

"Fiona," I repeated. It was a great name and one that fit her. "I like it."

"Thanks."

"So what's your story, Fiona? What are you doing in here alone on a Saturday night?" Holding my glass to my lips, I watched her over the rim.

Her shoulders sagged a bit as she sipped the whiskey. "It's a boring story. You really don't want to hear about it."

"I doubt anything about you could be boring. Tell me who Fiona is." I set my drink on the bar, giving her my full attention.

"What do you want to know?" She repeated my actions, placing her drink on the bar and swiveling around on her stool.

"Let's start with something simple. What do you do for a living?"

"I'm a nurse," she replied as she straightened her back.

"It's an admirable profession." An image of her in a naughty nurse outfit popped into my mind. A few buttons left open, showing off her amazing rack. The skirt too short, showing just enough thigh to drive a man wild.

"It's interesting, that much is for sure." A genuine smile spread across her face, almost touching her eyes. "What do you do? Sorry, I never got your name."

"It's Sam, and I'm in law enforcement." I didn't want to mention the FBI. It either wigged people out or they were filled with questions. There were two things I didn't want to talk about tonight: work and Izzy Gallo. It dawned on me in that moment that I hadn't thought about Izzy since I'd given my attention entirely to Fiona.

"Sounds dangerous. I've always loved a man in uniform." She smirked, and I swear to god my cock twitched.

"It has its moments, but there's a lot of downtime and paper-work." *Do not think of her sexually.* The last thing I needed right now was another woman in my life. "Do you live here?"

She rubbed her thighs together, and my eyes instantly caught the motion, watching them move back and forth. "Yeah, I went to college here and never left. I fell in love with the city and couldn't imagine living anywhere else. You?" She must've caught me staring because she placed her hands on her legs and rubbed her thighs back and forth.

I cleared my throat, trying to break the hold she had over me. The fact that she had on a skirt that rested around mid-thigh had me wishing for a peek of her underwear. "No, I live in Florida. I'm just visiting for a couple days."

"Work or pleasure?" The smirk was still plastered on her face. Maybe she liked me looking. The one thing I knew was that she didn't do anything to stop me.

"Pleasure." I grabbed my drink off the bar, giving my attention to something other than her lush thighs. I tried not to wonder what it would feel like for my hands to caress her skin or how she would react if I sank my teeth into her inner thigh. Would she call out my name or shudder in my arms?

"There's plenty of that around here. You don't have to look too hard." As she turned on her stool to face the bar, her skirt rode up, showing even more leg than I'd seen before.

Fuck, her legs were killer. If we stood, she would have to be almost as tall as me, especially with the heels she had on. The hint of red from underneath told me they were pricey. The name of the designer escaped me, but I knew enough about girl shit to know they were top-notch. "I'm finding that. What do you like to do for pleasure?" Licking my lips, I watched her eyes following my tongue as her lips parted. *Interesting.*

"That's a loaded question, Sam," Fiona said, almost purring my name.

"Humor me," I stated, gripping my glass a little tighter to stop myself from touching her. I wanted to reach out, wrap my hand around the back of her neck, and pull her lips to mine. The need was overwhelming and unexpected.

"I'm not usually a barfly. I prefer to enjoy the other things the city has to offer."

"Which would be?" I wondered if the whiskey would be sweeter if I tasted it from her lips.

"The history only New Orleans can claim. There's a darkness here that sucks you in. A beauty in the blackness and melancholy that no city can rival."

"You make New Orleans sound full of gloom and doom."

"No. I don't mean it that way. In New Orleans, there's an energy that becomes part of you."

"You still haven't told me what you like to do for pleasure," I stated, releasing my gin to rub my lips. I needed to do something to distract myself from the sinful thoughts I was having about Fiona.

"I like to walk around the city and soak in the energy."

I studied her, wondering what she meant by that statement. After a moment, I gave up. Figuring out the female mind had always baffled me. I wasn't going to gain some great insight today. "That's a different answer than I was expecting."

"You just haven't seen the city through my eyes."

I nodded, knowing she was right.

"What did you think I'd say?" she asked, turning her body in my direction as she grasped her drink.

"I don't know. Not that though."

She started twirling the damn straw in her mouth again, and all I could do was stare at her tongue. Watching it move was hypnotizing. "How about you buy me a couple more drinks, and I'll show you what I mean?" She smiled around the straw. The blue in her eyes caught the light from behind the bar and twinkled. Honest to God twinkled. I shit you not.

My body came to life at the thought of seeing the town with Fiona by my side. It had been ages since I'd walked around with a woman and enjoyed an evening. "You have yourself a deal, Fiona." I smiled, feeling hopeful for the first time in longer than I could remember.

Maybe my weekend wouldn't be about getting lost, but about finding myself again.

A fter I bought Fiona two more whiskey sours, we headed out of the Funky Pirate and onto Bourbon Street. It was after midnight, and I'd lost track of time while we sat at the bar, talking about life.

We each shared our stories, although truncated for humiliation's sake. She had recently become divorced after finding her husband of three years cheating on her with his secretary.

I couldn't image what the fuck the man was thinking. Fiona was stunning. She had a good job, killer body, and the face of an angel. What did she lack that made him look to someone else? If I had a woman like Fiona, there's no way in hell I'd ever stray. Shit. Even as Izzy strung me along for years, I rarely indulged in sex with other women. We weren't even in a relationship, and that shit ate me alive. How could someone do that to the person they vowed before God to love for better or for worse?

Most guys I knew were assholes. Spending months inside a

motorcycle club can fuck with your ideas of what normal and right are, but I knew that cheating wasn't in me. I wasn't built that way. As a child, it was ingrained in me to be faithful. Loyalty was important in my family. Joining the FBI was driven by that virtue. Loyalty to my country, dedicating my life to the service of the betterment of society was my main goal.

"Which way do you want to go?" she asked as we stood on the crowded sidewalk illuminated by the green lighting of the Funky Pirate. She intertwined her arm with mine, holding my forearm.

During our time at the bar, talking had turned into tiny touches. Small ones at first as our fingers found each other on the bar. As we drank and drank, the small grazes turned into full-on touches. When she laughed, she'd lay her hand on my arm. As she told me something personal, she'd lean in and place her hand on my leg. I tried to keep my hands to myself, trying not to scare her away. I didn't touch her legs, but I kept my hands to her hands or arms.

Looking both ways down Bourbon Street, all I could see were people. Masses of them filled the street. I don't think I'd ever seen so many people in one place before tonight. "You choose. I'm putting myself in your capable hands." I smiled down at her as she peered up at me. There were only a couple inches of height difference between us now, but if she kicked off her heels, I'd tower over her.

"Let's start in Jackson Square." She pointed to the right before pulling me with her as she began to walk.

"What's there?" I asked, trying to avoid knocking people over. We moved shoulder to shoulder with the other partygoers.

Even though we were tipsy, many of them were truly shit-faced and almost falling over as they stumbled down the street.

Music filled the streets as we walked past the bars, finally making it to Orleans Avenue. As soon as we turned the corner, the steeple of a church came into view. "What's that?" I asked as I took in the beauty of it lit up in all its glory. It was a one-eighty to the depravity on Bourbon Street.

"That's Saint Louis Cathedral in Jackson Square."

"It's stunning. I don't think I've ever seen it." Even though it was my second time in New Orleans, I'd never stumbled upon the church. Most of my time had been spent in the casino or on Bourbon Street getting shit-faced with the other tourists.

"Wait until you see the back of the church." Her grip tightened on my arm, her heels clicking against the sidewalk as we walked down the quiet street.

It's amazing how the sound of Bourbon dies as you drift away. After forty feet, the street grew hushed with just a few people wandering toward their destinations. We walked arm in arm, moving closer to the light of the church. As we approached Royal Street, the back came into full view.

I stopped dead in my tracks, entranced by the sight before me. Fiona walked one step before I caught her by the arm, dragging her back. "Wow," I whispered.

"It's pretty amazing, isn't it?" She looked at me for a moment before taking in the sight in front of us.

"It's unexpected." Standing before us was a giant statue of Jesus surround by white lights. The shadow of the figure was cast against the back wall of the church. It was as if Jesus was calling out, saying a prayer for the sinner before him. Extending his arms to reach the crowd on Bourbon Street. They probably needed the prayers the most. I started to laugh. The hilarity of the situation wasn't lost on me and I looked down at her.

"What's so funny?" she asked, looking up at me with her eyebrows knitted together as they formed a V.

"It looks like he's praying for the lost souls on Bourbon." Sliding my hand into hers, I gripped her hand, giving it a quick squeeze. "Don't you see it?"

She smiled, her forehead relaxing as a smile spread across her face. "I never thought about it that way. Maybe he is." She shrugged, resting her head on my arm as I looked back at the statue.

"Show me more, Fiona." I moved the hairs the wind had blown onto her face away from her eyes. "Show me the beauty you see in this great city."

"Gladly," she replied, moving her face into my touch. "Let's go to the square and people watch a little. It's one of the most interesting places in NOLA."

As she began to walk, she tripped, starting to fall forward. I moved quickly, grabbing her by the arms and pulling her upright. Her breath caught and her eyes widened when she looked at my face. Our lips were centimeters from each other. I could smell the whiskey on her lips as I inhaled.

I lingered, not wanting to move as her face softened. She opened her mouth, ready to say something, but I didn't give her the chance. The woman had intoxicated me more than the drinks. I couldn't go any longer without a taste.

As I held her in my arms, staring into her eyes, I placed my lips on hers, softly at first. Honestly, I wanted to make sure I wasn't going to be kicked in the balls for kissing her. Her actions throughout the evening said she wanted me, but I didn't want to be brought to my knees by her in the middle of New Orleans.

Her lips tasted of sweetened whiskey just like I imagined. I swiped my tongue across them as I kissed her. My touch was tentative to start, but with each second that passed, my need for her increased. I pulled her to my chest, crushing my lips against hers and devouring her mouth.

Her kiss stirred something inside me. It wasn't just my cock that was calling out to her, but something deeper. The only sound was of her breath as I kissed her with more passion than I had ever kissed another woman. I pulled her closer to me, and her chest rubbed against mine while our tongues tangled together.

She was an amazing fucking kisser. Not too much tongue, just the right amount of lip, and she wasn't trying to eat my face off. I pulled away, resting my forehead against hers. I was as winded as if I'd run a mile, but I hadn't. The sheer pleasure of kissing her had me struggling for air.

"I'm sorry," I whispered.

"I'm not." She looked up at me, her face hidden in the shadows.

I placed a kiss against her forehead, releasing my grip on her back slightly. When she straightened, she gained her footing again. Her blinks were slow and she smiled at me. Maybe she was in a trance like myself. "Let's go. I know exactly where I'm taking you next."

"Where?" I asked, being pulled me forward with my hand.

"There's an old woman in the square. You have to meet her."

She turned around, giving me a quick smile. The way her face lit up when she spoke made me feel warm inside.

Seeing her happy was different than how I had met her. We were both down in the dumps, looking to drown our night in the bottom of a liquor bottle. The night was now shaping up to be so much more than I ever imagined. "An old woman?" We walked on the side of the church, heading toward the square.

"You'll see," she said, keeping her eyes forward as she laughed. The sound of it gave me butterflies and hope for what would come next.

"This should be interesting," I mumbled. A genuine chuckle burst out of me.

"It'll be enlightening."

It wasn't what I expected. In my mind, I had seen a space filled with people, brightly lit, and teeming with life. I had been dead wrong. There were maybe twenty people walking through the square. It was hard to scc much of anything as I looked around. Directly in front of us there was a park surrounded by tall, black wrought-iron fencing. A few tables were set up near the front of the church where the light was the brightest. It was quiet as people spoke in whispers and hushed tones.

"This is the square?" I asked, totally unimpressed.

"Well, yeah. During the day, it's full of life. Artists set up around the square, hanging their artwork on the fence. People sit on the steps of the church and sip their coffees and watch the city go by."

"And the old woman?" I asked, looking around and zeroing in on an old woman sitting at table with a sign that said "Fortune Teller." I never believed in someone being able to tell me what was going to happen in the future. It was a clever way to swindle someone for twenty dollars.

"Right there," she replied, pointing to the gypsy woman sitting at the table I had spotted.

"Really? A fortune-teller?" I looked down at her.

She smiled as she bit her lip. "You have to sit with her and hear what she has to say. She's amazing."

"They always know exactly what to say to make you think they know. They're scam artists, Fiona."

She squinted, the smile on her face transforming into a grin. "Humor me, please."

"If you give me another kiss, I'll let her tell me my future." I thought it was an even exchange. At least I'd have something to look forward to while I listened to her drone on with a pack of lies.

"You got it, Sam. Now?" she asked, standing on her tiptoes as she moved her lips toward mine.

"No," I said, holding her by the arms. "Afterward. If it's horrible, you'll owe me more." I smiled, hoping she'd agree. I wanted more than a kiss. Being able to feel her body against mine sent goose bumps across my skin.

"That's fair. I'll wait here."

"What?" I asked before my mouth fell open. "You have to come with me."

"Oh no. No one else can know your fortune. I'll wait here on the bench where you can see me and I can see you."

I pulled her face to mine, letting my lips linger over hers. "You owe me big-time for this, Fiona."

"You wanted the New Orleans experience. Voodoo and magic are part of the charm. She just may surprise you, Sam."

"Big," I repeated, brushing my lips against hers before I released her. "This'll be quick."

"Okay," she whispered, holding on to my hand as our fingertips touched until our bodies were too far apart and our connection was broken.

I walked slowly. Dreading the next five minutes of my life. Listening to an old woman as she hustled me would be agony as I stared at her. Before I approached the table, I turned around, giving Fiona a quick glance. She gave me the thumbs-up with a giant smile on her face. Why did I think I was being set up?

4

"That'll be fifty dollars, sir," the old woman said with a smile.

"What?" I asked, looking at her with the most confused look. I thought I heard her wrong. When did the price of a few words skyrocket? Growing up I'd see fortune-tellers at the carnivals and never did I see a sign that read fifty dollars. Fiona better give me more than a kiss for the price of this bullshit.

I looked over the old woman's head and glared at Fiona. She tipped her head back, bursting into laughter. I could see her body shaking as her smile grew wider. Even though I couldn't hear her giddiness, I could see it. She was pleased with herself.

"A reading is fifty dollars," the woman repeated.

I shook my head, reaching in my back pocket for my wallet. "Here," I said on a sigh, kissing that fifty goodbye for no good reason.

Instantly, I pushed that thought from my mind. There was a good reason. Kissing Fiona was the reason. I'd do more to touch her lips again. To feel the warmth of her against me and the sweet smell of her breath as it cascaded across my face.

"Give me your hands," she asked, placing her palms up as she waited for me to comply.

I rubbed my palms against my jeans before setting them against hers. She flipped them over in her tiny hands and moved in closer. The table had a couple candles scattered about to help give extra light. I didn't see a need for the additional illumination. It wasn't like she was really seeing someone in my palms. I looked at them enough in my life and they never said a fucking word.

"Ah, I see," she mumbled, tracing the long line that hugged the ball of my thumb. "This is your life line. It's very long, longer than most I've seen."

"Okay," I replied, unsure of what else to say.

"You're going to live to be a very old man."

"Lucky me," I muttered as I tried not to fidget in my chair. The entire situation made me feel uncomfortable. I don't know if it was being swindled out of the money or the lies she was trying to sell me.

"I can tell that you've had your heart broken."

I wanted to interrupt her because, really, who hasn't had their heart broken at some point in their life? Most of us meander through our days, mending a broken heart, and looking for someone or something to give us hope for the future. If there was a person on this planet who had gone through life without heartache, they were the luckiest person in the world.

"What else can you see?" I asked, waiting to hear what fantastic bullshit she'd weave. I glanced at Fiona. She sat on the bench with her legs crossed. Her elbow was on her knee as she rested her chin in her hand. She watched us with a grin on her face. When I caught her eye, the corner of her mouth turned up a little more. She raised her eyebrows, giving them a quick wiggle.

The woman traced my love line, stopping at specific points. "It was recent and crushing," she replied, rubbing a small circle in the center of my palm. "The love was long and deep, but it ended suddenly."

I swallowed hard, taking in her words and how close they were to being accurate. It had been hours since I'd thought about Izzy. Spending time with Fiona, I didn't have the time or the urge to think about her. Fiona did that. Wiped Izzy from my mind and replaced her with laughter and happiness.

"She will not be your only love," the fortune-teller interrupted my thoughts. "Someone else will enter your life. Open yourself. Love is close by," she whispered.

My stomach dropped as my eyes flickered to Fiona. She hadn't moved. Her smile had disappeared, but her eyes stayed locked on me.

"How close?" I asked, buying into her words. Maybe it was the magic of the evening and spending time with Fiona. I knew she probably repeated the words to dozens of people every day, barely varying from her script.

"You must open your heart for you to accept what is right in front of you."

Could she... Did she know? There's a possibility that she saw us as we entered the square hand-in-hand. Her back was to us, but she could have caught a glimpse as I pulled Fiona into my arms.

"I see a change in careers coming too. Your job is no longer fulfilling, and a major shift will happen."

"What type of change?" I asked without thinking. I went from being cynical to asking her to explain her answer. Almost hanging on her words, I could feel myself buying into her statements.

If I had sat in this chair hours earlier, before Fiona sat down on the barstool next to me, I wouldn't have believed a word. But with Fiona waiting across the square from me with so many possibilities on the horizon, I felt myself wanting to believe.

"You need to break free from your past entirely. Starting over in a new city with a job that gives you pride. Something that will bring you peace…"

I sat there, letting the old woman's words sink in as I stared at Fiona. Was this my chance at happiness? Did fate step in and put Fiona at my side tonight? I had never believed in fate or some grand plan, but tonight I questioned everything.

I didn't feel there was anything back home for me. Izzy was the one person who kept me coming back for more, but now there was nothing. No reason to stay in Florida, or near Tampa, for that matter. I could go anywhere.

I didn't pay attention to the rest of her reading. I was too lost in her previous statements. Izzy was my past, and I needed to move toward my future. Shit happens all the time. How I move beyond it is what makes the man.

My future was in front of me.

"Do you have anything else you'd like to know, child?"

I blinked, sucking in a breath. "Um, have I met my future?" I didn't know what else to ask. The simple fact that she had worked her way inside my brain and made me believe was shocking and a little disturbing. What the fuck was I doing asking her a question when I didn't want to buy into her words?

"It sits before you, ready to be taken. The real question is, are you willing to open your heart and move beyond your past? If the answer is no, your future will escape you." She gave me a smile minus a few teeth.

I didn't move or respond. Staring across the square, I looked at Fiona. Was she my future? I know what you're thinking. I thought the same thing. There's no way I could have these thoughts only a few hours after meeting someone. I don't know if it was the old woman or Fiona who worked her way into my thoughts and made me doubt my heart.

Fiona seemed relaxed and carefree. There was a kindness to her. A side much like my own, caring and warm. I was drawn to her. It was something I hadn't felt from another person in years. Wanted. It's something we all want to feel. For once, I had it. Maybe I was reading her body language wrong or I had mistaken her kindness for a tourist for more than it really was, but I felt something there.

I wasn't about to fall to my knees and profess my love, but I wanted to spend more time with her. I didn't want to spend the weekend in the bars, wallowing in my sorrows and drowning them at the bottom of a liquor bottle. I wanted to explore this city, get to know Fiona, and see if I was crazy or not. Love at first sight wasn't something I bought into. But lust at first sight? Sure, why the fuck not?

"Thank you," I said as I stood from the chair.

"You're welcome, child." She gave me a quick nod of her head and waved.

As I walked toward Fiona, she stood and gave me a small smile. Clutching her hands in front of her, she bounced on her feet, rocking back and forth. "So what did you think?" she asked as I approached.

I shook my head, unable to stop the smile that crept across my face. "It was interesting."

"Does that mean you believed her?" Her eyes grew wide as her smile grew larger.

I shrugged. "I don't know what I believe." It was the truth too. Maybe I'd had more to drink than I thought.

"When I'm feeling down, I always go see her. For some reason, she makes me feel better. She gives me hope. Even if she's full of crap at least I walk away with a new outlook on life."

"So you think she's full of shit?" I arched an eyebrow, wondering if two people had just duped me.

She shook her head as she reached out and touched my arms. "No, I don't think it's all nonsense. Lately, her readings have given me more hope. She's typically pretty close to the truth."

I set my hands on her waist, pulling her closer to me. "Did she warn you about your heartbreak?" It was a shitty question to ask. Bringing up the reason she was so sad when I met her tonight. But it was valid.

"She did. It was the one thing she told me that I never bought into." Her eyes dropped to the ground. "I was madly in love with my husband and thought he felt the same. I didn't allow myself to believe what she said about the relationship coming to an end due to betrayal." Her shoulders sagged.

"Hey." I touched her chin and forced her eyes to meet my gaze, "I didn't need a fortune-teller to tell me how my heart would be broken. I knew it would happen, but I refused to believe it. Sometimes our hearts don't allow us to believe what our mind already knows." I moved forward, placing my lips on her forehead.

She wrapped her arms around my waist. "This is the first night in a long time I've felt like myself again. I don't want to talk about sad things. I want to enjoy the city and the man in front of me," she said as she peered up at me. "I don't want to waste another minute of my life being sad, Sam."

"Well, then," I replied, moving my lips closer to hers, "I think you owe me something, as per our agreement."

"I do," she whispered against my mouth as her eyes fluttered closed.

Without wasting another second, I kissed her as I cradled her face in my hands. I inhaled her whiskey-laced breath and the city fell away, growing quiet as we connected. I brushed my thumb across her jaw, feeling her body shudder against me.

The way she responded to my touch was mind-blowing. Never in my life had I had someone react to me as she did.

I wanted her. More than I could remember wanting someone in my whole life. I never believed in love at first sight. I always thought Izzy was my soul mate, destined to be with me for my entire life. But in that moment, as I kissed Fiona, something shifted inside me.

Maybe it was the crazy old woman filling my head with

nonsense, but I felt connected to Fiona. Like I was destined to be with her.

There was a high probability that the alcohol was impairing my judgment, but I didn't want to believe that was true.

After I released her lips, I rested my forehead against hers. "We need to keep moving or I won't be able to stop myself," I said through gritted teeth. My rock-hard cock made wearing pants almost unbearable. If I kissed her again, I wouldn't be able to control what happened next. The mix of alcohol and horniness wouldn't help me maintain my composure.

"From what?" she whispered as she stared into my eyes.

"I want you so bad. If I kiss you again, I won't be able to stop myself from wanting to fuck you tonight." I closed my eyes, trying not to visualize the act.

"I may want that."

My eyes flew open and saw the grin pulling at her lips. "Not tonight." I didn't want a one-night stand. What the fuck would I do the rest of the weekend? I'd be stuck in New Orleans for the next however many hours with nothing to do. I wanted to fill my weekend with her.

Sadness filled her eyes as they flickered toward the ground. "Hey," I said, using my fingers to lift her chin, "I want you more than anything right now. I just want to give you a reason to see me again tomorrow."

"Oh." Her magnificent smile returned and then vanished. "I have to work tomorrow. Shit."

Damn. I wasn't ready for it all to slip away. "After work?" I asked, hoping she wasn't just making an excuse.

"I work twelve to twelve, though." She sighed, leaning against me as she rested her hands against my chest.

"You get off at midnight?" I asked, feeling hopeful. I didn't care what time it was. I'd sleep all damn day if it meant I'd get to spend my night with her.

"I'm hoping." She laughed, digging her fingers into my pecs. "So muscular," she whispered, squeezing my chest.

"I'm big all over," I bragged. What a fucking idiot. That was definitely the liquor talking. I knew I could back that shit up, but it wasn't sexy to brag.

"You're too much, Sam, but I hope to find out." She smiled, her eyes looking into mine. "Walk me home?" she asked, raising an eyebrow.

"I'd love to, Fiona."

"You can stay the night if you want." Her other eyebrow joined the first, giving me a look of hopefulness.

"You need to sleep for work, and I need more than a few hours to worship your body."

She smacked my chest and laughed. "You're such a shit-talker."

"It's not shit when I've got the goods to back it up." I smiled down at her and grabbed the back of her neck. Holding her in my grip, I wiped the smile from my face. Bringing her lips to mine, I said, "I plan to take my time when I fuck you."

Fiona sucked in a quick breath as her hands stilled on my chest. "How is it possible?"

The question made me want to laugh, but I kept it in check. "Well, first I'm going to touch every inch of your body using my mouth and—"

"Stop," she pleaded. "That's not what I meant, Romeo." She giggled.

It was my turn to act surprised. "No?" I grinned, wishing we could stay in that moment forever.

She rested her forehead against my chin as her fingers started to rub my pecs. "I'm wondering if I'm truly here or if I'm passed out at home dreaming this."

"I'm real, sweetheart." I gripped her ass, pressing her against my body. "Does this feel like a dream?" My stiff cock should be enough affirmation that it was, in fact, very real.

"That feels real. Let me get a better feel though to be sure." She wiggled her lower half, rubbing against my pants and making the throbbing that much worse. "Yeah, huh," she whispered. "Sure as hell is for real."

I tossed my head back, laughing at her words. "You're just as wicked as I am, Fiona."

"You're the one who made it sexual, Sam. I wasn't even thinking that when I asked about this." She motioned between us with her hands.

"I know, but it was fun. Let's get you home so you're not asking yourself that question and regretting the entire evening."

She intertwined her fingers with mine and pulled me forward. "Not possible."

"All things are possible," I replied, following her away from the square.

The entire walk to her place was filled with flirtatious double-talk. The conversation flowed easily and never died. It was rare to find someone who made me feel completely comfortable with being myself. I didn't want the evening to end. I tried to tell myself "good things come to those who wait" as we approached her door.

"This is me," she said, glancing at the address above the door.

718 Saint Philip. I repeated in it my head, writing it on my memory. "Until tomorrow," I said, wrapping my arms around her body before I kissed her.

Her breathing changed as I pressed my lips against hers. She panted, moaning into my mouth as she fisted my hair in her hands. Listening to the sounds she made almost pushed me over the edge. If I didn't stop, I wouldn't be able to. This wasn't the moment to fuck her. No. I'd be back for more.

I nipped at her lips, finally removing mine from her mouth. "Fuck," I groaned, feeling my restraint slipping.

"I know," she agreed in a breathy tone, pressing her tits against me.

I grabbed her arms, holding her body away from mine. "We gotta stop," I said through gritted teeth. I knew what I said was right, but it was the last fucking thing I wanted to do. The only way to make myself feel better would be to bury myself inside her and not come up for air until my flight took off.

"Tomorrow," she whispered, peering up at me.

I looked down at her and nodded. Her entire face smiled. The corners of her mouth almost kissed her eyes. "Yeah. Give me your phone." She reached in her small purse and handed it to me without hesitation. I put in my number, saving myself as a contact. I hit send and waited for my phone to vibrate before hanging up. "I got ya now." I winked at her, turning off her screen before I handed it back to her.

She stared at the ground, kicking her feet against the sidewalk as she slipped the phone back into her purse and pulled out her keys. "Is this it?"

"For now, Fiona. I'll see you tomorrow night." I kissed her gently on the lips, holding her face in my palm.

"Promise you'll be there?" she asked against my lips.

I smiled, wishing I could explain how I felt about her without sounding like an absolute lunatic. "I promise."

She kissed me back, swaying a bit as she grabbed my arm. When she stopped, she glanced up at me. With a smile on her face, she said, "I don't know if I'm tipsy or just exhausted."

"Probably a little bit of both. I know I'm drunk on you." I swiped my thumb across her jaw, relishing the softness of her skin. God, I sounded like a cheesy asshole. Could I be any more of a tool?

"You're such a flirt, Sam. I'll hold you to your promise."

"And I'll get my payback you promised me for talking to the fortune-teller."

She blushed. Even in the virtual pitch-darkness, I could see the pink creep into her cheeks. "I thought maybe you forgot."

"A promise like that is unforgettable. I'll collect tomorrow." I dragged my hand down her jaw, touching her neck before I released her.

"Night." She waved before unlocking the door.

I gave her a goofy smile, feeling happier than I had in a long time. "Night, Fiona. See you tomorrow." I waited for her to enter the house and close the door before I started to walk away.

I fist pumped the air and whisper-yelled, "Yes!" as I headed back toward the action on Bourbon Street. I hope she hadn't watched me through the window, but the thought didn't occur to me until after.

Tomorrow felt promising. No longer did I feel like I was gliding through life, only trying to make it to the next day. I had a reason to be excited for tomorrow. Fiona, the golden-haired girl with eyes as blue as the Caribbean Sea on a sunny day. Her lips breathed new life into me.

There was a possibility that New Orleans wasn't just a place where people came to get lost and stay that way.

Maybe, just maybe, it was a place where someone could be found.

5

Throughout the day, Fiona and I texted as I enjoyed my time in the city. We learned a little about each other, or at least as much as either of us was willing to share. I learned that she was an only child. This little fact was refreshing to me. Izzy, the girl who crushed my heart, or at least I had thought so, had four brothers. Every single one of them hated me. Maybe not her brother Thomas, he and I had worked together and seemed to get along. But the rest—they were happy I was out of the picture.

I added multiple brothers to the list of things to steer clear of in a future mate. That was in addition to crazy, a drug addict, and crazy. Really, most women are perfection, but crazy wasn't my thing. They're fun to fuck, but not to spend time with in any way, especially as a girlfriend.

My job with the FBI didn't go well with crazy either. Everyone in my life had to go through a thorough background check. Sometimes I thought it was a pain in the ass, but in all actuality, it saved me a lot of hassle.

More and more, as the days passed by, I realized I no longer wanted to be part of the Bureau. It had lost its sparkle. Maybe it was the last undercover assignment I had, but it didn't make me happy anymore.

As I sat in the backseat of the taxi, I sent Fiona a text. I told her I'd pick her up at work, but a hospital is massive. She could be anywhere.

Me: Where do you want me to meet you?

I stared out the window of the taxi, watching the city pass by as I waited for her reply. The outskirts of New Orleans were like any other place on earth. The romanticism of the French Quarter disappeared quickly as you moved out into the city. Restaurants and bars fill the urban landscape, some new and some old. The mix of cultures created a unique city that offered something for everyone.

Fiona: Near the ER. Be there about 12:15

Me: Take your time.

I checked the time, seeing that it was only quarter to midnight. I was early, but I knew it was better than being late. The last thing I'd want her to think is that I didn't care. Tomorrow night I'd be at home, back in Florida and bored. Tonight, I'd be with Fiona, and there was no fucking way in hell I'd be late.

After handing the cab driver a twenty following the short drive, I strolled through the entrance of the ER. I didn't want to wander around looking for her; I figured she'd find me.

Not even ten minutes later she walked through the doors to

the waiting room. She had on her nursing uniform, and I was oddly disappointed. I wanted it to look more like a naughty nurse costume women wore at Halloween. Instead, it was a pink pantsuit thing and didn't fit the fantasy I used last night to jack off.

Her head turned from side to side as she scanned the waiting room, looking for me. I waited, watching her as she surveyed the room. A giant smile spread across her face as our eyes locked. She curled her finger, calling me to her.

Without hesitation, I sauntered in her direction, trying to keep my composure. Inside my body, everything danced, feeling the happiness and excitement as it coursed through my system.

"Hey," she said with a grin on her face. "You came."

I shot her my best cocky grin and a slow blink to go with it. God, the shit she said made it so easy to be dirty. "That's the plan."

She slapped me on the shoulder before placing her hand over her mouth to cover her laugh. "Dirty."

"You look stunning," I said, touching her cheek. My fingers itched to touch her. My lips ached to kiss her, but I couldn't. There were too many people around, and it was still her place of employment.

"Thanks." Her cheeks turned a rosy shade of pink, almost matching her outfit. "You ready to go?"

"Yes. You lead the way and I'll follow."

"Just have to grab my things in the break room." She swiped her card through the security system, unlocking the door into the ER.

I followed her through the doors, keeping up with her fast

pace. "I'm just along for the ride." Fuck, really? I didn't mean for it to come out dirty, but something told me she'd take it that way.

She stopped dead and turned to face me. "Do you always have sex on your mind?" she asked as the smile tugged at her lips.

"No. I could ask the same thing of you. I didn't mean it that way, but you took it that way. Who's the dirty one here?" I arched an eyebrow, throwing down the challenge.

She smiled before turning around and continuing down the hallway. "Point taken."

Crisis averted. I didn't want to be the creepy guy who only thought with his cock. I mean, I wasn't that guy right now. Tugging on it last night wasn't the same. It didn't dull the ache I had for her. It was a momentary Band-Aid that had been ripped off the moment I saw her again.

She opened a door labeled "Hospital Staff Only" and motioned for me to follow. Without thinking, I followed her inside. "What the...?" I asked as I scanned the room. It wasn't the employee lounge, but it sure as fuck was a storage room.

Before I could ask another question, she pushed me against the door. "I haven't been able to stop thinking about you." Her hands slid up my chest, feeling my pecs with her fingertips.

"Me either, Fiona." Reaching out, I grabbed her face and brought my lips down upon hers. The velvety texture was the same, but the taste was different. Last night they were laced with whiskey, but right now, the only thing I tasted was Fiona.

As I kissed her, she moaned into my mouth and squeezed my

chest harder. Tonight I wouldn't hold back with Fiona. I didn't have time for that luxury.

"Sam," she groaned as I ran my hands down her arms, brushing my thumb against her breast. Her body trembled under my touch as her breathing hitched. The simple sounds that spilled from her lips made the throbbing need in my cock almost unbearable.

When her hand made a beeline for my dick, rubbing it through my jeans, I almost exploded. The heat mixed with the friction of her palm almost brought me to my knees as she stroked my shaft hard and slow.

"Fiona," I whispered against her lips. It was a plea for relief. I wanted her both to stop and to keep going. The last thing I wanted was to come in my pants like a teenage boy. Fuck, that would be humiliating.

"Mmm," she mumbled into my mouth, the sound vibrating against my lips. She gripped my dick, her stroke growing more aggressive.

"Fuck," I groaned as my body shuddered in her grip.

Two could play at this game. Besides that, my fingers needed to touch her. The urge to touch her flesh and taste her became overwhelming. Sliding my hands away from her breast, I dipped my fingers inside the elastic waistband of her uniform. When they pushed through the top of her panties, it was her turn to quake in my arms and moan in my mouth.

Inside I found a landing strip that beckoned for me to go further. The closer I got to the Promised Land, the softer and damper the hairs became. Her need drenched my fingertips as I slid them between her legs. My fingers moved easily against her satin skin, laden with her wetness. Running my fingers through her lips, I savored the softness as she spread her legs farther apart.

I dragged my fingers backward, pulsing her clit between my fingertips. She hissed and bit down on my lip. Everything about that moment drove me wild with lust. The way she smelled, the feel of her pussy, the way she stroked me, it all had me on edge and fighting to keep control.

As she stroked me faster, I plunged my fingers inside her, unable to wait any longer. She cried out as her hand locked around my dick and ceased to move. Her lips popped off mine as she sucked in a harsh, shaky breath. "Oh God," she moaned as her head tipped back. "Yes," she whispered.

With my body against the door, I held her body close to mine using my hand. Digging my fingers into her pants, I used my other hand to stroke her deep. Feeling her pussy convulse around my fingers was sexy as fuck. Her breathing changed, growing more ragged as her hand finally started to move. Moving my face forward, I ran my nose against her neck before kissing the tender flesh.

Working in another digit, I stretched her body open and thrust them inside of her. She fit me perfectly, milking my fingers as I fucked her with my hand. She moved against my hand, not pushing it away, but smashing her pussy against my palm. I tried to focus on her, ignoring the pleasure and the feel of her hand as it rubbed my shaft through my jeans. I couldn't and I wouldn't come here. I wanted to feel her mouth as she took me deep, rubbing her tongue against the head. God, I wanted to feel something more than fabric and heat.

As her grunts turned into something different, a noise more primal, I touched her clit with the pad of my thumb. Her pussy quivered around my fingers and her mouth fell open. I wanted to tip her over the edge. Bring her to her knees with pleasure so intense I'd leave her winded.

I moved my fingers in tiny circles, increasing the pressure with each rotation. The more her pussy contracted, the more I quickened the pace. Even though I wanted to taste her flesh as she came, I wanted to see her face more. Watching a woman come is one of the most beautiful things in the world. Knowing I fucking did that to her is life-affirming. Life is nothing without pleasure. The way their mouths fall open and their breathing changes—it's heavenly.

Her hand locked on my dick, pulsing it as she sucked in a quick breath without exhaling. I watched her eyes flutter closed as her pussy locked down on my fingers. Her body swayed as the first wave of orgasm crashed over her. I didn't relent, fucking her harder with my fingers as she came on my hand. Increasing the pressure on her clit, I could hear the wetness of her pussy as my fingers moved inside of her. It was fucking fantastic.

As her body grew limp in my arms, she blew the air out of her lungs and then pulled in a breath. "Jesus," she whispered, raising her head to look at me.

I smiled and tried to ignore her hand that was still plastered to my dick. I didn't know if I wanted it to move again or for her to release me. "That was sexy as hell, Fiona. Watching you come is the best thing I've seen in New Orleans."

She laughed, letting her head fall back as she tried to swallow. "Give me a minute here." Her fingers flexed against my dick, and I knew my answer. I needed her to stop stroking me through my jeans before I would have to leave the hospital looking like I'd pissed myself.

We needed to detach from each other, or at least I needed her to move her warm, soft hand from my crotch. Slowly I slid my fingers out of her pussy and dragged them across her skin as I pulled them out of her pants. Her juices coated my fingers, and I couldn't help myself. I needed to taste her.

Her head came forward as she watched me lick herself off my fingers. Sticking them in my mouth, I closed my lips, trapping her slickness. It was better than I had imagined. The sweetness danced across my tongue and permeated my entire mouth. I soaked it up, wishing there were more and wanting nothing more than to plant my face between her legs and feast for hours.

When her hand released me as I licked my fingers clean, I instantly felt the loss. The warmth was replaced by nothingness, and my dick ached for her touch again. I groaned as my cock twitched, and my balls felt heavier than they had before we walked into the storage closet.

Her smells and taste surrounded me and drove me mad with need. I had planned to take her to a late, extremely late, dinner and then spend the night having wild, monkey sex. I wasn't about making love. I wanted to bang her brains out to the point that we both passed out. This put a kink into my plans, but a welcomed one.

Without warning, she dropped to her knees and started to undo my zipper. Although I should have told her to stop and wait, my dick did the thinking and told me to shut the fuck up. She licked her lips as she unfastened the button and peeled the material away from my skin. I made it easy on her. I never wore underwear. Clothing alone was constricting enough without adding an extra layer to suffocate my cock.

She palmed my hot flesh, moving it between her two hands, and I swear I almost died. The intensity of her soft skin against my hardness had my knees wobbling. As she moved forward, opening her mouth, I sucked in a breath. I couldn't look away. Who the fuck would want to anyway?

I stared at her as her tongue darted out and swiped against the tender spot underneath the head. "Fuck me," I said through gritted teeth, tangling my fingers in her hair. As her lips closed around my tip, I shuddered. Honest to God, my body reacted of its own volition, moving forward to push my cock deeper into her mouth.

She moaned around the shaft, causing the vibrations to shoot straight to my balls. I gritted my teeth and tried not to yell out all the things I felt or a string of curse words. My fingers dug deeper into her hair as she worked my dick. Sucking, licking, and stroking with her hand slick from her spit. It was a thing of fucking beauty the way she swallowed me whole and peered up at me. This was the second-best thing in the world next to seeing a woman come from something I did. It was a very, very close second.

"So fuckin' good," I whispered, my voice harsh. I rested my head against the door and braced myself. I'd like to think I could last hours as she sucked me off. But there was no way in hell I'd last more than a couple minutes from start to finish.

She increased her stroke, and when her mouth pulled away, she used her hand to swipe the tip. The softness of her hand against the hard, sensitive spot, my sweet spot as I call it, pushed me over the edge.

My thighs locked as my hand fell away, releasing her hair. I rested my palms against the door, enjoying the feel of her lips as I released everything I had into her mouth. My body quaked with each stroke, the aftershocks just as intense as the first wave that smashed my last bit of resistance.

When her lips left my dick, it bobbed in the air and immediately missed the heat of her. I stood there, unmoving, and drew in quick breaths. My heart banged against my chest, outpacing the air I tried to suck into my lungs. She sucked a mean dick. Although it may have been the best blow job I'd ever received, there was nothing more that I wanted than to be buried balls-deep inside her.

She grinned as she rose to her feet. My cock twitched, loving the look on her face. She wasn't done with me as much as I wasn't finished with her. I grabbed the back of her neck, crashing my lips down on hers. Our mouths tasted of each other, mixing together on our tongues. The smell of sex and orgasm hit me like a ton of bricks and made me want more. More than I could get in one night. She was intoxicating.

When I released her from my grip, she peered up at me and bit her lip. "What's wrong?" I asked. The look on her face confused me. Was she worried about something? I hoped she didn't regret anything we just did because it was fucking spectacular.

"This was always a fantasy of mine." She blushed as her eyes glanced down.

"I plan to make a few more come true before the night's

over." I smiled down at her, brushing my lips against hers. "The night's still young, doll."

"Let's get the hell out of here," she said as she pushed away from me and started to adjust her clothing.

I nodded, pushing my dick back into my pants and zipping them up with great caution. The last thing I needed right now was an injury. My pecker and I had plans for tonight. They involved Fiona and not a wound that would put it out of commission.

She stepped back and put her hands down at her sides. "Do I look good?" she asked, sighing as she blew a puff of air upward and moved the tiny wisps of hair that had fallen free when I fisted her hair.

"You look fuckin' beautiful, Fi." She did too. As the overhead light bathed her in a white halo, she looked almost angelic. If I didn't know her abilities, I'd swear she was an angel sent to rescue me from my weekend of pity.

She blushed again and smiled. "You may want to button that." She pointed at my dick and giggled.

I laughed, fastening the button that just a few moments ago I couldn't wait for her to open. "Do I look like you just gave me the best damn orgasm of my life?"

"The best?" she asked, looking shocked.

"Of. My. Life," I admitted and nodded. I couldn't stop the giant smile from growing wider on my face. I don't know if I'll be able to get rid of this smile the entire night. It may be permanent, and I hadn't really been much into smiling recently.

"Well, shit. I could've done better than that," she replied, putting her hands on her hips.

"What?" I blurted out. "There's no way it could be better than that."

"I have a few tricks up my sleeve." She grinned, looking at me from under her eyelashes.

I closed my eyes, trying not to picture her mouth on my dick again. I didn't want to walk out of here with a boner. I finally felt a sense of relief, or at least I wasn't in discomfort like I had been just a few minutes earlier.

"I don't need tricks. I just need you. I just want Fiona without any bullshit."

"You'll get her, but first let's grab my stuff."

I reached back, moving my body away from the door as I turned the doorknob. She walked out in front of me, pretending that nothing had happened. She looked cool as a cucumber, but she fidgeted with her hair. It was a bit haphazard and had that freshly fucked look about it as we walked down the hallway. She kept peeking over her shoulder, giving me a tiny smile as we walked down the hallway.

I winked at her, watching her face turn a brighter shade of pink. The excitement I felt was written all over my face. The sadness I had last night had vanished. It was replaced by a sense of hopefulness and eagerness.

How could I go back to my life in Florida after spending a few short hours in New Orleans with Fiona? The bigger question was how did a woman like Fiona work her way inside, change my view of the world, and cause me to examine my entire future?

Were my feelings true, or were we a classic case of rebound?

6

After I returned home to Tampa and got back to my job, I knew it wouldn't work. Not Fiona, but my life in general. The restlessness I felt working for the FBI had become suffocating and inescapable. Living in a town that held so many memories fucked with my head. I was miserable.

The only bright spot in my day was Fiona. Talking with her, video calls, and texting kept me sane day to day. The western coast of Florida even lacked spirit. The area was bland. It lacked the culture and history that saturated New Orleans.

Everything felt wrong. Every damn thing. I didn't belong here. The linchpin that kept me here had always been Izzy. I rarely thought about her anymore. I didn't wish for what could've been. We were friends from childhood, and she was no longer the woman I loved.

I wanted to be with Fiona. Nothing brought me greater joy than seeing her face and hearing her voice. I was ready for a new start. I'd never been a pussy when it came to change. Some people may have thought I was overly cautious or a little too in control, but for once I was ready to say "Fuck it."

Even if it didn't work out with Fiona, I'd get a fresh start. I deserved that. I earned the right to find my happiness. There was no better place in the world to try to do that than a city like New Orleans.

"Fi," I said after she answered my call on the first ring.

"Sam!" she yelled. "I've missed your voice."

"Hey, baby. I'm thinking about taking a trip." I flicked at the balled-up paper sitting on my desk and watched it fall to the floor.

"Oh, where ya going?"

"Well," I said as I pulled a piece of paper out of my desk, ready to write my letter of resignation. I closed my eyes, praying she wouldn't freak the fuck out. "I think I need New Orleans."

"Oh my God, really?" she screamed into the phone, causing me to move the earpiece away from my head. "When? For how long?" she asked quickly.

"Now and forever."

Those three words were filled with so much hope for what lay ahead. Sometimes you find someplace, someone that makes you feel at home, and you just need to grab it by the reins and hold on for the crazy-ass ride called life. Everything comes with chances, and if we don't take a risk, we may miss out on the best thing in our life. I was ready for anything. Fiona made all things possible.

"Those are the sweetest words I've ever heard," she whispered. "I'll be waiting, Sam."

"On my way, doll. Talk later."

"Later, babe."

I disconnected the call and wrote out a short letter, stating that effective immediately I was no longer an employee of the FBI. I had a life to live and nothing would hold me back.

Love.

Life.

Laughter.

I had a future that would be filled with all of those things, and I wouldn't let anything get in my way. Fiona and New Orleans had changed me. Made me a better man. Brought me more happiness than I thought possible.

I always thought I was in love until I met Fiona. I knew when I touched her that no other woman could ever compare. I wasn't in love with Izzy Gallo. I loved her, yes, but she wasn't *the one*. The time with her wasn't wasted. It brought me to the Funky Pirate in New Orleans. The stool next to me had sat empty, waiting for Fiona to fill the space at the bar and the void in my life.

For once, I believed in fate.

7

"What's wrong?" Fiona asked after she set her purse down on the kitchen counter.

I'd been sitting at the table, staring out the window for an hour in total disbelief. Never in a million years did I think I'd be debating going back to Florida. "Nothing, baby. Come here and give me a kiss." I held out an arm, waiting for her to come to me.

She walked slowly, staring at me cautiously with every step. "I can tell something is off. Just tell me. Did I do something wrong, love?"

I smiled, slowly shaking my head as I curled her into my side. "Fiona," I said, brushing my nose against the tiny patch of skin on her arm, "I can never be mad at you."

She ran her fingers through my hair, slowly raking her fingernails against my scalp. "You look like you've seen a ghost, Sam."

I pulled her closer, wrapping both of my arms around her waist and resting my head against her stomach as she stood between my legs. "Thomas called."

"Oh." Her body stiffened slightly in my arms and her hand stilled. "What did he want?"

Mindlessly, I stroked the smooth skin of her back after I slid my hands underneath her shirt. "He offered me a job."

"And?"

"And, what?"

"What did you say?"

"Nothing, Fi. I told him I couldn't, and he told me to think it over and get back to him." I nuzzled her stomach, inhaling her scent and letting it soothe me. Fiona had become my place of calm in the last year. When life seemed to be going haywire, only she could bring me back to center and wash away any panic I felt.

Slowly, her hand began to work through my hair in long, broad strokes. "Do you miss it?"

I looked up at her in confusion. "Miss what?"

"The guys. I know you were close to them."

Even though it was hard to admit, I did miss them. Often they were tools, but it was almost like being the little brother. I had grown used to them harassing me. Getting a call from Thomas was like an invitation back into the family. No matter what shit went down between us or with his sister, he still wanted me around. "I miss them sometimes, yeah."

"Do you want to say yes?"

I didn't know how to answer the question. Would she think that all I wanted was to be near Izzy again? Fiona knew my history, the love I'd had for Izzy Gallo, and how that led me to her. But hopefully over the last year I had showed her how much I loved only her. "A small part of me does."

She smiled and moved to sit in my lap. She wrapped her arm around my neck and began to stroke my shoulder. "If you want to go back, I'll go with you."

My eyebrows shot up and I was completely caught off guard by her words. "You would?"

She nodded quickly. "As long as I'm with you, I don't care where we are."

"Fiona, you can't mean that." I held her face in my hand and stared into her eyes, studying her. "I know how much you love New Orleans."

"I do, but I want you to be happy too."

"I am happy here." It wasn't a lie. I was happy in New Orleans—more because I was with Fiona than at my surroundings. But living in New Orleans and visiting as a tourist were two very different things.

"Listen," she said softly, pushing her face into the palm of my hand. "I don't have any family here besides you. But you, you have a family in Florida that you've left behind."

"I could never ask you to leave your job."

Her small fingers brushed against my five-o'clock shadow. "You didn't ask; I'm offering."

My thumb stroked her cheek, touching the edge of her mouth. "It's a big step, and I like our life."

"We can make a life anywhere, Sam."

I leaned in, placed my lips on hers, and kissed her gently. "As long as you're with me, I'm a happy man," I said against her mouth.

"I think we should do it."

I pulled back and held her face in my hands. "You do?"

She nodded. Her smile touched the tips of my thumbs. "Yes." She turned, straddling me fully and pushing her lips against mine.

I breathed her in, wrapping my arms around her and holding her tightly. This was the thing I loved about Fiona. She never had demands of me, nor did I of her. Things were just easy with us.

If she was willing to go with me back to Florida, I was more than ready to go home. My family had missed me, and with my parents growing older each day, I felt like I should be there for them.

It was time to go back to my life and stop running away from the past.

8

_____

"We have to get some shit straight." James didn't hide his anger toward me.

I didn't think he'd welcome me with open arms, but after all this time, I didn't expect the hostility. "Shoot." I figured I'd let him blow off some steam and spew his macho bullshit while I paced around the living room.

Fiona and I had spent the last week packing up our small New Orleans apartment. We had another week before she could leave the city after putting in her two weeks at the hospital. But being a nurse, a week equaled only three more days of work before we headed toward the Sunshine State.

"I want you to stay away from Izzy."

"Why?" I asked, pausing from the pattern I had started to wear into the hardwood floor.

"Cause you've done enough damage. We're in a good place and—"

"Hold it right there, James," I said, interrupting him and figuring it was the perfect time to set his ass straight. "Izzy and I have been friends for most of our lives. No matter what happened in the past, we'll always be friends. I'm at a really good place in my life. I'm in love with an amazing woman, and I'd never do anything to jeopardize my relationship with her."

"Good," he mumbled.

"So whatever issue you have, or whatever you think will happen when I come back, put it out of your mind. I'd never do anything to get between you and Izzy. I realized a long time ago that she never loved me. In all honesty, when I met Fiona, I realized that I'd never really loved Izzy the way I should. She wasn't my forever. Fiona is the person I was meant to be with."

"Fine."

"What the fuck are you so worried about, man?"

"I'm not. I just don't think I've ever forgiven you for putting her life in danger."

I sighed and started pacing again. "I know I fucked up. I was an idiot for bringing her around the club, but if it weren't for my fuckup, you probably wouldn't be married to her right now."

I'd thought about it a million times since the day I realized Izzy was in love with him. I put them together. My idiotic move of bringing her to Bike Week placed her right in James's hands. I didn't regret a moment, though. Without those events, I wouldn't have Fiona in my life.

I know, in James's book, he "won" Izzy. But there was never a competition. She wasn't a prize I was meant to win. "Whatever issue you think we have, you need to get the fuck over it."

"You have to put yourself in my shoes, Sam."

"I have. I can't change what's happened in the past, James. What's done is done. I want to move forward. I have the love of a good woman, and all I want to do is come home and be part of a team again. If you don't want me there, tell me now and I'll make other plans."

"No." He breathed hard into the phone. "We need you."

I laughed. "That was hard to say, wasn't it?"

"Don't be a chump."

"I can see you're still a cocky bastard."

"Just get your ass settled and stop in the office when you get to town."

"I'll be there."

"I'll let Thomas know."

I wasn't about to tell him I'd already spoken to Thomas. James and I would always have a tense relationship, and I was trying not to rock the boat. Eventually, we would have to work our shit out and put it to bed forever. I wasn't about to let him hold shit over my head for my entire life.

"Thanks, man. I gotta run."

"I have to go feed the kids."

"See ya soon," I said right before he disconnected the call.

The thought of Izzy as a mom had my head reeling. She was probably supermom and ultraprotective. I'm sure having twins changed her. It had to, after all. The funniest part of it was that God graced her with boys.

Before I could set my phone down, Fiona texted me.

Fiona: Meet me on Bourbon after work.

Although we lived within walking distance, we rarely spent

time among the tourists. So her request was out of the ordinary, but I'd meet her anywhere she asked.

Me: *I'll be there at 9. Where?*

Fiona: *Where we first met.*

The thought of going back to where we began brought a smile to my face. When I thought I'd hit my lowest point, Fiona entered my life and changed everything.

I texted Thomas, letting him know I'd be in the office in a week. The wheels of change were moving, and Fiona and I were about to start a whole new life. But first, I wanted to relive our first night together.

I SAT ON THE SAME BARSTOOL I HAD LAST YEAR AND WAITED FOR Fiona. The bar was crowded, but it was every night, I'm sure. It was a hangout not only for tourists, but it was also a great place to listen to local musicians. Tonight was no exception.

"Is this seat taken?" Fiona asked from behind me.

I glanced over my shoulder at her and smiled. "I'm saving it for my woman."

She touched her bottom lip with her index finger, and her cheeks turned pink before she smiled. "She must be very lucky."

I shook my head, slowly turning in my seat. "I'm the lucky one," I said, pulling her between my legs and snaking my hand around her waist as I studied her face. "I never knew what love was until she sat next to me."

She rested her hand on my shoulder, slowly stroking my neck with her thumb. "She sounds amazing."

"She's everything."

Fiona leaned forward and kissed me. "If you're a good boy, maybe you'll get lucky tonight."

I smirked against her lips. "I plan on it."

She backed away and gawked at me. "You do?"

"I plan to get her tipsy, fuck her here, and then head to my favorite fortune-teller."

"Oh, you don't believe in that nonsense, do you?"

"Let me buy you a drink and explain why I believe every word." I patted the stool next to me before she took a seat.

After a few drinks, I couldn't help but look around the bar, filled with nostalgia. This was where Fi and I began. The very spot where I started to live again. "Aren't you going to miss this?" I asked, using my Hand Grenade to motion toward the reflection of the crowd in the mirror behind the bar.

"Nah." She shook her head. "We can always visit when we miss it."

"So many great memories, babe."

"I wouldn't change a thing. You know?"

"Yeah." I knew what she meant. We'd talked about it before. All the bad shit we went through in our lives brought us to each other. If one thing had gone differently, we wouldn't be together.

"So how about that fuck?" she asked, brushing her fingertips against my neck where they had rested for the last ten minutes.

I leaned forward, watching her eyes try to focus on me when I moved. One Hand Grenade was her usual limit, but tonight she was halfway through her second. "You want it, Fiona?"

"Yes." Her voice was breathy and filled with need.

Reaching between her legs, I slowly ran my hands up her

inner thighs, resting them near her panty line. The sundress she was wearing would make fucking her in the bathroom a breeze. Our backs were to the crowd, and the bar in front of us would give us privacy for what I'd planned. "Finish your drink."

"Sam," she complained, pressing her legs together and trapping my hand.

"If you can finish your drink without moaning, I'll take you to the bathroom and fuck you senseless."

She pursed her lips, eyes sparkling, and swayed a little on her seat. "I can do that," she said, seeming a bit cocky.

Fiona quiet during sex never happened. Fiona quiet while I finger fucked her wouldn't be possible, but I was more than happy to see how it went. "Drink up, beautiful."

When she brought the cup to her lips, I slipped my fingers inside her barely there lace panties. She started to choke before she could get down her sip of Hand Grenade. "You're playing dirty," she rasped out.

I moved her panties to the side, holding them with my pinkie finger while I continued to stroke her pussy. "I am." She squirmed on the stool, and I could see her struggling not to make noise. "Keep moving and we'll get caught, Fi."

"Fuck," she muttered around the rim of her green plastic cup. "This is hard."

"I'm hard, baby, and the longer you take to finish the drink, the longer I have to wait to fuck you." My girl was wet and ready. Slowly, I inched a finger into her greedy pussy and gave her a taste of what she wanted. My thumb toyed with her clit, but not enough to bring her to climax. Just enough to have her ready to rip my clothes off in the middle of the bar.

Before I could add a second finger, she slammed back her drink, set the cup down, and turned to me. "Now!" she demanded, clearly audible over the loud music.

Her eyes burned for me. Even though I loved teasing her, I needed her more than I wanted to keep playing this game. The first night I met her, I wanted to fuck her. I would've done it here if given the chance. If we had, though, we wouldn't be here right now.

Without hesitating, I removed my hand from under her dress, stood, grabbed her hand, and headed to the courtyard. Through the small doors at the back of the Funky Pirate was the most amazing starlit patio leading to the bathrooms. She followed behind, holding on to my hand and walking on wobbly legs, wanting this as much as I did.

"What if we get caught?"

"Fi," I laughed, turning to face her in the middle of the flower-lined courtyard, "live a little."

She nodded and bit her lip before looking over her shoulder. "Hurry," she said when she faced me.

I dragged her toward the bathroom while she still had a buzz and before my balls exploded. "I can do quick, but later I'm taking my time."

Once inside the cramped space, I locked the door before quickly undoing my fly. I'd like to say it was pretty and sexy, but this was sheer need and nothing more.

Fiona watched, filled with giggles and smiles until I turned her around and bent her over the sink. Moving her panties to the side, I rammed my cock inside her, unwilling to wait another minute.

She cried out, the usual loudness I'd grown to love, and gripped the edge of the sink as I pounded into her. Over and over again, I sank my cock into her. Holding her hips for traction, I battered her ass with my body, shoving her into the sink and allowing my dick to go as far as possible.

When her body began to shake and she was close, I swiveled my hips and hit her G-spot with my cock. Moments later, she started to mumble gibberish as if she were possessed and speaking in tongues. When her pussy began to milk my cock, I couldn't hold out any longer and let the orgasm I'd been trying to stave off break free.

In the frenzy, and with enough alcohol in our bloodstreams to inebriate a small family, we fucked and came in under five minutes. It may have been a new record for me, but the way Fiona looked, the amount of love I had for her, and knowing this was where we started had me sprinting toward the finish line at breakneck speed.

BY THE TIME WE GOT TO THE SQUARE, IT WAS WELL AFTER midnight. I wanted to visit with the old woman who told me my future was right in front of me over a year ago, but she was gone.

"Where is she?" I asked, turning around in circles and feeling a sadness I hadn't expected.

"She's not here." Fiona squeezed my hand.

"Damn." I wanted to end our time here the same way it began, but it wasn't going to happen. Most things never do end up the way we plan.

She snaked her arm around my neck and rested her head on my chest. "It's okay, Sam. She said everything you needed to hear last time."

I buried my face in her hair and smiled. "I know. I just wanted to hear her say that everything was going to work out."

She peered up at me, touching my cheek with her hand. "Are you worried it won't?"

I sighed. "There's a lot that could go wrong."

She stood on her tiptoes and gave me a soft kiss. "Nothing will go wrong, Sam."

I wrapped my arms around her, holding her tightly as I looked across the square. "I hope so, Fiona."

Out of nowhere, the old fortune-teller walked behind us and caught my eye. She stopped walking and, before I could speak, she said, "You future is not here."

Fiona released me and turned around, just as much in shock as I was that she had shown up. "Thank you," Fiona said and tipped her head at the old woman.

She smiled and walked away before I replied. Her words caught me off guard. Days before we were about to leave New Orleans the words rang true. Our future wasn't here.

Even though I wanted to believe everything would turn out okay, moving to Florida and being near the Gallos might stir up so many feelings and past hurts that problems would be inevitable.

One thing I knew for sure. No matter what, with Fiona at my side, I could get through anything. Even James's shitty attitude and seeing the girl I thought I'd loved again.

Life was about to get really interesting.

MEN OF INK2ED
CHRISTMAS NOVELLA

FROM THE *USA TODAY* BESTSELLING AUTHOR

CHELLE BLISS

1

MIA

S tone's clapping as Pop bounces him up and down on his knee. "Stone, my boy. This is a special year." Stone laughs, drool running down his chin like a ribbon of melting snow, but Pop doesn't care. He loves Stone too much to care his pants are covered. "You don't realize it, but this has been the best year of our lives," Pop tells him, beaming with excitement. Stone claps again, his little head bobbing with each dip as Pop raises him higher and into the air.

They're adorable together. Stone loves his grandpa the most. Sometimes I think even more than he likes Michael or me. As soon as we walk in the door, he reaches for Pop to take him and won't leave his arms until we leave. It usually involves tears, as if we're taking away his favorite blanket.

"Not only were you born, but the Cubbies won the World Series too," Pop tells Stone with a smile that stretches from ear to ear.

I place my hand over my stomach, missing the feel of him moving inside me. It's hard to believe he's already nine months old. Time flew after Lily was born, but with Stone I thought it would move slower. Instead, it moved so fast it's almost like I'm watching it all take place before my eyes at double speed. It feels like yesterday that I found out I was pregnant. It was a shock to me, but even a bigger shock to Mike. After she nagged him mercilessly, he finally gave in and got a vasectomy. He was one of the unlucky one percent who went through the procedure unsuccessfully.

When he found out we were having another baby, he was excited. He claimed this proved that his manhood and virility couldn't be stopped. Naturally, he'd think it was a good thing.

"Baby, you want anything?" Mike asks, taking a seat on the armrest of the chair and wrapping his arm around my shoulder.

I glance up at him, and he's staring at Stone with the biggest smile. There's something about a man and his son. When the doctor announced that we had a boy, I thought Mike was going to beat on his chest and hold him high in the air, beaming with pride. The man prayed every day for a boy.

Don't get me wrong.

He loves his baby girl. God, Lily has him wrapped around her little finger. She always has. From the moment she was born, Mike was a goner. The little princess can do no wrong in his eyes, and she knows it. He doesn't realize it, but soon she'll be a teenager, and he's going to be in for a rude awakening.

"I'm good, love. Just watching your dad and Stone." I smile up at him, watching him as he gazes at them with the biggest grin. There's pride in his eyes every time he looks at his son.

"They love each other, huh?" Mike's thumb strokes the exposed skin on my shoulder that is peeking out from my new sweater. I still don't get why it's missing part of the sleeves, but the sales lady told me it's all the rage. I feel like I paid the same amount for a portion of the clothing.

"Yep, it's weird, almost."

"Yeah."

I place my hand on his knee and rest my head against his rock-hard chest. "Where's Lily?" I ask him, closing my eyes for a moment, listening to the steady beat of his heart

Two kids and years later and I'm still utterly and completely in love with this man. He still has the ability to make my insides quiver with anticipation when he's near.

People said we wouldn't last. A fighter and a doctor. Hell, it was probably a bet I would've taken before I really knew the man.

On the outside, he's a massive wall of muscular testosterone, but on the inside, he's nothing but a soft, loving human being. Except when he's in the ring. Then he's a beast. He transforms into someone I don't know. Someone who would pound another man's face in without even blinking. I'd never admit it, but watching him fight turns me on.

"Somewhere in the backyard with Gigi and Nick." He leans down, placing his mouth next to my ear. "We can sneak upstairs and do it in my old room." His teeth find my lobe, tugging gently. "Everyone is busy, the kids are being looked after."

I melt into him as the noise around us fades.

His lips skid across the skin of my neck before his teeth dig into my favorite spot. "Come on, Doc. I need your special medicine."

My skin breaks out in goose bumps, and I'm more than eager to steal a few moments away with my husband. Time alone has been minimal since Stone arrived. And sneaking away for a quickie sounds perfect.

"You're on, big boy," I whisper.

Mike stands and grabs my hand, pulling me up from the couch and heading toward the foyer. Pop's so engrossed in Stone that he doesn't even see us leave. Everyone else is sitting outside, watching the kids play and chitchatting while dinner is in the oven. Ma's in the kitchen, cooking and still trying to teach Suzy how not to burn food.

I giggle softly as Mike drags me up the first few steps. When I don't move fast enough for him, he hoists me over his shoulder and jogs up the grand staircase, taking two steps at a time. I bite down on my lip to stop the squeal bubbling from my throat that would be loud enough to draw attention to us.

When we're inside his room, Mike kicks the door closed and we both freeze, holding our breath because we figure our cover's blown.

"Shit, that was close," he whispers, choosing now to be quiet. Mike loosens his grip, making my body slide down his front. It's like cascading down an old-fashioned washboard.

I can feel every ripple and dip of his abdominal muscles until my feet touch the floor. Even then, my body is plastered against his, humming with excitement at his nearness. "Training has done a body good," I tell him with the biggest smile, while my hands dig into his rock-hard sides.

When I met him, I thought he was built like a brick house, but I was wrong. Over time and with more training he seems to be getting bigger and harder. There isn't an ounce of fat on the man. A year ago when he told me he wanted to get back in the ring, I was worried. After such a long absence, I wasn't sure his body could handle the grueling training and snap back.

But, damn. Mike proved me wrong.

"Whatcha thinking, Doc?" He quirks an eyebrow with a smirk. "You look like you want to eat me."

A slow, easy smile spreads across my face as I stare up into his caramel eyes. "Just thinking about how lucky I am to have you."

"Baby," he whispers before leaning forward and placing his lips against mine. He snakes his arms around my back, one hand tangling in my hair and holding me still as he kisses me deeply.

More than anything, I want to savor him, take my time making love to him, but we can't. Backing away, I say, "Michael, we don't have much…"

"Shh," he murmurs, tightening his grip on my back before he trails a line down my neck to my chest with his soft lips. He pulls my hair gently, and my body follows, giving him better access to the opening in my V-neck sweater.

I grip his biceps, digging my fingernails into the skin just underneath his T-shirt sleeve. I'm hot, but not from the overly humid December Florida air. Instead, it's from the way my husband is touching me. I shouldn't feel as needy as I do. He woke me up in the middle of the night last night, spreading my legs wide and slipping inside of me before I could fully wake. The hazy memory of it makes my skin tingle.

Reaching under my skirt, he pulls my panties down and tosses them over his shoulder before I quickly undo his pants, pushing them to his ankles. He turns us, pressing my back against the wall next to the door. His kiss deepens, growing more demanding as he presses his hot erection against me.

Lifting me by the ass, he boosts me into the air, lining our bodies up perfectly before crashing his mouth against mine. I'm breathless and needy, wanting to feel him buried inside of me and needing another orgasm like it's part of my life source. Mike runs the tip of his cock through my wetness before pushing inside, and my legs wrap around his back, taking him deeper and wanting all of him.

He starts with long, languid strokes, causing my slow-burning desire to ignite into a wildfire of lust. The heels of my bare feet dig into his ass and try to pull him forward quicker. The leisurely pace teases me, taunting me with an orgasm that's just out of reach.

"Faster," I moan, digging my shoulder blades into the wall and bearing down on him.

Mike smirks and grips my ass cheek rougher in his palm as he increases his strokes. He's pounding into me; the photo on the wall next to my head bounces with each thrust. My toes begin to curl, and my muscles strain with the building orgasm.

Mike's grunts become deeper and his hips move faster, slamming into me so roughly that my back begins to ache from the assault against the wall. The mix of pleasure and pain, along with his massive cock inside me, sends me over the edge.

Mike covers my mouth with his when I get a little too loud and quickly follows with his own climax. Even after we both catch our breath again, we don't move. It's too quiet, too comfortable to pull apart and go back downstairs. We both have the same thought. We want to stay in this bubble of bliss for as a long as possible.

"Mike!" Joe's voice echoes through the hallways outside the door.

We both make a face at each other, knowing our moment is gone.

"I love you," I whisper to my husband, who is still buried deep inside of me.

"Love you too, Doc." He smiles and slowly lowers my feet to the floor. He starts to pull up his pants when there's a knock at the door.

"Yo, asshole. Get your cock out of her and come downstairs."

Our eyes meet, and we both break out into laughter. We weren't as sneaky or probably as quiet as we thought we were. Joe doesn't care. He and his wife, Suzy, have snuck away more times than I can count to do it all over the house. In reality, every person in this house has, at one time or another. Gotta get it when you can.

"Coming," Mike tells him as he fastens the top button on his jeans.

"Do I look okay?" I ask as I shimmy my panties up my legs and try to right myself.

"That shade of pink is amazing on you."

I give him a "What the hell are you talking about?" look and move my hands over my outfit, showing him there's not a thread of pink on me. "Pink?"

He steps forward and rests his hand against my face, stroking my cheek with his thumb. "You have that well-fucked glow about you." He smiles.

The pink he's referring to turns into the brightest shade of red. "Damn it," I grumble.

He kisses me with tenderness, his hand still on my face, and the embarrassment that flooded me moments ago vanishes. We're not kids anymore. We weren't sneaking off to have premarital sex. The one thing I've learned about the Gallos, even his parents, is that everyone has a healthy sex life.

"We better go," I tell him when I feel the dull ache between my legs starting to return.

He nods and adjusts himself in his pants. "Going to be a long day. I may pull you into another room later."

I press my hand between his solid pecs and smile up at him. "I may just let you."

***

When we walk down the staircase, trying to act like nothing happened, Joe's waiting in the foyer with the girls. His arms are crossed in front of him with Lily and Gigi on either side of him, and from the look on his face, I'd say the girls are in trouble... again. They're staring at the floor as tears trickle down their splotchy red cheeks.

I drop to my knees as soon as I'm in front of Lily. "What happened?" I move my eyes between Joe, Lily, and Gigi. My heart's racing because I can't imagine what has them in tears.

They've grown up so fast. Too fast for my liking. The biggest problem is they're thick as thieves and usually getting into some sort of trouble, but rarely are they in tears.

"Our lovely children thought it would be funny to convince Nick to strip down naked and run through the neighbor's yard."

I'm shocked. "What?" I gape.

Mike places a hand on my shoulder as if to steady himself. "Why in God's name would they do that?"

Joe blows out a breath and clenches his fist. "Well, I guess Nick has a crush on the neighbor girl. Our innocent little girls told him that the way to get her attention would be to run through her yard naked, singing 'Jingle Bells.'"

I have to bite the inside of my cheek not to laugh. Jingle Bells? These two little mischief-makers will be the death of Joe and Mike. They have no idea what's coming because we haven't even hit the teen years. It's going to be hell.

Mike digs his fingers into my shoulder. "What the heck were you two thinking?" His tone is biting.

"Dad," Lily says with a sniffle.

"Don't Dad me, li'l girl. Why did you tell Nick to do that?"

Joe glances down at Gigi, quirking an eyebrow, waiting for her to respond. "You have anything to say, Gigi?"

"Well..." she says, kicking at the tile floor with her eyes downcast.

"Lily, why?" Mike pipes in when Gigi pauses.

"Listen," Gigi says and looks me right in the eyes. "When my mom and dad want to show each other how much they like each other, they always get naked. We wanted to help Nick get Poppy's attention." She glances up at her father with a sad smile. "We didn't know we did anything wrong, Daddy."

"You too, Mommy," Lily says to me. "You and Daddy wrestle sometimes, and you said it was just how you show each other you love one another." And I'm horrified and a little embarrassed.

Joe's face is pale, and he looks more uncomfortable than I do. "We'll talk about this later. You and Lily go wash up for dinner. We'll see if Santa comes tonight. You two just earned a spot on the naughty list," Joe tells them.

"I told you it was wrong," Lily tells Gigi with a snarl. "I'm not going to get my tablet for Christmas because of your stupid idea." Lily rolls her eyes and starts to walk away, dragging her feet with each step.

Gigi peels away from Joe, walking next to Lily, and swings her arm over her cousin's shoulder. "Don't worry," Gigi whispers. "Santa's already in the air, and our gifts are in his sleigh. You'll get your presents."

The girls seem to forget that we can hear them. Even though they try to whisper, they're doing a shitty job of it. They've never been able to be quiet a day in their lives.

"You think?" Lily asks, glancing at Gigi.

Gigi nods. "Next year, we have to be extra good now, though."

"Darn," Lily says.

"I know. It's going to suck."

Joe, Mike, and I look at each other and bite back our laughter until the girls disappear to the back of the house, and then we lose it.

Joe sobers first and rubs the back of his neck. "We're in so much fucking trouble with them."

"Ya think?" I laugh.

Mike shakes his head, rubbing his forehead with his fingertips. "So much fucking trouble."

"Where's Nick?" I ask.

"Getting his ass chewed out by Thomas." Joe smiles. "I'd hate to be him."

Mike pulls me into his side and kisses the top of my head. "Poor kid."

"What are we going to do, Joe?"

"I think we're going to have to talk to them about nudity and sexuality."

"Fuck," Mike groans. "They're ten, for shit's sake."

"Dude, they just made Nick run around with his cock waving in the air. I think it's time for that talk," Joe laments.

"Jesus," Mike says. "This is Mia's department."

I slap his stomach to give him a reality check. "This is an us department, jerk. I'm not talking to Lily about sex by myself."

Suzy strolls into the hallway, glancing into the living room behind her. "Why do Gigi and Lily look like they've been crying?"

Joe wraps his arm around her waist when she's close enough and hauls her into his side. "You don't wanna know, sugar."

"Can't we have one day of peace?" she asks, hugging him tightly.

"I don't think I'll ever have another day of peace with three girls to raise."

We all laugh because we know his words are a sad, sobering truth.

"Wait til they date," Suzy says, looking up at her husband.

The moment Lily starts dating, I know everything is going to spiral out of control in a hot minute, and I dread the day. Mike isn't going to let a boy near his baby girl without a fight.

"I'm locked and loaded when that day comes."

"Me too," Joe tells Mike with a nod.

"You two are crazy," Suzy says with a small giggle. "Boys aren't that bad."

"Walk with me," Joe tells Suzy, placing his hand on the small of her back and ushering her out of the hallway. "Let me tell you what Nick just did."

Mike and I are trailing behind them, waiting for when she finds out exactly what our innocent angels encouraged their little cousin to do.

Joe whispers in her ear, and I know the moment he says the words because she stiffens. She stops walking and turns to face him. "What the frick? Seriously?"

"Afraid so."

"Oh, my God. We're horrible parents," she says, covering her face with her hands.

"No, we aren't," I tell Suzy, knowing exactly how she feels. "We're human. But it's time for the birds and the bees."

"This is bullshit," Mike says, being the pain in the ass he is. "Pop never gave us that talk. I don't even know what to say to a girl."

My eyebrows draw downward as my head jerks back. "He didn't give you that talk?"

Mike and Joe both shake their heads.

"Well, what the…"

"Pop just said to use a rubber and gave us each a box of forty-eight when we turned sixteen."

My mouth falls open. "You can't say that with girls," I tell them. "So, you better figure something out because I'm not doing it alone."

"They're ten," Mike reminds me, as if I forgot that little fact, and crosses his arms in front of his chest.

"Naked," I remind him. "They think that's how you show someone you like them."

Mike winces. "Don't remind me."

"What's going on?" Izzy asks as she rounds the corner and almost barrels straight into Suzy.

"The girls got in trouble," Suzy says but leaves out all the gory details.

"Thank God I have boys." She smiles proudly, finally not complaining about having a baby girl to love.

"Hey, Izzy. Did Mom or Dad give you the birds and the bees talk?" Joe asks.

I'm sure she got a different treatment than her brothers. There has always been a double standard when it comes to parenting children.

"Mom did. I think I was like twelve."

"What did she say?"

"I didn't even know half the shit she was talking about. Basically, she told me to wait until I was married to let anyone touch me down there. She told me that it was the most sacred gift you could give anyone."

Mike almost chokes. "She did?"

"No, ya dumb fuck. She told me to wait until I got married because men are assholes and will say anything to get in my pants. She gave me a box of rubbers and brought me to the gynecologist and put me on the pill too. She figured it didn't matter anyway. With four brothers, I'm sure she assumed I'd never get laid, so why worry."

That isn't an option for Lily and Gigi.

We aren't ready for that yet. Lord, I don't know if I will ever be ready for that.

"Izzy!" James's voice carries through the house like a roar. "I need you."

"Goddamn it. I swear, Trace thinks everything should go in his mouth. I bet he's eating the Christmas ornaments again. He should be over this phase at his age."

"Oh, gawd," I groan and dread the day when Stone starts to eat everything in sight, including Legos and other objects that aren't meant for consumption.

"Fuckin' James takes pictures of it for his Instagram. Asshole thinks Trace is the funniest little thing ever. I'm going to junk punch him soon."

"Bullshit," Mike coughs out. "I'd like to see you try. Bet your ass gets whipped."

Izzy winks, smiling at her brother. "Only if I'm lucky."

Mike's face scrunches at her words. "Yuck."

"Oh, stop the bullshit. You know you love to spank my ass," I tell him with a small giggle, but my cheeks heat at the thought of him buried inside me and his hand coming down on my ass repeatedly.

He places his hand on my ass cheek and gives it a firm squeeze. "Fuck, I love making that ass pink, baby. When I do, your pussy grips…"

"Hey," Joe says, motioning around the room. "There are children around here, man."

"Right," Mike says and bites his lip. "Have kids, they said." He rolls his eyes and groans. "They'd be fun, they said." His lip curls and he growls. "All fucking lies."

Suzy interrupts Mike's pity party. "You guys should really stop swearing so much around the children."

"I'm sorry. You're right. I'll make an announcement before dinner."

"This should be interesting," I mutter because swearing has become almost a second and more expressive language since I've become a member of this family.

"It's best for everyone if we find big-people words to use instead of the dirty ones."

"Yes, Mrs. Gallo," Mike teases her in a whiny, little kid voice because she just pulled out the teacher tone.

"You better behave, Michael, or I'm going to have Mia give you detention."

Mike stares down at me with a cocky smirk. "Only if there's oral involved."

"Boys only think about one thing," I say, shaking my head. But to be honest, when Mike's around, it's always on my mind too.

He beams with pride. "Yep."

Ma walks in with the biggest tray of appetizers I've ever seen. "They're almost here," she says with excitement. "I never thought I'd see the day when Franny got remarried."

Two weeks ago, Fran and Bear tied the knot.

"They've been gone forever," Mom says as she sets the tray

down on the coffee table near Pop, who's still holding Stone and watching the video replay of the Cubs winning the World Series for the hundredth time.

"Ma, it's been ten days since they left for their honeymoon. Calm down," Anthony tells her, coming out of the kitchen with another tray of food.

His words earn him a glare from Ma. "Hush your mouth. My best friend has been without any type of cell reception or internet for ten days. Do you know how that killed me?"

"Killed me too," Pop says sarcastically over his shoulder.

Ma gives him a death glare. "Shut up, Sal." She pushes us out of the way when there's a knock at the door, making a beeline for the foyer.

Mike and I settle onto the floor of the living room just as Fran and Maria start squealing with delight in the foyer. Joe and Suzy walk away, heading toward the front door, while the rest of us stay put. Pop's still holding Stone, Izzy and James are off with Trace somewhere, Max and Anthony are curled up on the sofa, and Thomas and Angel are standing in the backyard, watching Nick "the Streaker" like a hawk.

The kids are running around the house, their screams of happiness while playing carrying through the sprawling two-story house. The cacophony only dims when they run out the open sliding doors lining the back of the house, but they quickly return and do it all over again. They're making a circle pattern—up the staircase, around the top floor, back down, out, and back again. I'm exhausted just watching them and more than a little jealous of their endless energy.

Mike's hand is resting against my middle, stroking my

stomach slowly. "Maybe I knocked you up again, Doc," he whispers in my ear, and I can feel his smile against my skin. Diapers and sleepless nights weren't my favorite, but they definitely weren't Mike's thing.

"If there's a baby inside me, Michael, I'll never have sex with you again," I whisper back, but we both know it's a lie.

"There's the big guy," Anthony says when Bear and Fran walk into the room with Ma close behind. "What the hell do I call you now? Uncle Bear?" Anthony scratches his head in confusion.

"You're an idiot," Thomas tells Anthony and shakes his head in disgust.

Pop climbs to his feet, placing Stone on his hip, and wraps his sister in a half hug. "Franny, you look relaxed."

Fran steps back, laughing nervously as she slides back under Bear's arm. "I spent ten days in bed with this big lug. I should be in a coma."

Stone yanks on Pop's beard and giggles, distracting him from Fran's statement. "You little stinker." Pop lifts him in the air, exposing his stomach, and gives him a sloppy raspberry against his belly button.

"Why don't the girls go into the kitchen and work on dinner, and the boys can stay out here and watch the kids," Ma says, hooking her arm with Fran's and trying to pry her from Bear's body.

"Sure," I say, climbing to my feet after kissing Michael. I've been in the family long enough to know "work on dinner" is code for drink and gossip.

"We'll hold down the fort out here," Joe tells Suzy when she stands as I pass by her and pull her with me, needing a glass of wine and a little girl talk.

By the time Suzy and I step foot in the kitchen, Fran already has seven wineglasses on the island and Ma has started to pour the wine.

"Sit," Ma says, motioning toward the stools with her chin. "Fran, we want to hear all about it."

"I'm going to need more wine if we're going to talk about old-people sex."

"Stop being a brat, Izzy. You're not too far off from being old," Ma teases.

Izzy gasps with wide eyes. "I'm in my thirties, Ma. I'm far from a senior citizen."

"You're no spring chicken anymore, sweetheart," Fran says, grabbing a glass from the countertop and lifting it near her mouth. "Just yesterday, I was in my thirties. Goes by in the blink of an eye. You'll all be old soon enough."

Each of us grabs a glass, silence falling over the room as we all take a larger than usual sip, contemplating Fran's words.

Every year, time moves faster, and nothing I do makes it slow.

"So, how was the honeymoon?" Suzy asks first as the rest of us continue to drink.

Fran rests her elbows on the counter, leaning forward and holding her wineglass in one hand. "I've never experienced anything like it."

Izzy sighs loudly before guzzling the wine, holding it with both hands.

"Bear is an animal in the sack. I can't believe I can even walk after it all." She snorts against the back of her hand. "The man should've been an acrobat."

"Sounds like you had a great time," I say, feeling slightly awkward hearing about their sex life. She's not my mother or aunt, but I've grown to think of her as a friend and I love her.

"Girl, there's something about a big, muscular guy twirling you around and bending you like you're a Twizzler."

"You mean a pretzel," Max corrects her, finally entering the conversation.

"Whatever. Who knew I was so damn flexible?"

"Anthony does this thing with his..."

Izzy grunts. "Not enough wine in the world for this conversation." She grabs one of the bottles off the counter and heads back toward the living room. "I'm going to sit with the guys and watch the World Series for the millionth time. At least that won't make my stomach turn."

When Izzy storms out of the room, we giggle loudly.

"She's such an uptight princess sometimes," Max says, rolling her eyes. "We have to hear about her chains and whips all the time, but Lord forbid we talk about one of her brother's cocks."

"I don't like hearing about Sal and Maria. It took me years not to want to throw up every time Maria would talk about their sex life," Fran admits.

"Well, shit. Who else was I going to tell? You're my best friend." Maria fills our wineglasses before refilling her own. "Fran, later you can tell me all the steamy details. We don't want to make the young ones in the room faint."

"Thank you, baby Jesus," Max mutters into her glass.

"It's time." Ma pushes a stack of plates in front of Suzy and me, and we know the routine. It's the same every week and is like a well-choreographed machine. Half of us set the table and get the troops set, while the other half prep the food and carry it out.

Someday, the men will do something more than watch sports and bullshit.

2

MIKE

I get Lily situated at the children's table before coming to sit next to Mia and Stone at the adults' table. "Did you get her something to drink?" Mia asks just as my ass touches the chair.

I climb to my feet again even though I'm so hungry I feel like I could pass out at any second. "No," I grumble. "She's ten. Her legs aren't broken."

I know I'm a whiny bitch. I love my kids and wife, but there's a limit to my selflessness and it seems to be when I'm hungry. Keeping my body in tip-top shape isn't easy.

"Just do it," Mia orders me with a piercing stare while she cuts Stone's food into the smallest pieces possible. By the way she's stabbing at the meat, I'd say I pissed her off.

After pouring Lily a glass of milk, I collapse into the chair next to my lovely wife and begin to fill my plate without talking.

Everyone is chattering around me, but I'm too hungry to do more than grunt.

"Should you be eating all those carbs?" Izzy asks, pointing at my plate with her fork.

"It's Christmas. This is my cheat day." I narrow my gaze at my nosy sister. "Mind your own business."

"When's the next fight?" James asks as he hands me the giant pan of lasagna.

"In a month," I tell him, scooping out the biggest helping I can get away with without getting yelled at by Ma.

"We'll all be there, son," Pop says, which makes me smile.

My big and sometimes annoying family has been nothing short of amazing. They've always supported my choice to fight, and even after I quit and decided to go back, they followed my every move. Even Mia. I thought she was going to have a coronary when I told her I missed it, but the woman told me to follow my dream, even if it included pounding someone's face in. I remember when we first met, she hated the idea of me being a fighter. She said it went against her oath or some bullshit as a doctor to watch me beat the piss out of another man. But I saw the fire in her eyes the first time she saw me fight. It turned her on, and she couldn't deny it. Even to this day, she protests violence, but I always get pussy after a match.

Max wipes Asher's face. I've never seen a baby eat as much as that little man does. When he gets older, he just may give me a run for my money.

"Let me do that, baby. Just eat," Anthony tells her, taking the napkin from her hand.

His unusual selflessness and tenderness earn him funny looks from the entire table. Anthony isn't known for his soft side, but he's changed over the years. Between Max and his kids, he's turned into a smartass teddy bear instead of the reckless manwhore he used to be.

If I'm being completely honest, all of us have changed. I'm still an asshole, but Mia makes me want to be a better person. I'm still a work in progress, but I'm getting there.

"Fine spread you have here, Mar." Bear jams a chunk of meatball into his mouth and moans. His lack of table manners sometimes makes me look like a gentleman. I think it's why I like him so much.

"Thanks, Bear." Ma smiles. "Shit. We didn't say a prayer and our thanks. Sal, sweetheart, can you start?"

There's a collective groan before forks clank against everyone's plates. I bow my head and hope the kids get so out of control that we eventually skip finishing and go back to eating.

"Behave," Mia says and puts her hand on my knee.

"Higher," I whisper with a smirk.

"I'll go first," Fran says, standing up and looking around the table. "I'm thankful for my family and my new husband. I never thought life could be this good."

"Babe, I love the hell out of you," Bear tells her and then stands. "I'm thankful for my wife and friends around this table and those who couldn't be with us tonight. And thanks to Maria for the amazing food that's getting cold."

I knew I liked this guy. My stomach rumbles, and in order to speed shit along, I stand next before Bear can put his ass in the chair. "I'm thankful for my family and my little surprise, Stone."

I glance over at my little man as he shoves lasagna in his mouth with both hands.

The kids are eating at the next table, but no one seems to care. Back in the day, Ma would've knocked us into next week for not listening and saying thanks, but not the grandkids—they always get a pass.

I tune out after Mia says her thanks and stare at my plate. It's like the food is taunting me, the aroma wafting up from the dish, making my mouth salivate.

Pop stands, clinking his fork against his wineglass, even catching the attention of the kids. "Let's bow our heads for a prayer."

Everyone grows quiet, even the kiddos, and we bow our heads and wait. Pop clears his throat before he speaks. "Today, as we're gathered here together, I want to thank God for the amazing lives we have and that everyone is happy and healthy. Not only am I blessed with such love, but…"

He pauses and gets choked up. I roll my eyes because I know where he's going before he even says the words. There's only one thing Pop loves as much as his family. The Cubs. I'd never seen him as happy as he was the day they won. His life had been made.

"But my Cubbies winning the World Series was the best day of my life. I can die a happy man."

"For the love of God," Ma mutters. "I wish everyone a happy and healthy New Year. May we continue to be blessed in the coming year. Amen."

Joining everyone else, I say, "Amen." And I quickly do the

sign of the cross before grabbing my fork and digging back into my food.

After twenty minutes of gorging ourselves on an obscene amount of food, the women clear the table and kick our asses happily back to the living room, putting us in charge of the kids. We spread out around the room, leaving enough space for our other halves when they return.

I settle into the couch with Stone in my arms. He's in that familiar food coma too. His eyes are heavy and his blinks long and drawn-out. He's fighting it, unlike me. I prop him on my shoulder and rub his back, making tiny circles until he's fast asleep

I doze off somewhere in the middle of the conversation about the Cubs. The topic has become boring to me, although Pop is still as excited as the night it happened.

"Daddy." Lily yanks on my pant leg.

"Yeah?" I don't open my eyes.

"Can I snuggle with you, or are you still mad at me?"

I glance down at her and smile. She's chewing on her index finger and staring at me while she turns her body from side to side. I pat the cushion next to me, careful not to wake Stone. "Come here, sweetheart. I always want your snuggles. I love you."

A giant smile spreads across her face. She looks so much like her mother that she takes my breath away sometimes. She climbs on the couch, settling in the crook of my arm and resting her tiny hand on my stomach. "Do you have a baby in there?" she asks into the fabric of my shirt.

"No, Lily. No baby. It's only food. Only girls can have

babies. Remember Mommy and I told you that when she was pregnant with Stone."

"That's not fair. I don't want to ever have a baby. Men should be able to have them too."

Joe chuckles next to me after hearing Lily's statement, and I pull her closer to my side.

"Just stay away from gross boys, and you won't have to worry about getting pregnant."

She sticks out her tongue and makes a gagging noise. "Boys are gross, Daddy."

"That's my girl." I pray she'll always feel this way.

"I'll never love a boy the way I love you," she says, melting my heart into a pile of goo.

I lock this memory away because I know soon she'll be dating and will forget the words she just spoke. Someday, I'll have to have a man-to-man with her new beau, and it isn't going to be pretty. Soon, probably sooner than I want, I'll be threatening the life of some asswad horny teenager about putting his filthy hands on my daughter, and Lily will hate me for it.

If she's ever going to get married, it'll take a hell of a man to survive my hazing. I don't know of many fools who will willingly subject themselves to me for a piece of ass. The way I figure it, if he sticks around after dealing with me, then he'd have to be doing it for love.

When the ladies return, gift opening starts. Only the kids get gifts anymore. The main event, as I call it, takes hours. There are so many gifts in the room we'd need twenty Christmas trees to set them under. It's obscenely beautiful. The kids are glowing as they take turns opening their presents.

"We have a great life," Mia says, curling into the spot where my little girl had been an hour earlier.

"I wish we could freeze time, Doc. I don't want them to ever grow up."

"I know." She kisses my cheek, nuzzling into my neck with her face. "I love you, Michael."

"Love you too, Mia." I pull her closer, careful not to smash Stone. Somehow, he's sleeping through all the noise and shrieks as each present is opened.

"We gotta wake him up." She strokes his cheek. "Stone, baby, wake up, sweetheart," she whispers. "He'll keep us up all night, otherwise."

"We're going to be up all night setting up Lily's presents anyway. Might be nice to have him with us."

"I thought we could make love by the fire." She smiles up at me and bites her lip.

She doesn't have to say another word. I pull Stone from my shoulder and cradle him in my arms. "Stone," I whisper repeatedly until his tiny eyes flutter open. He smiles up at me in a sleepy haze before Mia takes him from my arms.

I glance around the room, taking in the moment. My parents are on the floor with the kids, happier than I've seen them in years. Ma's beaming with pride, and Pop's already trying to make sense of the chaos of wrapping paper, boxes, and presents.

Joe and Suzy are snuggled on the floor beside the tree with Rosie, Gigi, and Luna. I don't envy the man. There's so much estrogen in that house, I'm surprised he hasn't gone mad.

Max and Anthony are whispering to each other with Asher and Tamara in front of them, ripping open their presents and throwing the wrapping paper backward onto them, but they don't seem to care.

Thomas and Angel are next to us on the couch. She's sitting in his lap with her legs hanging over the side closest to us. Nick's by Pop, showing him the new baseball glove as they talk about how someday he'll play for the Cubs.

Izzy's leaning against James as she sits between his legs with the kids near her feet. Trace, Mello, and Rocco are like three hellions, throwing things and tossing presents to their cousins like wild animals.

When I look to Fran and Bear, they're oblivious to the chaos in the room. They're into each other. It's nice to see them both finally happy. I never would've imagined that they would be a perfect match, but they are. He balances her nutty with his crazy, and somehow, they work perfectly.

Even my cousin Morgan showed up with his beautiful wife Race. They were late, which is normal for them. Their excuse this time is Race's ovulation schedule. Instead of being here with us, they've been at home fucking like animals, trying to get pregnant. It's a reason I can get behind.

I take it all in and try to memorize this moment. The room is filled with so much love and happiness, it's almost too much to comprehend.

I wish I could hit pause and keep us here, in this moment, forever.

How I've become this lucky is beyond me. I know the moment is fleeting. Time moves on. We're getting older. The kids are growing up and will soon take our place.

DELUSION

WHAT IF NOVELLA

USA *TODAY* BESTSELLING AUTHOR

CHELLE BLISS

PROLOGUE

I'm a simple woman. I grew up in a house with four brothers and loving parents who have remained married even after more than thirty years together. They showered us with love and affection. I'm the youngest of their children.

I have four very annoying older brothers. They're overprotective, and even though I'm an adult, that's never changed. They chased every man I ever liked—fuck the L-word—away as they screamed bloody murder and ran for their lives. Some would call the Gallo men alphas but not me. I call them pains in my ass.

They helped mold me into the woman I am today. I don't take shit from anyone. I know how to throw an amazing right hook, just the right angle to knee a guy in the balls so he'll never have children, and how to keep my mouth shut.

A couple years ago, we opened a tattoo shop together. We simply named it Inked. Our family has money, but we were raised to not sit on our asses like spoiled brats. We get up each day and go to work. It's our goal to stand on our own two feet. So far, we've been successful. Even though we fight like cats and dogs, we love each other fiercely and are very careful who we let into our little Gallo Family Club.

Thomas, my eldest brother and an undercover DEA agent, is the only one who doesn't work in the shop. He's a silent partner, and we pray that, one day, he'll get sick of his undercover work and settle down. He's been working inside the Sun Devils MC for some time. Moving up the ranks, he's made his mark and is on the verge of bringing the entire club to its knees.

Joe is one badass motherfucker. He's kinda my favorite, but I'll never tell him that. Shit, I'm not stupid. He's an amazing artist and tattooist, and he will be an amazing father. A while back, he rescued a hot little blond named Suzy. She's sweet as pie and used to be innocent. His badass biker ways ruined her, but naturally, I rubbed off on her, too. Some of his friends call him City because he was born in Chicago. The name fits him, but he'll always still be my Joey.

Mike is our shop's piercer, and he's built like a brick shit-house. He trained for years to be an MMA fighter. He was moving up the ranks and making a name for himself. That was until he literally knocked the woman of his dreams on her ass. He traded in his fighting days to help the love of his life, Mia, with her medical clinic. I'd almost say that he lost his balls some-where along the way, but that would just be my jaded, fucked-up perception of love talking.

Anthony. What can I say about him? He's my partner in crime most of the time. He and I are the single ones out of the group. Thomas doesn't count, because we never know anything about his life. Anthony wants to be a rock god. He wants ladies falling at his feet, professing their love, and freely offering their pussies to him with no strings attached. It makes me laugh, because honestly, he's already arrived if those are his criteria. He's stunning. One day, someone is going to steal him from me, and I'll end up being a lonely ol' biddy.

Then there's me—youngest child who still uses the word *Daddy*. I'm not talking about some sick fuckin' fetish shit either. I melt into a puddle of goo when my father's around. I've always been a daddy's girl. I don't think that'll ever change.

I live by no one's rules—well, maybe my daddy's at times—and I try to cram as much fun as I possibly can into my one shot at this life. I don't make apologies for my behavior. I shoot straight and tell it like it is. I never want to be tied down. Fuck convention. I don't need a husband to complete me a la Tom Cruise in *Jerry Maguire*.

Men are only good for a few things. One—they're handy when you have a flat tire or some other thing that requires heavy lifting. Two—their cocks are beautiful. Three—did I mention cock? Four—fucking. Wait... That's still cock-related.

I take it back. They're only good for two things in life: lifting heavy shit and fucking. Walks of shame are for pansy asses. I proudly leave them hanging, walking out the door, and I make no apologies for it. I'm not looking for a prince charming or knight in shining armor. I want to be fucked and then left the hell alone.

That is where my life was headed. I was blissfully happy and unencumbered. Life was grand—one big fucking party, and I was the guest of honor.

Ever have a man walk into your life and alter your entire universe?

I'm not talking about the small shit. I'm talking about the "big fuckin' bang." You're minding your own business, enjoying yourself, and then *WHAM*. Everything you think is right suddenly spins on its axis and bitch-slaps you in the face.

The party came to a screeching halt the night of my brother's wedding.

He changed everything. He fucked it all up.

World altered.

Party over.

Standing in the reception line had to be the most mind-numbing experience of my entire life. Greeting people I didn't know, welcoming them, and thanking them for coming to my brother's wedding—totally fucking exhausting.

Then there were the people who liked to pinch my cheeks like I was still a five-year-old girl. It took everything I had not to slap their hands away and to keep a smile glued to my face. By the time the line waned and I was able to hit the bar, my face hurt from my fake smile and my feet were screaming for relief.

I kicked off my shoes, pushing them under the bar and held my hand up to the bartender.

He sauntered over with a giant smile on his face. "What can I get you, darlin'?"

I leaned against the bar, putting my face in my hands, and stared him down. After the hour of awesomeness that was the receiving line, I wanted a drink and nothing more. I didn't feel like flirting or small talk.

"Jack, straight up," I said without cracking a smile.

"Single or double?"

"Double, please."

As he walked away to pour my drink, I turned and took in the room of people. The wedding was massive. Between Suzy and my ma, I think they had all of Tampa Bay crammed in the room.

"God, I need a drink," Mia said as she walked toward me.

"As bored as I am?" I asked as I leaned back, taking the pressure off my feet.

"At least you know all those people," she replied, motioning toward the bartender.

"The fuck I do. I know maybe half, and even then, I'm sketchy on their names."

"There's a small army here," she said. "Martini, please. Make it dirty with two olives."

"Someone looking to get a little buzzed, like me?"

"Just need to take the edge off," Mia replied. "Weddings make me itchy."

"Like you're allergic?"

"No, Izzy." She shook her head and laughed.

"Well, what the fuck? Clue a sister in."

We turned toward the bar, picking up our drinks and clinking them together.

"I feel like I'll always be a bridesmaid and never a bride."

"You have Mike." I sipped the Jack, letting it slide down my throat in one quick swallow.

Mia sipped her martini and winced before her lips puckered.

"I could be an old hag before he finds just the right way to ask me to marry him."

"Fuck tradition. Ask him already."

"He'd die," she said, bringing the glass to her lips and looking at me over the rim.

I held up my hand, snapping my fingers for a refill. "He'll get over it. Make a deadline, then. If he doesn't ask by a certain date, then you ask him."

"Maybe," she replied, setting her drink on the bar. "I wouldn't walk away if he doesn't ask. I love him too much."

"He loves you too, Mia. It's really sickening how often I have to hear about you." I laughed, tapping my fingernails against the wooden surface as I waited for my drink. "I love you, of course, but Jesus. The man talks about nothing else except for you and the clinic."

She hit my shoulder, causing me to laugh. "Would you rather him talk about Rob and working out all the time?"

Rob was my brother's trainer before he quit fighting. Rob and I had had a "thing" for a short time. It'd ended badly. Mostly for him, though, since my knee had found its way to his balls, and he'd ended up on the floor.

"Well, lesson one is don't refer to women as bitches."

"I'm sure he learned his lesson," she said and laughed. "I've heard more than once about your wicked, bony-ass knee. I think he still has a thing for you, Izzy."

I turned, holding my glass near my lips. "Ain't no way in hell am I ever dating him. Never. Ever. He's a total asshole."

Mia's laughter turned into a fit of giggles as she held on to the bar to maintain her balance. Tears streamed down her face and her dark eyes twinkled in the lighting. "I know he is. Total douche, but he has a soft side."

"Mia, stop trying to get me to hook up with Rob." I sipped the Jack Daniel's, the feeling of the first shot already making its way through my system. My legs felt a little wobbly and my core warmed. "I don't want a boyfriend, and I certainly don't want him."

"Someday, Izzy, you're going to meet that guy. One who makes your belly flip and toes curl. The electricity between you two will be undeniable. You just haven't met the right one."

"He's like a unicorn, Mia. Totally fictional bullshit."

She shook her head, finishing the last sip of her martini. "He's not. You just haven't found him yet. I feel those things when I'm with Michael."

"You're obviously mentally impaired," I chortled.

"I can't wait to see the day someone has you all in a fluster. You're going to be totally fucked."

"Mia, babe, there ain't no man tough enough to handle all this," I said, motioning down my body.

"Uh-huh," she clucked, her shoulders shaking with laughter. "I can't wait to see the damn day."

"It's dinnertime, ladies," my ma sang as she walked through the bar area. "It's time to take your seats."

"I could use a little food and a damn chair," I said, wondering how I'd make it to the table with my feet feeling like someone was rubbing hot coals on them as I slipped on my shoes.

"Me too," Mia said, following behind me.

We both walked gingerly toward the table that was placed on the dance floor and facing the entire room. I felt almost like a zoo animal as I sat down and looked around the large ballroom.

I ate my food and chatted with Mia throughout the dinner. Joe and Suzy were interrupted so many times with clinking glasses that I didn't have any idea if they were able to consume half their meal. It was cute, and at some point, I thought Joe would tell them to use their fucking forks to eat, but he didn't.

Suzy did that to him. She chilled him out at times when he was ready to burst. I knew he wanted the day to be special, and he did everything in his power to make sure it was perfect. Even held his tongue when I know he had to be biting it so hard that he drew blood.

"I'm hitting the bar again after dinner," I told Mia, hoping she'd join me.

"I'm in," she replied. "Until Michael drags me onto the dance floor."

"I wish you luck with that." I laughed, placing the last bit of pasta in my mouth.

I didn't get up immediately. My mother would have given me the stink eye if I'd looked too eager to run to the bar. I sat there staring at the crowd, smiling and making small talk with the others at the table. Sipping my wine, I counted the minutes until I could stand again on my aching feet and drink myself into oblivion.

Weddings, even my brother's, were bullshit. There was no fucking way in hell I'd be standing on the dance floor later, knocking over girls to get a bouquet of flowers. I wasn't looking for some symbolic nonsense that I'd be the next one walking down the aisle and giving up my freedom. Fuck tradition.

2

After downing countless drinks and chatting up Mia and all the long-lost family members who'd shown their asses at the wedding, I turned to see a very red-faced Suzy enter the ballroom. Joe stood by her side, but he looked calm—besides the small smirk on his face.

"Hey, sister," I said as I walked toward her. "I'm so excited to be able to say that and have it be true. I've always wanted a sister." I wrapped my arms around her, squeezing her a little too tightly.

"Can't breathe," she whispered.

"Man up," I said, releasing her.

"I'll be back, ladies. I'm going to grab a drink at the bar with my boys," Joe said before he kissed her cheek and left us alone.

"Where's your sister?" I asked, looking around the crowd.

Suzy had a sister, but they weren't close. The Gallos were

closer to her and more of a family than hers would ever be. I felt bad for her, but it made me love her more.

"Don't know and don't give a shit either." She shrugged and looked at the floor.

"You know you've turned into a badass with a potty mouth, Suz."

She smiled, shaking her head. "City. It's all his fault."

"I'd like to think I played a part in it, too." I laughed.

"You're always getting me in trouble, Izzy."

"Me?" I asked, holding my hand to my chest.

"Always."

A man cleared his throat next to us, and we both turned in his direction. "Excuse me, ladies. I don't mean to interrupt."

"Well, then don't," I slurred, looking the stranger up and down. Handsome, well-built, great hair, and totally doable. Maybe I shouldn't have been such a bitch, but then again, Jack was talking after I'd consumed more than necessary.

"Don't be rude, Izzy," Suzy said, turning to face him. "How can I help you?"

"I'm a friend of Thomas's, and he asked me to drop off a gift on his behalf." The man held out an envelope and waited for her to take it.

I took this moment to study him further. His muscles bulged underneath his suit as he held out his hands. His eyes were green, but I couldn't tell the shade. His jawline was sharp and strong.

"Is he okay?" I asked. I hadn't seen my brother in so long, and information wasn't flowing freely lately. I wanted him home, safe and sound.

"He is, and he's very sorry he couldn't make it," he said, looking down at me.

"Don't mind her," Suzy said to him, her eyes moving from me to him. "Thomas is her brother."

"Ah, you're *that* Izzy," he said, his lips turning up into a smile. "I've heard a lot about you."

What the fuck did that mean? I snarled, not entirely liking the shit-eating grin on his face. "And you are?" I asked, holding out my hand for him to take.

"James." He slid his hand along my palm and stilled. "James Caldo."

"Never heard of you, Jimmy," I said, trying to knock him down a peg. I didn't like that he had heard of me, with his "*that* Izzy" comment, and I'd never even heard his name.

He brought my hand to his lips and placed a kiss just below my knuckles. "Perfect."

His lips scorched my skin. An overwhelming sense of want came over me. I felt the urge to jump into his arms and kiss his very full lips. My toes curled painfully in my shoes as I stared at his mouth against my skin. As he removed his lips from my hand and brought his eyes back to mine, I wiped all evidence of want from my face.

Suzy coughed, ruining my fantasy and bringing me back to reality. "Thanks, James. I'll give this to Joseph for you. Why don't you stay and enjoy the wedding?" She smiled at the man.

"What?" I asked, turning toward her. Suzy played dirty. Her angel act was just that—an act.

"We have plenty of food, and I'm sure the Gallos would love

to talk with you about their Thomas," Suzy said, grinning like an idiot.

I gave her the look of death. What in the fuck was wrong with her?

"You can keep James company tonight, Izzy. You didn't bring a date."

She did not just say that. If it weren't her wedding, I swear to shit I would've smacked her. I could feel my cheeks turning red as his eyes flickered to mine.

"I'd love to stay. Thank you. Izzy, would you like a drink?" he asked, still holding my hand in his.

"Only because Suzy would want me to be a gracious host," I said, looking at her out of the corner of my eye.

"I don't want to put you out or anything. I'm a *big* boy and can handle myself. I just thought you could use a drink to unwind a bit. You feel a little tense, and that mouth of yours could get you into trouble."

Obviously, he was full of himself. Trust me when I say I can smell a cocky bastard from a mile away. I grew up with enough of them to sniff them out across a room.

"I don't need a babysitter, Jimmy, but I'll take the drink."

"It's James," he said, squeezing my hand.

"You two kids play nice," Suzy said before she waved and walked away.

"Bitch," I mumbled under my breath as I turned back toward the bar.

"Excuse me?" he asked, gripping my arm as he pulled me backward.

I stopped and faced him. "Are you going to release me anytime soon?"

"Highly unlikely." He smirked.

"Jimmy, listen. I don't know what your deal is or who the fuck you think you are, but no one touches me without permission."

With that, he released me, but not before squeezing my arm. "You'll be begging for my touch."

I glared at him, floored by his cockiness. "Obviously you know nothing about me then." I left him in the dust.

I leaned against the bar, feeling him behind me as I motioned to the bartender. At this point in the evening, I no longer had to verbalize my order. He knew it.

"Like what you see?" I asked as I kept my eyes forward.

"Your brother didn't do you justice."

Resting my back against the bar, I asked, "What exactly do you think of me?"

He smiled, stepping closer as he invaded my personal space. He brushed the hair from my cheek, running his fingertip down my face. "You're prettier in person. You are tough as nails, just like your brother said, but I can see the real Izzy underneath."

I snarled, feeling all kinds of bitchy. "There's no hidden me underneath. This is who I am. I make no apologies for my bitchiness or candid comments."

"Oh, little girl, you're so much more than a smart mouth." He leaned in, hovering his mouth just above mine.

I held my breath, silently debating if I wanted him to kiss me. I had to be crazy. There was nothing about this man I liked, besides his face. His words were infuriating, his attitude was obnoxious, and the fact that he thought he had me pegged made me want to slap his face when he spoke.

His eyes searched mine as I stood there not breathing and just keeping myself upright against the bar.

"You're an asshole, Jimmy."

He didn't back away. Instead, he held his ground, pressing against my body. "It's James," he murmured.

I swallowed hard, my stomach flipping inside my body like I'd just gone down the giant hill on a roller coaster. "Still an asshole," I whispered, my tongue darting out to caress my lips and almost touch his.

"Doll, I never claimed to be nice." His lips were turned up into a grin so large that it almost kissed his eyes.

"Can we drink now?" I asked, wanting to move our bodies apart. The heat coming off him was penetrating my dress and causing my body to break out in a sweat. The pop and sizzle I felt inside was more than just the alcohol. James, the asshole, did naughty things to my body, and I needed distance between us.

"Don't you think you've had enough?" he asked without moving out of my personal space.

I placed my hands against his chest and pushed. He didn't budge or falter as I pushed again.

He tipped his head back and laughed. "Is that all you got?"

"Fucker. First off, I have more, but I don't want to cause a scene at my brother's wedding. Second, I haven't had enough. You aren't my father, and you don't get to tell me when to stop drinking. Last time I checked my driver's license, I was old enough to make that choice for myself." I crossed my arms over my chest, trying to put some space between his torso and mine.

"Let's get one thing straight, Isabella." His hot breath tickled the nape of my neck as he put his mouth against my ear and spoke. "I will have you in my bed tonight."

I rolled my eyes and pursed my lips, trying to hide exactly how excited that statement had made me. I didn't want to date the man, but shit, I wanted to fuck him.

"You're quite sure of yourself, *Jimmy*." I emphasized his name, knowing it would drive him crazy.

"There are things I'm very sure of."

"Like what?" I spat.

"From the moment I saw you, I knew I wanted to be inside you. When I touched you, I felt something, and I know you felt it, too. There's something between us. I think I need to fuck you out of my system."

"Is that the best line you have?" I hissed, feeling his lips against my ear. I groaned, closing my eyes to let the feel of his mouth on my skin soak into my bones.

"I don't need lines, Izzy," he growled with his teeth caging the flesh of my ear.

My toes curled inside my heels; I felt him all over my body. No one had ever affected me in this way.

"I'm down for a challenge."

"Doll, there's no challenge with a willing participant."

I pulled back, feeling his mouth slip from my skin, and looked him in the eye. "I was referring to your ability to keep up with me."

Again, he laughed and held his stomach. "Izzy, Izzy. Baby, if you can walk right in the morning without still feeling me inside you, I'd be shocked. I have no doubt I can keep up with you. You'll never be the same after I've fucked you."

"You better buy me a drink, then. I'll go easier on you." I smiled, turning my back to him and facing the bartender. Then I snapped my fingers, pointing in front of me as he smiled and grabbed the bottle of Jack.

Over my shoulder, James called out, "Make it two." He placed one hand on the bar to my right and stood to the left of me. His forearm pressed against my back, holding me in place and leaving me no escape. "What shall we drink to?" he asked.

"My brother," I replied. Thomas was our link. The connection that James and I shared. "What did he say about me?" I asked.

James smiled, turning his head to face me. "That you're his favorite sister."

"Jackass, I'm his only sister."

"I know." He laughed. "He told me you're hard to please."

I shook my head. "I'm not. I'm just picky, and I don't settle."

"Can't fault you there. He's proud of you."

"For what?" I asked, looking at him, stunned.

"He's proud of the strong woman you've grown into, and I'd have to agree with the little bit of you I've experienced."

"Ha," I said. "I learned everything I know from my four brothers."

The bartender placed our shots on the bar and started to walk away.

"Hey, can we get two more?" I asked before he could get too far.

He nodded and grabbed the bottle, making two more drinks.

I lifted my glass, waiting for James to pick his up before I spoke. "To Thomas." I tipped my drink, clinking the glass with his before downing the liquid.

I watched over the rim as James swallowed it and didn't wince. His features were so strong and manly. I mean, what the fuck was that? I'd never thought of anyone as manly. *Maybe I shouldn't have another drink.*

"Tell me who you really are," James said as he placed his empty glass on the bar.

"What you see is what you get," I said before I licked the Jack off my lips.

"I know there's the Izzy everyone sees and the real woman underneath."

"James, what you see is what you get."

"Are you always so hard?" he asked, brushing his thumb against my hand as it rested on the bar.

"I don't know. Are you always so damn nosy?"

"I think you haven't found the right man to tame your sass."

I turned to glare at him. "Hold up. I need a man—is that what you're saying?"

"No," he said, shaking his head. "I think your tongue is so sharp because you haven't found the man who makes you whole. Someone who crawls inside you so deep that you finally figure out who you are, what you were always meant to be."

"What the fuck?" I asked, scrunching my eyebrows in confusion.

"It's for another day, doll. Sometimes, we just need someone to bring out our true nature."

"Either I've clearly had too much to drink or you're talking out of your ass. I'm going to go with option two."

He cupped my face in his hand, rubbing the spot just behind my ear with his fingertips. "Sometimes, we don't know who we really are until we find the perfect partner to bring it out."

"Jimmy, I think we were talking about one night. You and me fucking each other's brains out and then walking away. Now, you're talking crazy if you think I need you in my life to complete me. I'm certainly not Renée Zellweger, and you're no Tom Cruise. I don't need any man to complete me. I'm quite happy with my life."

"Fine. Tell me who you are." His stare pinned me in place.

Swallowing, I didn't take my eyes off him as I thought about my reply. I'd never had to explain myself to anyone. "Who are you, James?"

He shook his head, a small smile on his face as he laughed softly. "I'm a protector."

I cut him off. "Do you think I need protecting?"

"I don't know," he replied.

"I have four older brothers who have made it their life's mission to make sure I'm protected. It's the last thing I need in my life."

"Can I finish?" he asked, taking a deep breath and tilting his head.

"Yes," I said, gulping hard and searching for some moisture in my now parched mouth.

"As I was saying, I'm a natural protector. That's why I joined the agency. I'm loyal to the core. I know what I want in life, and I never give up until I get it. There's nothing better than a good chase. Once I have my mind set on something, I'll stop at nothing to get what I want."

"Am I your goal?" I asked, smirking and feeling a little playful.

"What if I said yes?" James asked, moving his face closer to mine.

"I'd say you better have a new game plan."

"Are you a secret lesbian?" he teased, the corner of his mouth twitching.

"No! Fuck!" I hissed. "I mean, more power to anyone who loves vag, but I'm all about cock, baby."

He closed his eyes, his breath skidding across my face as he blew the air out of his lungs. "If you talk about cock one more time, I'm taking you upstairs and fucking you until you can't scream anymore."

"That sounds creepy."

His chest shook as a laugh fell from his lips. "You have to be the most difficult female I have ever met."

"Maybe I'm more woman than you can handle," I purred, running my hand down his chest. Underneath my fingertips, I could feel his muscles flexing. I splayed my palm against his shirt, letting my hand rest against his rock-hard pec.

"Doll, I'm more man than you've ever had. That, I can guarantee."

The air between us crackled. Like it did in the movies. Sparks were probably visible to any guest milling around the bar area.

"Izzy," Mia said, interrupting my moment with James.

I blinked slowly, looking over his shoulder and smiling at her. "Hey, Mia."

"Who do we have here?" she asked, a grin on her face.

"Mia, this is Jimmy, Thomas's friend."

His eyes flashed before he turned to face her. "Mia, it's nice to meet you. I'm James." He held out his hand, waiting for her touch.

"James, I'm Mike's girl." She slid her hand into his palm, shaking it slowly.

"I'd say you're more than a girl." He pulled her hand to his mouth and placed a soft kiss on the top.

She laughed, her cheeks turning red. Did he have this effect on all women? "You know what I mean," she said, batting her eyelashes.

Thank Christ Mike wasn't here to see Mia blushing and flirting with Jimmy boy.

"Mike's a very lucky man," James replied, releasing her hand.

I sighed, rolling my eyes before glaring at Mia. "Where's Mike, anyway?" I asked, feeling a bit jealous of his flirting.

I was bothered that he was flirting with her, but why? I shouldn't have been. I didn't like him. I wanted to use him. That was all. I wanted to have my way with him for one night and walk away unscathed. Jealousy wasn't an emotion I was used to experiencing, and I sure as hell didn't know how to deal with it.

"He's dancing with his ma," she replied, winking at me and mouthing, "Wow," as James turned to look at me before returning his attention to her.

"Would you like a drink, Mia?"

She smiled, nodding. "Always."

James motioned to the bartender as I walked to stand next to Mia.

"He's sexy as fuck," Mia whispered in my ear.

"He's an asshole, though."

"Nah, he couldn't be. He seems to be a perfect gentleman."

"Maybe you shouldn't have another if you think he's not a total prick."

"You're just too damn hard on men, Iz."

"He's cocky, Mia. He makes Mike and Joe seem like teddy bears."

"I like him," she said, her eyes raking over him.

"Hey, slutty Aphrodite, you're taken."

"I can look, *putana*. I'm not dead. I can tell you like him."

My mouth dropped open. "What?" I whispered. "I do not."

She smiled, nodding at me. "You do."

"All right, ladies," James said as he held out two glasses of Jack.

"To love," Mia said. "And passion."

"For fuck's sake," I blurted, bringing the cup to my mouth.

"I'll drink to that," James said, holding me in place with his stare.

I didn't respond as I slammed back the drink, letting it slide down my throat. Instead, I started to picture sex with James. There was a simmering tension between us. An animal attraction that was undeniable. I wanted to slap him and fuck him at the same time. I wanted to let loose and show him what Izzy Gallo really had.

"Thanks for the drink, James. I'm going to find Mike. You

two have a fun night," Mia said, winking and smiling as she waved and walked away.

"Traitor," I mumbled, turning to face James.

"You want to fuck me?" James asked, taking the drink from my hand.

"What?" I asked, wondering if he would be so bold.

"You in or you out?" he growled with his hand on my hip, gripping it roughly with his fingers.

"I don't even know you," I replied, his hold on me starting to feel like a branding iron under my dress.

"What do you want to know?" he asked, still touching my body.

"You could be a bad man." That sounded stupid and childish, but I was trying to not seem too eager to jump in the sack with him.

"Would your brother send me here if I were a total asshole?"

He had me there. "No," I admitted.

"Do you know everything about every man you sleep with?" he asked, running his free hand down my arm.

"No."

"Do you want to fuck me?"

I bit my lip, blinking slowly and processing my thoughts. Did I want to? Fuck yes, I did. Was it a good idea? Hell no, it wasn't a good idea. But then again, mistakes sometimes leave the biggest mark on one's life.

"Maybe," I squeaked out.

He released my hip, moving his hand to the small of my back. "Ready?" he asked, cocking an eyebrow.

"Now?"

"Are you scared, little girl?" he teased.

"Of you?" There wasn't a man on this planet who scared me. The fear I felt was from within. It was pointed directly at me. A man wasn't the issue. James was, and the way my body reacted to him had me on high alert.

"Yeah," he said, the side of his mouth turning up into a grin I wanted to smack off his face.

This was where I should've called a time-out. The words I should've spoken didn't come out of my mouth.

"James, I have four older brothers. You hardly scare me."

"But they want to protect you and love you. While I, on the other hand, want to bury my dick so far inside you that I ruin you for eternity."

"You say such beautiful things." I'd be lying if I didn't admit to myself that he made my pussy clench with his words.

"You in or you out?"

"The real question, Jimmy, is am I going to let you in?" I turned back toward the bar and signaled for another drink.

Let the games begin.

3

W hat the fuck was wrong with me? This wasn't how I normally treated a woman I'd just met. There was something different about Izzy, though. I'd felt like I knew her the moment we met. Thomas had filled my head with stories about his little sister and made her bigger than life. Seeing her in person only drove the point home that she was different than other women.

If he'd heard how I was talking to her, he'd have my nuts in a vise, making sure I'd never be able to get another hard-on in my life. I needed to slow my shit down.

"I'm a patient man, and you'll be in my bed before the night is through."

She laughed, her head falling back as her teeth shone in the light. "I can't leave yet," she said, grabbing her drink and swirling the contents inside. "I have to do all the bridesmaid bullshit."

"I can tell by your comment that you believe in true love."

"Fuck love. Don't get me wrong. I'm thrilled for Joe and Suzy, but the shit isn't for me. Don't say it," she warned, her eyes turning into small slits as she glared at me.

"What? That you just haven't met the right man?" I stood next to her at the bar and leaned my arm against the wooden surface as I faced her.

"Yes. It's not about that. Love makes shit messy," she explained before bringing the glass to her lips.

"Can I get a beer?" I asked the bartender as he walked by, and his eyes flickered to us.

His eyes raked over Izzy, and I saw the hunger burning inside them. I felt an overwhelming urge to rip them from his skull just so he couldn't eye-fuck her again.

He looked to me and snarled as he reached into the cooler, popped the top of a Yuengling, and placed it in front of me. Grabbing the cool bottle, I let my fingers slide over the wetness. Then I wished I could squelch the internal burning I felt for Izzy.

"You sound like a woman who came from a broken home. Thomas speaks very highly of your parents and the love they feel for each other. What turned you off love?" Bringing the bottle to my lips, I watched her as she swallowed hard and played with the glass in her hand.

"It's not love that I have an issue with. It's the battle that ensues because of it."

After pulling the beer from my mouth, I shook my head, trying to make sense of her statement. "What battle?"

"The one every girl I've ever known has gone through. They

have to decide how much of themselves they're willing to lose to be with the man they love."

"That's bullshit."

"There isn't a female I know who didn't change after being in 'love,'" she said, making air quotes and rolling her eyes.

"Maybe they brought out the real woman who was always lurking under the surface and too scared to show."

"You can have your opinion, Jimmy, but I know what I see."

"Ladies and gentlemen," a man called through the microphone. "If we could have the bride and groom on the dance floor and all the single ladies and gentlemen join them."

"You going?" I asked with a cocked eyebrow.

"It's stupid," she said before taking a sip of Jack.

"You're such a party pooper. Get your fine ass to the dance floor."

"Or what?"

I smiled, shaking my head slowly. "Let's place a bet."

"Whatcha got in mind, Jimmy?" Izzy cooed, rubbing the lapels on my suit jacket with her fingers.

"If I catch the garter, then we ditch this place and head to my room. No questions asked and no lip from you." I'd knock every motherfucker on the dance floor over to get the garter and have Izzy underneath me within an hour.

"Okay, and if I catch the bouquet, then I don't have to go anywhere with you. You leave, and I get to spend the rest of the night in peace." She tilted her head, waiting for me to accept that challenge.

"Fuck yeah. I'm game," I said. Then I gulped the last bit of beer as she downed her drink and placed it on the bar. Setting my hand on the small of her back, I guided her away from the bar.

She stood stiffly next to me as we watched her brother use his teeth to remove the garter from underneath the dress of his new bride. The crowd cheered when he emerged from the dress victorious. Twirling the small scrap of material in his hands, he raised his arms in victory.

"You ready to lose?" I asked, looking down at Izzy.

"One thing I'm never good at is losing, Jimmy."

"Single gentlemen first. All others, please clear the floor," the DJ said as everyone moved away, leaving about fifteen of us to jockey for the garter.

I looked around, sizing up the competition. I was the biggest besides Michael, Izzy's brother. I took my spot to the side, knowing I could move quickly in front of the crowd and snatch the material before it turned into a free-for-all.

As the DJ started the countdown, Joe turned his back, practicing his throw, and the men moved with his motion. I readied myself as my heart hammered in my chest louder than a drum at a Metallica concert. I kept my eyes locked to his hand as he moved, waiting to see it fly through the air.

As his hand jerked back, the material flew through the air only feet to my right. I moved quickly, stepping in front of everyone else, and snatched it easily. The wedding attendees cheered as I turned to Izzy with a sinful smile, and nothing but seeing her ass in the air, waiting for my dick, filled my mind.

"Fucker," she mouthed at me as I walked toward her.

"It's all on you now. Better catch that bouquet," I said, running my index finger down her cheek.

She closed her eyes, swallowing hard before opening them. Inside her baby blues was a fire burning so hot that I could see her pupils dilate as she looked at me. She nodded before making her way toward the crowd of women now standing at the ready.

She whispered to Mia, and their eyes flickered to me. A giant smile spread across Mia's face as Izzy glared at me. Winking, Mia tipped her chin in my direction as her smile grew wider. I said a silent prayer as Suzy readied herself with her bouquet and turned her back on the crowd. Mia bent at the knees like an athlete waiting for the gunshot to sound.

Silently, I prayed that Mia could take Izzy down and make sure she didn't grab the flowers. I wouldn't want to lose a bet to Isabella Gallo, and certainly not one as important as this. I didn't need a bet to bed a woman, but I had a feeling Izzy needed to feel like the choice was out of her hands. She needed an out. Needed something to tell herself to make it all okay to spend the night with me.

I should have felt guilty about the bet, but I didn't. Not one fucking bit.

The countdown began, my heart matching the drum roll blaring through the speakers. "Come on, Mia," I whispered.

My palms grew sweaty as I formed my hands into a tight fist, trying to shake out some of the nervous energy. If Izzy caught the fucking bouquet, I'd have a very long night filled with fantasies and jacking off like a twelve-year-old boy.

As the flowers traveled through the air, Mia held out her arm, pushing Izzy backward. Mia jumped in the air, Izzy looking at Mia in horror. The flowers grazed Mia's fingers, sailing over her head to the woman standing behind her.

The redheaded beauty closed her hands around the flowers, jumped up and down, and squealed.

"Fuck," Izzy hissed, turning to me and glaring in my direction.

I smiled, shrugging as I held up the garter and twirled it in my fingers. "You're mine," I mouthed before licking my lips.

The hunger I felt inside when looking at her was unlike anything I'd ever felt before. I'd lusted after women in the past, but the want for her was so intense that I wasn't even sure one night with her would be enough to satisfy the craving.

She turned to Mia, saying a few things, with her hands flapping around. Clearly Izzy was angry, but all Mia did was shrug and smile. Then Izzy turned her back, quickly moving toward me.

"Mia totally fucked me," she said as she stood in front of me, looking up into my eyes.

My lips curved into a smile as I stuffed the garter in my jacket pocket. "I don't care how I get you, but tonight, I'm the only one fucking you, doll."

"Fine," she said, standing with her legs shoulder-width apart and her arms crossed over her chest.

"I'll give you one out. Kiss me, and if you feel nothing, I'll let you out of the bet." It could all blow up in my face, but I couldn't be a total prick. I didn't want her to be an unwilling participant.

"Just one kiss?" she asked as her face softened.

"Yes," I said, holding her face in my hand and running my thumb across her bottom lip.

"I'll take you up on that offer, but I don't welsh on my bets."

"It's your only out. So use it if you need to, or else we're going to my room. No more waiting."

"Come on," she said, grabbing my hand and pulling me toward the ballroom exit.

I laughed as I followed behind her, letting her lead me into the corridor.

"Over there," she said as she pointed down the hallway near the elevator bank.

"Anywhere you want, doll."

The crowd thinned as we walked to a small cutout near the bathrooms.

"Why don't we go outside for a moment? Grab some air," I said. I didn't want to kiss her outside the bathroom. There were too many wedding guests, and it was not sexy at all.

"Are you pussying out?" she said as she stopped and turned to face me.

"Fuck no. I just don't feel like kissing you outside the bathroom. I've never been a pussy a day in my life."

"Fine, but fuck, these shoes are killing me," she said as she reached down and pulled one off her foot. When she removed the second one, she sighed, closing her eyes like she'd had a weight lifted off her shoulders. She shrank by at least three inches, making me feel even bigger than I was.

"Are *you* pussying out?" I asked, teasing her for taking a moment to enjoy the newfound freedom of being shoeless.

"You're fucking crazy. Just know that once my lips touch yours, there's no turning back. Come on, Jimmy boy. Show me what you got," she said as she pushed open the exit door in the hallway.

We stepped outside into the cool night air, into privacy. The back of the hotel was deserted as the parking lot light flickered above us.

"So now what?" she asked, turning to face me.

I looked down at her, taking in her body before staring into her eyes. I didn't respond as I stepped into her space and pulled her toward me. Holding her neck with one hand and her back with the other, I molded my body to hers. Pushing her against the brick façade, I hovered my lips above hers.

Her eyes were wide, the deep blue appearing black in the darkness. Her warm breath tickled my lips as her breathing grew harsh. I waited a moment, letting the anticipation build, knowing that the kiss would alter everything. There would be no turning back.

I crushed my lips to hers, feeling the warmth and softness, tasting the Jack as I ran my tongue along the seam of her closed mouth. A small moan from her filled my mouth, causing my dick to pulse. Pulling her closer to me, tipping her head back farther with the grip on her neck, I devoured her mouth.

Her hands slid into my hair, trying to grab hold, but the cropped cut made it impossible. She dug her nails into my neck, kissing me back with such fervor that I knew I had her. Skimming my hand down her dress, I pulled the material between my fingers and hiked it up enough to touch the skin above her knee. Then she broke the kiss, backing away as she stared at me and tried to catch her breath.

Before she could respond or tell me to stop, I plunged my tongue into her mouth, stripping her ability to speak. Her hands found their way into my suit jacket, gripping my back and kneading the muscles just above my ass. I ground myself against her, pinning her against the wall as I kissed her like a man possessed.

The ember of lust that had filled my body when I'd first touched her turned into an out-of-control wildfire. She shuddered as my fingers slid up her inner thigh, stopping just outside her panties. I rubbed my finger back and forth, touching the edge where the lace met her soft flesh. Her body grew soft in my arms as she moaned into my mouth.

Not waiting for approval, I pulled the material aside and dipped my fingers into her wetness. I slid my fingers up, circling her clit with my index and middle finger. A strangled moan escaped her lips as my touch grew more demanding. She pushed herself against my fingers, wanting more pressure from my touch.

Gliding my fingers down, I inserted a single finger inside her pussy. She was tight, slick, and ready. Her inner walls squeezed against my digit, sucking it farther inside. Moving my thumb to her clit, I finger-fucked her, bringing her to the brink of orgasm without breaking the kiss. She held on to my shoulder, digging her nails in so hard that I could feel the pinch through my suit jacket.

Just as her breathing grew more erratic and her pussy clamped down on my finger, I pulled out. She sucked in a breath as her eyes flew open.

"What the fuck?" she hissed as she glared at me.

"You want to come, doll?" I asked, sticking my finger in my mouth and groaning.

This was just as much of a fucking tease for me as it was for her. To taste her and feel her against me made my body blaze with need and want, and I wasn't sure one night could extinguish the flame.

"What kind of question is that?" she snapped.

"It's simple. If you want to come, you'll follow me to my room, or I walk away and never look back."

She placed her hands against my chest, slightly pushing me away from her. Staring into my eyes, she stated firmly, "No strings attached."

"I didn't picture myself getting down on one knee and proposing." I instantly regretted the words. It wasn't that I wanted to propose, but I didn't want her to feel cheap and disposable. Then again, she'd set the stage for that type of statement. Izzy Gallo didn't want to be tied down, and I didn't want to have to explain shit to her brother. I liked my life and balls too much to tell him that I wanted her in my life.

"Music to my ears," she said, dropping her hand to my chest, sliding it down my abdomen and grabbing my dick. "Let's see if you're as good as you claim, Jimmy."

"Babe, I'm going to rock your world so fuckin' hard, you're going to get down on one knee and propose to *me*."

She threw her head back and laughed. Her beauty was amplified when she smiled. With a small burst of giggles breaking free, she tried to speak. "You obviously think highly of yourself." She squeezed my hardness and bit her lip, stifling the laughter.

"I'm done talking," I said as I pulled her toward the door. "Time to put up or shut up, doll."

"I like a challenge," she replied as she touched the door handle.

Reaching in front of her, I placed my hand over hers. Pulling the door open, I waited for her to step inside. When she walked, she shook her hips, and the movement made it almost impossible to keep my hands to myself. I nestled my palm against the small of her back, helping her toward the bank of elevators.

"Last chance to chicken out," I teased in her ear.

"I may have a pussy, Jimmy, but I'm sure as hell *not* one."

"Usually, a mouth like that I'd say is crude, but hearing you talk dirty just makes me want to jam my cock inside to quiet you," I whispered, trying to avoid the attention of the people passing by us.

As soon as the elevator doors closed, I had her against the wall. I claimed her mouth, her tongue sweet from the Jack lingering on the surface as I devoured her. Caging her face in my hands, I stole her breath and replaced it with my own.

When we reached my floor, I broke the kiss. Her body was still as her eyes fluttered open, and her breathing was ragged. I grabbed her hand, pulling her toward my room, a little too eager to feel her skin.

The chemistry was off the charts. As soon as the door closed behind us, I pushed her against it, capturing her lips. The need I felt to be inside her bordered on animalistic as our heavy breathing and panting filled the room. I grabbed the purse she had tucked under her arm and tossed it over my head, removing any distraction.

I dropped to my knees, looking up at her, and said, "I need to taste you."

She was a vision. She had on thigh-highs that connected to a garter belt and lace panties.

She didn't reply, but she did spread her legs. I cupped her ass, ripping the thin lace material from her body and bringing her forward before I swept my tongue against her skin. I could smell her arousal. I wanted to worship at her altar.

I lifted her with my hands, placing her legs over my shoulders as I feasted on her. I sucked like a starved man, licking every ridge and bump as she chanted, "Fuck yeah," and "Oh my God." I didn't relent when she came on my face, her legs almost a vise around my head. I dug in deeper, sucking harder as I brushed her asshole with my fingertip. Her body shuddered, the light touch against the sensitive spot sending her quickly over the edge for the second time.

I gave her a moment to catch her breath before I peeled her off me and stood. As soon as I did, her lips captured mine; the tiger inside her had been unleashed. Her tongue danced inside my mouth, intertwining with mine. She wrapped her legs around my waist, digging her pussy into my already hard and throbbing cock.

The wetness from her pussy soaked through my dress shirt, searing my flesh. I walked toward the bed, unzipping her dress and resting my palm against her back. I wanted to rip her dress off, take her fast and hard, but I knew I needed to take my time with her. This would be my only shot to have Izzy Gallo, and I wouldn't waste it. I wanted to spend all night inside her and hear her scream my name.

My first instinct kicked in as I pulled her dress down her shoulders. She released my hair, removing her arms from the small scraps of material that encased her. Holding her body with one arm, I slid my other hand up her side and cupped her breast.

Rolling her nipple between my fingers, I pulled her body closer and left no space between us. I toyed with the hoop piercing, gently tugging on her nipple to see her pain threshold.

Her breathing grew erratic as her body shuddered against mine. Biting her lip, I moaned into her mouth as I tried to keep myself upright. I had never kissed someone and felt weak-kneed, but with her, it was like my first kiss. World-ending. Life-altering. Completely fucked up.

She sucked the air from my lungs, capturing my moans as she rubbed her core against me. Unable to wait any longer, I reached between us and plunged my fingers back inside her. Her body sucked them in, pulsing around their length as I dragged them back out. Curling them up, I rubbed her G-spot with each lash of my digits.

Her fingers moved to my shoulders, digging into my flesh as I brought her close to coming. Claiming her mouth, stealing each other's air, and driving each other absolutely mad, I knew I was fucked.

That's the thing about sex. Touching someone for the first time is so intense that you feel like you'll never be the same. I felt that way with her in my arms and my fingers inside her. I knew I'd be changed forever. Izzy was my equal. Her wit, sass, and sexuality couldn't compare to any other woman I'd ever met. How could I go back to average when I'd had spectacular?

I removed my fingers, hearing her hiss at the loss of friction. I shrugged off my suit jacket; my body cooled, but not my need for her. I laid her down, her chest exposed and the bottom of the dress a mess as I pulled off my tie and started to open my shirt.

A small smile crept across her face as she fondled her tits.

Taking a deep breath, I tried to calm my insides as I watched her touch herself. Giving up on the slow-ass fucking buttons, I ripped my shirt open, and the buttons flew everywhere.

Fuck slow. I needed relief. I needed her.

The smile melted from her face as I stared down at her. She pulled at her nipples, her eyes raking over my chest. Moving forward, I unzipped my pants. I grabbed her ankles, yanking her to the edge of the bed. Unable to wait any longer, I pushed down my pants, letting my cock spring free.

Her eyes traveled down my body, landing on my dick. Then her eyes perked up and the corner of her mouth turned into a devilish smile.

"Impressive," she said as she cupped a breast in each hand and squeezed.

"Fuck," I hissed, realizing I didn't have a condom.

What a fucking idiot. I hadn't planned on taking her to bed, or else I would've been prepared. This hadn't been in the cards for this weekend, but I'd take the jackpot and ride the wave.

"I got it," she said as she rolled over and grabbed her purse off the floor, pulling a strip of condoms from inside.

Normally, the sight would disturb me, but not with her. "Planning on getting lucky?" I asked, staring down at her.

She laughed for a moment before her smile faded. "I'm not trashy, Jimmy. They're from the bachelorette party."

4

IZZY

I know how it looked. Like I was the type of girl who carried around a box of condoms because I never knew whom I'd be fucking from night to night. It was the furthest thing from the truth. Don't get me wrong. I'm not a prude, and I never put down any woman, no matter how many partners she's had. Men can do it without being looked at with disdain, and I wanted to high-five every lady out there getting what she wants.

I had distanced myself from sleeping around. Men were a complication I didn't need or want. Flash was my standby. The one I called when I needed some cock and a quick goodbye. Lately, that in itself had turned into an issue and a fucking headache. I loved him, but as a best friend. We had passion and the sex was fantastic, but the spark wasn't there and neither were the feelings.

Flash was like my favorite teddy bear as a kid, but he ate

pussy like a pro. He was comfortable. Maybe a little too easy for me, and I'd grown complacent with just okay instead of fucking amazing. I knew I needed to make a change and kick Flash's ass to the curb, but I had to be gentle about it.

Looking up at James, I didn't see anything comfortable or easy about the man. He stared down at me with such passion and burning that I worried he'd burst into flames before my very eyes.

Sitting up, I tore one condom from the strip and threw the rest on the floor. I'd brought a bunch of them to the bachelorette party as party favors and to throw around at the girls. I'd wanted to make sure every cock was covered and that all the girls were safe. It was something I always preached.

"Must've been one hell of a party."

"Oh, it was," I said before tearing open the package with my teeth.

I motioned with my finger for him to step closer, batting my eyelashes at him. I needed to taste him before I covered it. I moved, kneeling on the edge of the bed and waiting for his dick to come to eye level. The glimmer of shiny metal made my insides twist and my pussy convulse. There's something about a man with a piercing in his cock.

I grabbed his ass, bringing him closer to my face as I took in all his glory, feasting on him with my eyes. I opened wide, laying his hardness against my tongue and closing my lips around his length. The velvety firmness mixing with the saltiness made my mouth water. I swallowed around his dick, pulling it farther into my throat, and fought the urge to gag. It hit the back of my throat, cutting off my airway as my eyes watered.

Squeezing his ass, I sucked him deeper before pulling out and repeating the process. I looked up into his eyes, watching his head fall back in ecstasy. Digging my nails into his rock-hard muscles, I flicked the underside of the tip with my tongue. His body trembled beneath my fingertips and my body warmed. I felt powerful with him at my mercy.

The apadravya caressed my tongue and tapped my teeth as I worked his cock. Just as I felt him grow harder and his body shake uncontrollably, I released him, a popping noise filling the room.

His body jerked, his cock lurching forward as if it was searching for my mouth of its own volition. His teeth chattered as he sucked in air and glared at me.

I shrugged and smiled. "Sucks, doesn't it?" I said and began to giggle.

He pushed me back before grabbing my feet and yanking me to the edge of the bed. I screamed from happiness—his strength had shocked me. I don't know why. The man was huge. He looked like a giant next to me, but I hadn't thought he could move me around like a fucking rag doll. Holding the condom up for him to take, I bit my lip. His cock was red and bulging as it bobbed in the air.

The shiny metal looked like it was ready to pop free on both sides. I couldn't wait any longer to feel it stroking my insides. He slid the rubber over his cock, paying careful attention to the piercing, while I took in the sight of him.

He had strong, broad shoulders covered in tattoos. I wanted to lean forward and get a better look, but I remained in place. If I hadn't known better or had seen a picture of him first, I would've bet money that he was airbrushed. He was too perfect, with all his rippling muscles, hard body, and flawless skin.

He caught me looking and winked at me. My cheeks turned pink and heated. I don't know why. I was half dressed, had had his dick in my mouth, and he'd tasted me. At this point, what was there to be embarrassed about?

He grabbed the bottom of my dress as I lifted my ass and let him remove it. It flew across the room, landing near the door, where we had begun. I held out my arm, looking to touch his skin, and he gripped my wrist and pulled me off the bed. Then I wrapped my legs around his body, trying not to fall to the floor, and instantly captured his lips.

He grunted, grinding his dick against my pussy as I clung to him. Reaching underneath my leg, he grabbed his dick, rubbing it back and forth twice before jamming it inside me.

I cried out, not having expected to feel so full and stretched. But then he stilled, letting my body adjust before he turned and pushed my back against the wall. The rough wallpaper scratched my skin with each thrust. I reached out, trying to grip the wall, and knocked over the lamp. The sound of glass shattering as it hit the floor didn't stop James.

The pictures on the walls rattled as he pounded into me. My tailbone felt like it was being beaten with a bat each time my body slammed up into the wall. With my back on fire, my ass in pain, and my head bumping against the wall, James pummeled me. Sweat trickled from the edge of his hairline, slowly running down his face.

Sweat and I didn't always get along. With him, I wanted to reach out and taste it. See if it had the same salty taste as his dick against my tongue. Just as I leaned forward, going for the wetness to alleviate the dryness inside my mouth, he placed his lips over mine.

Reaching between us, he flicked my clit with his fingers. It wasn't a gentle touch. There were no tentative feels to see if my body was sensitive. Each stroke felt like a slap against my pussy. My insides clamped down, the edge coming nearer as I sucked his tongue into my mouth.

His strokes became harsh and erratic, matching his breathing. I began to bounce off him, my body flying away from his due to the forcefulness of his thighs. Slamming back down on his cock over and over again mingled with the flicks, sending me spiraling over the edge and screaming his name until my throat burned. My eyes rolled back in my head, my head slamming uncontrollably against the wall as my entire body went rigid.

He didn't let up his brutal assault on my pussy as I came down from an orgasm that left me dizzy. While he pummeled me over and over again, I gripped his shoulder, letting myself get lost in the moment.

He stilled, his abs clenching harder as he grunted and leaned his forehead against mine. Then he sucked in a breath, his body shuddered, and he gulped for air.

"For fuck's sake," he muttered, swallowing again.

I rested my head against the wall, my entire body feeling like jelly. "Yeah," I said, not able to say anything else.

He held me there for a moment before carrying me to the bed and placing me on top of the mattress. He collapsed next to me, his chest heaving as he wiped his forehead.

"Tire you out already?" I asked as I turned to face him.

"Izzy," he said as he pushed the hair that had fallen behind my shoulder. "I'm just getting started, doll."

I rolled onto my back and stared at the ceiling. The room was spinning slightly from the amount of Jack I'd had at the reception. As I was lost in the passion and booze, he'd consumed my entire world and made everything else vanish.

My eyelids felt heavy as I lay there listening to his breathing slow. My mind was cluttered and I wanted to shut it off and drift off to sleep, but my body had other plans—and so did James. The bed dipped and sprang up as he climbed off the bed. A squeak from the stiff mattress pulled me back to reality. I opened one eye, watching him walk over to the minibar and grab something inside.

"Want a drink?" he asked, dangling a bottle of Jack.

At this point in the night, there were two options. I could either stop drinking and fall asleep or have another and party to the point that, tomorrow, I wouldn't remember what had happened in this room.

"Yes," I said, sitting up on my elbows.

He twisted off the cap, plopped some ice cubes into a glass, and poured the amber liquid inside before handing it to me. I took shallow sips, not wanting to swallow it too quickly. The wetness on my tongue and burn down my throat helped breathe new life into me. We stared at each other, sipping our drinks stark naked. He leaned against the small bar area, while I sat on the bed with my shoulder back, giving him a full show.

Unable to take the silence, I sloshed back the rest of my drink, shaking the glass, causing the ice cubes to clink together.

A small grin spread across his face as he placed his cup on the bar and walked toward me.

"What?" I asked before I stared down into my empty glass.

"Gave me an idea," he said as he grabbed his tie off the floor. Then he removed the knot from the silk material. "Lie back."

"Why?"

"Jesus, just lie the fuck back," he growled, taking the glass from my hand and setting it on the nightstand.

The growl had been a little bit scary, but sexy as fuck. A shiver ran down my spine as I crawled up the bed backward before placing my head on the pillow.

"Give me your hands," he commanded, straddling my body.

I swallowed hard, my mouth feeling dry again as I held up my hands and offered myself to him.

"Hold them together. Clasp them."

"What are you going to do?" I asked out of pure curiosity.

"I'm tying you to the headboard, doll." He smiled, snapping the tie between his hands.

My natural reaction in this situation should have been "fuck no." But since I'd had more Jack than I could remember, and James was hot as fuck, I said, "Okay," before clasping my hands together and holding them in front of him without a care.

James twisted the tie around my hands, securing it in a tight knot and drawing them over my head to the headboard. "You okay with this?" he asked, leaning over me with his dick in my face.

"Yes," I said, reaching forward with my lips to lick the tip of his cock.

He shuddered as he fastened the tie to the headboard before

grabbing a spare pillow and placing it under my head. "This should help your arms."

"It's not my arms I'm worried about." Really, I wasn't. I knew he wouldn't hurt me. Thomas would kill him, and then the rest of the Gallo men would be in line to revive him and kill him again.

He laughed, nudging my legs apart with his knees. "Wait. Something's missing," he said as he climbed off the bed. He walked to his suitcase, riffled through the contents, and returned with another tie. "For your eyes. Lift your head."

"I want to see," I said, pissed off that he wanted to take away my sight.

"It'll be better."

"I've been blindfolded before, Jimmy. I'm not a virgin."

"Did you like it?" he asked, studying my face.

"Y-yes," I stammered, hating myself the instant I said it.

"Good. Head up."

I sighed, lifting my head from the pillow and watching as he drew closer to me before darkness came.

"Comfortable?" he asked as he tied the knot around the back. "Can you see?"

"It's fine. I may fall asleep. Just warning you now," I lied with a smile.

"Impossible," he whispered against my lips, running his tongue along the seam.

I opened my mouth, trapping his tongue between my teeth. Sliding his hand down my torso, he cupped my pussy.

I smiled, still holding his tongue as his hand left my skin. Suddenly, shooting pain radiated from my core, spreading down my legs. The smack of his hand against my pussy sent shock waves through me.

Instantly, I released his tongue and shrieked, "Fuck!" as I tried to free my hands. I wanted to rub my pussy, hold it, and make the sting go away. "Asshole," I hissed.

"Doll, I'm in control. You can challenge me all you want, but I'll get my way."

I grumbled, twisting my body to change the sensation and pulsating heat between my legs. My breathing was fast from the shock of his assault. Laying his hands against my legs to hold them down, he waited for me to calm.

"Can you handle me, little girl?"

"Fuck you," I seethed. "I can handle anything you give." My ability to make rational statements or judgment calls was clearly off.

I wanted to see his face. Being robbed of my vision made it impossible to read his emotions. The tone of his voice didn't betray his intentions. I hadn't expected him to smack my pussy, and without seeing his hand move, I couldn't prepare for it.

"Does it burn?" he whispered, the bed jostling as he moved.

I nodded, not able to speak without my voice trembling. The sound of something moving against the wood grain of the nightstand made me turn to the side. I needed to be able to hear what was about to happen, especially if I couldn't see, but how I'd turned just blocked one of my ears.

I faced forward, waiting for the next sharp sting, when I heard the sound of ice against the glass. I cried out as the cold penetrated through the burn. He held the ice against me, letting tiny droplets of water drip between my legs.

The heat of the slap melted the ice, and the sting of the cold gave way to a feeling of relief. I ground my body against it, craving the coolness of the ice against me. Drawing tiny circles, he moved the hardness around my clit, making sure to keep it far enough away from the one place I wanted it most.

Goose bumps dotted my flesh as he slid the ice cube up the center of my body, stopping at my belly button, dipping it inside, and resting it there. Then I heard the sound of more ice before a second cube touched my skin and both started their ascent toward my breasts.

My nipples were rock hard, throbbing with need, and the thought of the ice touching them had me on edge. I wanted warmth, the feel of his mouth sucking on my tit. My body shook as he circled my breasts, tightening the ring until it landed on the center. The ice instantly cooled my piercings, sending the bite deeper into my flesh.

"Your mouth," I snapped, craving the heat.

"You don't call the shots."

Water dripped down each breast, pooling in the center of my chest. My skin felt like it was on fire except for the spots he touched with the ice and the small stream running down my torso.

Suddenly, his warm tongue blazed a trail up my stomach, sucking the water that had collected on my skin. I lurched forward, trying to offer him my nipple, but he pushed me back down with his palm.

"Be still," he warned, holding me against the mattress.

I gulped, trying to find an ounce of wetness in my mouth, but came up empty. After licking a path to my left breast, he sucked it between his warm lips and drew it into his mouth. My other nipple was still being blasted by the cold, the opposite sensations causing my eyes to roll back in my head as I lay there immobile.

Once he released my left breast, he placed the ice back on my nipple and moved to my right. The sensation overwhelmed me. No longer could I tell if it was water or my own moisture dripping off my pussy.

Squirming, I needed to find something to stop the throbbing and intense need I felt. With the earth-shattering orgasm I'd had minutes ago, I hadn't thought he could have me so close to the edge that fast.

The ice, cupped in his hand, slid down my body to my core and rested against my clit. I sucked in air, the cold more than I could bear without wanting to claw his face off.

After letting the ice slip toward my center, he pushed it against my opening. As he moved his fingers inside me, the ice slid inside too, burning a path as it slid deeper. I hissed as his cold fingers pushed against the ice, filling me completely.

Water started to trickle out between his fingers as he worked them in and out. He adjusted, moving his body farther down mine and lashing at my clit with his hot tongue. I shook my head, ready to explode from the overload of hot and cold. When he added a third finger, a burn settled between my legs and he lapped at my core.

I pulled against my restraints, feeling the need to move, but it was no use. I was his prisoner as he devoured my body, sucking and finger-fucking me.

I began to chant softly, calling his name at first. As my orgasm neared and he curled his fingers inside me, I began to yell, "Yes!" and "Fuck!" over and over again. I couldn't stop pushing myself down on his hand, feeling his tongue slide across my clit. I felt my toes curl as my body grew rigid. Then I held my breath, riding out the wave of pleasure.

Behind the blindfold, my world filled with colors. Vibrant yellows, reds, and oranges danced inside my eyes as I finally gulped air.

I didn't move as he left the bed. My hands were still above my head, growing tinglier by the second. My chest heaved, the hot breath from my body skidding across the droplets of water. The rip and snap alerted me that he was putting on a condom.

He wasn't done with me yet.

Since I hadn't caught my breath, I couldn't speak before he was between my legs again, rubbing the head of his sheathed dick against my cold opening.

"So fuckin' amazing," he growled as he pushed inside.

I mumbled some bullshit even I didn't understand in my post-orgasm haze. He grabbed my legs, placing my knees over my shoulders as he rammed his dick to the hilt. His fingers pulled on my piercings, sending an aftershock from my tits to my pussy as I gripped him tightly, milking his cock.

Linking my feet behind his head, I held his body to mine and pushed against his thrusts. The man was a beast. No other way to describe him. There wasn't a moment I felt in control of the situation, and for once, I liked it. Maybe it was the alcohol that had me going against everything I believed in and had allowed me to give up control so easily. I liked to think it was Jack and not James causing me to give in and become complacent.

What seemed like a lifetime passed before his rhythm slowed

and his body convulsed against me. His weight crushed me as he collapsed, drawing breath as if he couldn't get enough.

"Hands," I mumbled as I shook them, hoping to give them more blood. The prickly feeling wouldn't allow me to be comfortable.

He lifted off me, untying my hands before removing the blindfold. I blinked and squinted, the light blinding me. I closed my eyes, trying to stop the pain caused by the brightness.

"Fuck," he hissed as I heard the familiar snap of the condom as it was removed.

My eyes flew open as I saw James staring at the rubber. "What?"

"The fucking condom broke."

"Jesus." Shit like this had happened before—hazards of forceful sex and big dicks.

"Please tell me you're on the pill."

"Nope. But I'm sure it'll be fine, James," I said, closing my eyes again. I was too tired to bother, and I'd make sure to grab the morning-after pill tomorrow on my way home.

MY STOMACH TURNED AS I MOVED. IT FELT LIKE SOMEONE WAS hammering a nail into my skull. *Tap. Tap. Boom. Tap. Tap. Boom.* I winced, trying to pry my eyes open from their sleepy state. The little construction worker inside my skull didn't relent as I looked around.

I swallowed, not recognizing the room before closing my eyes again. Where the fuck was I? Last night was a blur. I remembered the boring-ass reception line, dinner that had seemed to go on forever, and then drinks at the bar. Not just any drink, but my best friend Jack, sliding back and wrapping me up in his warmth.

I tried to smile when looking back on the evening, but everything hurt—even my cheeks. *What the fuck happened?* I slowly shook my head, trying to clear the fog that clouded my thoughts. My head fell to the side, and I opened my eyes to get another look around the room.

I blinked twice, clearing the haze from my vision, and saw *him.* James. My stomach fell as I looked down his body and then to mine. We were naked, our clothes thrown around the room haphazardly. I'd fucked him. My pussy ached, the muscles in my arms burned, and my nipples throbbed at the memory of the night before.

I thought I'd dreamed being awoken from my sleep for another go, but nope, I hadn't. James was insatiable. Even while asleep, his dick was semi-hard, staring at me as a reminder of the multiple orgasms he'd brought me.

I stared at James, watching him sleep. He looked peaceful and kind and not like the man I'd met the night before. James had a sharp tongue, a commanding tone, and an air of authority about him. Everything that made me run for the hills and hide. My body liked him, though. Fuck, even my mind tried to tell me that he was a great guy.

I knew better than that. No man, especially one like James, would make me change my mind on love and relationships. He'd promised me a night with no strings attached, and that was exactly how I wanted it.

Saying goodbye was overrated. I didn't feel the need to chitchat and thank him for the amazing fuck. Once I had a good grip on the side of the bed, I slowly pulled myself up, praying that the room would stop spinning. Then I turned toward him, waiting to see how heavy a sleeper he was and if I could slink out unnoticed.

I climbed to my feet, holding my head as I collected my dress and panties from the floor. I had to pee like a motherfucker, but I couldn't risk him waking and finding me in his room.

After placing my panties in my purse, I opened my dress and stepped inside. I zipped it, keeping my eyes locked on him and holding my breath. Then I slipped on my heels, looked around the room one last time to make sure I hadn't left anything behind, and made my way toward the door. Before I twisted the handle, I turned and stared at James.

He really was beautiful when he was sleeping. His rock-hard body covered in tattoos, his cock ready for more, and his beauty enough to suck any girl in, but not me.

A wave of guilt overcame me, but I pushed it aside as I opened the door, trying to avoid waking him. As I entered the hallway, I exhaled and clicked the door closed. I swear, fucking hotels and their loud-ass doors pissed me off more than anything.

A man passed by, looking me up and down, and I felt like a tramp. Dressed in my gown from the night before, my hair a mess, and probably with makeup out of place, but fuck it. I straightened my back, standing tall as I walked to the elevator.

Pushing the elevator button, I glanced back toward his room, silently chanting, "Please don't come out," over and over again.

I couldn't calm my breath as my heart pounded inside my

chest at the thought of him finding me in the hallway trying to sneak out.

When the doors opened, I ran to the back of the elevator and held the walls as if they were my lifeline. I'd made it inside without being discovered. I relaxed, almost sliding down the faux-wood walls, allowing the enormity of the situation to hit me.

I'd fucked my brother's friend. I'd fucked him more than once. I'd left without saying goodbye. Would he come after me? Was he a man of his word? There was so much I didn't know about James.

I'd never been the type of girl to sneak out without so much as a goodbye. The night before started flashing before my eyes. Being tied to the bed, the feel of his fingers inside me, the way he'd fucked me, how he tasted—instantly, my body responded. I wanted more, but I closed my eyes and tried to cool off. There was no way in hell I'd allow myself to go there again.

I needed to forget James Caldo.

5

My eyes flew open as I heard the click of the door closing. Reaching over, I felt the empty space that was still warm from her skin. Groaning, I rolled over and stared at the door. My first instinct was to run after her and drag her back to my room, but I fought it. It wasn't right. Izzy and I weren't meant to have more than a night together... at least not yet.

I'd have my time with her again. There was a connection that couldn't be denied, but she wasn't ready. She still had wildness to her. A rebellious attitude that felt the need to fight against the norm, and that included relationships. Izzy wanted to be the badass chick who didn't need anyone in her life, but that was the furthest thing from the truth.

Her tough shell seemed impenetrable, but I'd witnessed the small crack and peered inside. I could see the fire in her eyes, love in her heart, and the wild animal waging a battle inside. I needed to break down the walls, but timing was key. I couldn't chase after her. I was all about the chase, but not yet.

Her brother Thomas and I were tied together through work. We had a mission, and I couldn't do anything that may put his life in danger. Izzy would have to wait until the Sun Devils MC was removed from the equation and Thomas was free from the club.

Throwing my arm across my face, I could smell her on my skin. Inhaling deeply, memories of the night before flooded my mind. I'd never felt weak in the knees before *her*. The electricity in the air as we touched could've lit an entire house and possibly blown out a few light bulbs in the process.

If I said that it didn't sting a little that she didn't stick around to say goodbye, I'd be lying. Izzy was as affected by me as I was by her, and she had to slink away before she would have to confront the feelings I evoked in her last night.

I knew I'd have her again. She couldn't escape the inevitable. The connection we felt was undeniable. I'd let her go...for now.

I knew in the end I'd get exactly what I wanted—Izzy Gallo.

6

As I stood up from my chair, the room started to spin. I felt like I was in a tunnel as the room began to dim and everything looked fuzzy. I tried to grab on to the chair and hold myself up, but I hit the floor with my head landing first.

My brothers stood over me, their mouths moving, but I couldn't make out the words. As their figures became darker, I thought about how fucked up things had been for the last couple of months.

Everything in my life had shifted since Joey's wedding. About a month ago, I had my annual lady parts appointment. Color me shocked when the doctor walked in and made an announcement that would forever alter my life.

"Congratulations, you're pregnant."

"That's funny, Doc. You almost gave me a heart attack," I replied with my legs in the stirrups.

"Izzy, I'm not joking," she said as she rolled the stool over to the side of the bed.

"There has to be a mistake." I instantly began to cry. Not happy tears, but tears of total devastation.

She rested her hand on my arm. *"I'm sorry. We ran the test twice. You're definitely with child."*

I fought through the tears as my lip trembled. *"It can't be."* I wiped my cheeks with the back of my hands.

"We just have to see how far along you are."

"Oh, God. I can't be pregnant."

"Let's see how far along you are, and then we can figure out your next step."

I shook my head, knowing there was no other step. *"I have to keep the baby. I just can't believe this."* My family would shit a brick if I aborted a child. I wasn't raised that way, and my mother was dying to be a grandmother. Either way, it was still a piece of me, but I just wasn't ready.

"Let me go grab an ultrasound machine, and we can get a better idea. When was your last period?" she asked, looking at me with a sympathetic smile as she stroked my arm.

"November," I replied, feeling my stomach begin to roll.

I hadn't thought anything of it. Missing a period happened often for me. If I became too stressed or worked out too much, I'd miss a month or two. I never realized I'd missed three.

She walked out to grab the equipment, leaving me with my thoughts.

It's not that I don't like kids, but I like when they're other people's. I'm too young, unattached, and enjoying life to have a baby at this time in my life.

Plus, I'd be tied to Flash the rest of my life. I mean, I liked the guy, but shit, I didn't want him to be the father of my children. He'd be over the moon, but I wouldn't be.

As she moved the wand around my belly, measuring the baby, she chattered on about children and pregnancy. I didn't hear a damn thing she said. I was too paralyzed by the fear and anger that I'd allowed myself to get knocked up.

"Based on the size of the fetus, it looks like you're about twelve weeks along."

"When is that around, Doc? I can't calculate that in my brain." My head started to ache with everything I was trying to process.

"It puts the time of conception around Thanksgiving."

"Thanksgiving," I repeated.

That was Joey's wedding and the night I'd fucked James. James. I still couldn't remember everything that happened that night, but I couldn't imagine I'd let him fuck me without a condom. I never let anyone fuck me without one, but here I was knocked up.

The problem was I also fucked Flash that weekend. Either of them could be the father. I thought that shit only happened to people who ended up on the Jerry Springer show.

I made a decision in the doctor's office that I'd wait to share the "happy" news with my family and especially the men in my life. If anything, I'd exclude them for as long as possible.

I could raise a baby on my own or at least with the help of my family. I didn't need a man to help me. They'd just use it as another excuse to tell me what to do, and I wouldn't have any of it.

I woke in the ER. Lying on a gurney with Anthony sitting next to me. I blinked a couple of times, trying to clear the haze from my eyes.

"Izzy," Anthony said as he moved closer to me.

"Yeah," I replied, swallowing through the dryness in my mouth. An IV had been attached to my arm with a clear bag feeding into it.

"Thank God you're awake."

"I'm fine, Anthony."

"No, you're not. You passed out at the shop."

Suddenly my heart began to pound. Maybe something happened to the baby. Lord forbid, the doctor told my brothers about the baby I was carrying.

"What did the doctor say?" I asked as I prayed that they didn't know about my bundle of joy.

"Nothing yet. They said that you probably passed out from overexertion, but they had to run more tests." He gripped my hand, giving it a light squeeze.

"That's probably true. I didn't eat today." I exhaled, feeling like I just dodged a bullet.

"Let me go tell everyone you're awake," he said as he started to move out of his chair.

I grabbed his hand, stopping him from leaving. "Everyone?" I asked through gritted teeth.

"Naturally, Izzy. The whole family is in the waiting room, worried about you."

"For the love of God," I whispered. "I'm fine," I barked.

My nosy family probably already badgered the doctor

enough that they were given information that wasn't their right to hear.

"Stop being bitchy," he snapped. "I'll be right back." He pulled his hand from my grasp and walked out.

I slammed my fists against the mattress and screamed with my mouth closed. I didn't want them to find out like this. It's my right to tell them when I felt ready. Probably the day my belly grew too big to conceal I'd have to spill the beans, but I wouldn't do it until I absolutely had to tell them.

"Baby girl," Pop said as he walked in the room with my mother behind him.

"Hey, Daddy," I replied, giving him a small smile.

"Are you okay?" he asked as he approached the bed.

"Oh, Izzy. I was so worried," Ma said before I could reply.

"I'm fine, Ma. I forgot to eat today."

"You work too much, Izzy. You need to take better care of yourself," Pop chastised me.

"I know. I'm sorry," I said as I shrugged. "What did the doctor say?"

"Nothing. They said they were still running tests and they'd be in soon. Your mother kept asking for more details."

"They gave me some Hippo nonsense."

"HIPAA," Mia corrected as she strolled into the room.

My eyes grew wide and I felt my heart skip a beat. Mia worked at the hospital and knew how to read a chart. I'm sure she wouldn't have an issue peeking at my chart and seeing exactly what was going on.

"Hey Mia," I said, trying to read her face.

"Hey, Iz. You sure scared the shit out of everyone."

"It wasn't my intention. I'll make sure it never happens again. I need to remember to eat."

"Yeah," Mia replied, but I couldn't tell if she was agreeing with me or not.

My head was still fuzzy from passing out and trying to process everything that could explode in my face. I rubbed my temples, feeling the dull ache making its way to the front of my skull.

"Good evening," an older gentleman in a lab coat said as he knocked on the door. He flipped through the chart before looking up. "Ms. Gallo?" he asked.

"That's me," I replied. It wasn't hard to figure out since I was the one lying in the bed.

"May I have a moment to speak with Ms. Gallo alone before we release her?" he asked as he scanned the room.

My mother glanced at me, maybe waiting for me to ask her to stay. "So you're going to be releasing her?" she asked.

"Yes, ma'am. I just want to go over a few medical items with Ms. Gallo before she's released."

"I'll be okay, Ma. Give me a few minutes. I'll tell you every-thing he says," I lied.

"Fine," she said in a clipped tone.

I knew when she was pissed, and she was just about at her breaking point. God love her, but she wanted to know everything about everyone. I wasn't any different, but I couldn't have her hear this.

After they left the room, the doctor closed the door and took a seat next to me. "Ms. Gallo, I don't know if you know this, but you're pregnant."

I nodded. "I do."

"We can't find anything medically wrong with you, ma'am. You need to make sure to eat regularly and hydrate. You're going to need to follow up with your OB/GYN for a checkup, but everything seems fine."

"That's it?"

"Yes, but you need to rest and eat better. Don't overdo it the next couple days, and make sure to see your doctor as soon as possible."

"The baby is okay?" I asked, hoping that I hadn't hurt it by passing out or not eating right.

"As far as we can tell, you're both fine."

"Doc?"

"Yes, Ms. Gallo?"

"Did you tell anyone in my family about my condition?"

"No. That's against doctor-patient privilege and would be a violation of the HIPAA laws."

"Phew," I whispered.

"You aren't going to be able to hide the fact much longer, ma'am. You're going to start showing soon."

"I know. I just want to do it on my own terms."

"Any other questions?"

"No, Doc. Thanks," I said before he walked out of the door.

After a while, the ER nurse came in and unhooked me from the IV so I could sign the paperwork and leave. Anthony stayed with me that night to make sure I was okay. He was sweet like that to me, but I didn't even clue him in on my secret.

From that day forward, I ate regularly, drank lots of water, and tried to rest as often as possible. I'd have one last hurrah with Flash in Daytona before adulthood slammed me in the face and I'd finally have to let my secret out.

7

IZZY

Rolling into Daytona was an unforgettable experience. The entire beachfront was lined with row after row of bikes, babes, and badass boys. Flash and I checked in to the shitty, seedy-ass hotel, but at least it seemed clean and had a bed. I chuckled when I caught a glimpse of the old coin-operated machine that caused the bed to vibrate. We'd find a way to make that useful.

After throwing my bag down on the floor, I collapsed on the lumpy mattress. The vibration of the three-hour bike ride still hadn't left my system as I stared at the brown spot on the ceiling. Being pregnant made everything more grueling. I often found myself exhausted and needing a nap.

"Hey, baby." Flash crawled on top of me, crushing me with his weight. "I want to taste you before we head out." He planted soft kisses on my neck before biting down on the tender flesh of my ear.

I moaned, tangling my fingers in his hair. "You know how I like it," I whispered, pulling on his scalp. "Do me good." I pushed his head down my body, not wanting to waste any time.

"Don't I always?" He licked his lips as he unbuttoned my jeans.

"Mm-hmm. Usually." I smirked as I lifted my ass, allowing him to slide the denim down my legs.

Flash was a beautiful man. He didn't resemble the scrawny kid I used to play kickball with at recess. His blue eyes, killer smile, and chiseled body made my mouth water. I was sure I wasn't the only girl out there who enjoyed his beautifully bent cock—not broken, just curved. It wasn't too wide or thick, just total perfection. Each stroke hit just the right spot, and I'd never found another one since. It was the reason I always welcomed him in my bed.

He threw my jeans across the room before he nestled between my legs. "No panties," he mumbled as he kissed the skin on my lower abdomen. "Landing strip too. You know how I like it."

"Just for you," I lied.

It was the start of bikini season in Florida. I wouldn't be caught dead with stubble or razor burn. I pulled my knees up, planting my feet flush with the comforter to give him better access.

He inhaled, a gleam in his eye. "You smell better than I fucking remember. You have the sweetest pussy, Iz. Fucking fantastic." Sticking his tongue out, he flicked my clit as he gripped my hips, holding me in place.

A jolt of pleasure shot through my body as I arched my back, pushing my head into the mattress. Warmth cascaded across my body as he latched on to me, sucking my flesh. Letting my knees fall toward the bed, I lay before him, spread-eagled and wanting more than his mouth.

His hands slid under my ass as he squeezed it roughly, kneading it with his fingers. He sucked and licked my core while he stared into my eyes. Our gazes were locked as he rubbed his fingers against my opening.

"You're so wet, baby. I can feel how much you've missed me."

"Stop talking, Flash." My body was overly sensitive from the long bike ride. The slightest touch of his lips sent tiny shock waves down my legs, causing my toes to curl. "Make me come, and maybe I'll let you stick your cock in me."

"I'm taking that shit," he muttered against my flesh as he thrust two fingers inside me.

I cried out, the pleasure too intense as he latched on to me. He rhythmically sucked and finger-fucked me until I screamed through the breath-stealing orgasm.

"It's my turn now, Izzy." Flash patted my thigh as he sat up.

"I said maybe." I closed my eyes, lost in a post-orgasm haze.

"I'm taking it. No maybe about that shit. I earned it," he murmured as he nudged my legs farther apart.

I smirked, closing my legs. "You didn't earn shit. Eating my pussy *was* your reward."

"I'll stick it in your ass, then, but I'm taking something," he said as he flipped me onto my stomach.

I reached back, covering my ass with my hands. "Oh no, you

don't!" I yelled. Then I felt a sharp sting on my ass as the sound of the smack he'd just landed filled the air.

"You know you want my sweet cock, Izzy. Don't play hard to get. It's not a good look on you."

I laughed into the blanket as the bed sprang back from the loss of his weight. He opened his bag on the old wooden desk next to the television. The man could wear a pair of blue jeans. He looked in the mirror and caught my eye before turning with a condom in his hand.

"Liking what you see, baby?"

"Eh, it's all right," I mumbled, putting an unimpressed look on my face. I did, but no fucking way would I ever tell him and let my foot off his throat.

With a smile, he unbuttoned his jeans and pulled them down before kicking them off. His cock bobbed as he straightened, waving at me in all its hard glory. He tore the wrapper open with his teeth, sheathing his stiff, curved member before walking toward the bed.

"Not even going to take your shirt off?" I asked, staring at his cock. Then I forced myself to look at his face.

"You didn't." He pointed to me with a shitty smirk.

I didn't even care. All I'd wanted was his mouth on my pussy and the orgasm that had been just out of reach during the trip to Daytona. "I'll fix that. You, off the bed and totally naked," I commanded, pulling my tank top over my head.

After grabbing the back of his collar, he pulled it over his head, exposing his washboard abs. Fuck. He was a sight. Then he crawled up the bed, his cock swaying and a shitty-ass grin on his face.

"I know you want it. You need my dick more than you'll ever admit, Izzy. No one makes you come like I do," he whispered in my ear as he rubbed his hard length against me. "You want it?"

"If you think you're man enough to give it," I challenged. I loved when Flash felt like he needed to prove himself. He worked harder at it, fucked me better, and outdid himself each time.

"I'm busting that shit, Izzy. I'll show you how a real man fucks." He stood on top of the bed, pulling me up by the hips. "Ass up, princess," he said as he smacked my other cheek.

I giggled into the comforter. Dipping my stomach toward the bed, I pushed my ass in the air, wiggling it.

"Don't move," he said as he landed another blow to my already stinging flesh.

My laughter became uncontrollable as I buried my face deeper into the blankets, trying not to hurt his pride. Flash was hot. But controlling? Not one bit. I'd let him play the part for the pleasure of feeling his cock in me.

He pushed into me in one quick thrust. His fingers dug into my hips as he pounded me. I moaned each time the head of his cock stroked my G-spot. I fisted the sheets, closing my eyes, and tried to remember to breathe. His body bounced off mine, slamming into me to the hilt before he withdrew. As our bodies collided, my ability to keep my upper body in place began to slip. I reached back, wrapping my hands around his ankles, holding our bodies together.

He rested his palm against my lower back and placed his finger against the one hole I'd never given him. I opened my eyes, looking behind me. He towered over me with a hand on my hip, his abs clenching and relaxing, and a trail of spit falling from his lips. I squeezed my eyes shut, trying to get my body to relax as he rubbed the saliva against my flesh.

"Fuck," he muttered as he pulled out his cock and pushed his thumb inside my ass.

I whimpered, wanting the feel of his cock as I dug my fingernails into his ankles. He rammed his cock into me, filling me in both holes. Pleasure shot through my body as he worked one in and the other out. Moving out of sync and in absolute fucking perfection.

"Who's fucking you, Izzy? I want to hear you scream my name." He stilled.

I mumbled, not able to form words.

His thumb dug deeper, pulling upward, hooking me. "What's my name?" he growled, taking out his cock.

"Flash. Fucking Flash," I answered in one quick breath, burying my face in the comforter.

He pummeled me, his balls slapping against my clit, the curved shaft stroking my G-spot, his thumb caressing my ass. The second orgasm tore through me without warning as I chanted his name.

I lay there panting as the world came back into focus. My grip slipped from his ankles as I became putty in his hands. Flash picked up the pace, slamming into me a couple of times before resting his chest against my back and twitching. He gasped behind me, trying to catch his breath. Our bodies were stuck together by sweat-soaked flesh.

"Fuck, darlin'. I've missed ya," he panted in my ear as his cock slipped out.

"I missed your cock, Flash." I chuckled, earning me a swift smack on the ass. I started to crawl off the bed, ready to hit the town and get out of this shithole of a room.

Flash grabbed my foot. "Where are you slithering off to?" he asked as he pulled me against his body.

"I wanna shower and go out. I'm ready for a little fun." I sighed.

"Just lie here for a minute. I'm tired and I want to hold you." He jerked me back, holding me tighter to his chest, and nuzzled his face in my neck.

I relaxed against him. He did feel really good. Flash and I had never had that type of relationship, but I was so tired. We drifted off together, and the only thing I thought as I fell asleep was I'd have to tell him soon and I dreaded it.

When he'd said that he'd take me out and show me the town, I hadn't thought that included the shittiest biker bar in all of Daytona Beach. The place reeked of cigarettes; the air was hazy with the smoke. A band was playing behind a cage like in that movie *Roadhouse*. I walked through the door with Flash at my side. The floors were filthy and the men inside didn't look much better.

"None of your mouthy bullshit that I love so much when we talk to these guys, got it?" Flash cocked an eyebrow at me, standing like a statue as he waited for my answer.

"I'm not mouthy," I insisted, crossing my arms over my chest.

"Darlin', ya are, and I fuckin' love it." His smile grew wider, giving me a glimpse of why they called him Flash. He had a perfect smile filled with shiny, pearly-white teeth, one that could charm the pants off any girl. It did funny things to my brain, and I couldn't say no to him. "In this bar, with these guys, it's not the place. Understand? I'm a prospect, and that shit won't fly here."

I slid my arm around his waist, looking up into his baby blues. "I got it. I'm to be seen and not heard?"

He grabbed my shoulders and stared back at me. "That's how these guys are. You don't like something they say, just keep quiet."

The last thing I wanted to be was a piece of arm candy that faded away in the background. It was not how I'd been raised. "Let's get one thing straight, Flash. I know you're badass and all, but I don't stand in the shadows for anyone. *Understand?*"

"Fucking hell," he muttered, rubbing his face.

"I'll play the part this once, for you, but hear me now, mister. I'm not a club whore, and I sure as hell ain't your old lady. I don't know what in the hell we are exactly, but if you want to be more than whatever the fuck this is"—I waved my hand in the air between us—"I will not stay quiet and be a mindless twat."

"Calm the fuck down, woman," he croaked as he wrapped his fingers around my wrist. "I don't think of you that way. This is for them." He turned his attention to the table full of rough-looking men about twenty feet away. I could handle big and burly. I hadn't grown up a pussy. "Just please do this for me, and

I'll make sure to make it worth your while," he said, waggling his eyebrows and giving me a cocky-ass grin.

"I won't make a scene and walk out, but you owe me big-time." I tore my wrist from his grip.

"Whatever you want, Izzy. You know that." His eyes softened as he looked down at me.

"I'm going to use my *silent* time to come up with something really *big*." I swiped my fingers across the small hint of chest hair just below his throat.

"I can do big." He laughed and grabbed my hand to pull me toward the table.

"Fucker," I muttered to myself as I followed behind.

He looked over his shoulder and said, "I heard that."

When he stopped suddenly, I ran into his back, and it felt like hitting a brick wall. I used his body as a shield from the men at the table. I didn't know if I had an off switch, but this wasn't really the place for me to test it. I just needed to keep my eyes down and pray their little hello didn't last long.

Flash leaned over the table, shaking their hands as I stood behind him pretending to be invisible—something I'd never done for anyone. Ever.

When he'd said that he wanted to take me to Bike Week in Daytona Beach for the weekend, I hadn't been able to imagine anything better than the feel of the wind in my hair, the sand between my toes, and a shitload of hot bikers. What could be bad about that?

I hadn't expected this, and I didn't like it one bit. Flash would have to pay and pay dearly to make up for this "be seen and not heard" bullshit.

"And who do we have here?" a rough voice asked, pulling me out of my thoughts of how to torture Flash.

Flash shifted and reached around to grab my hand, tugging me to his side. "This is Izzy, my woman." He tightened his grip on my waist.

I glared at him.

What the fuck? I wasn't his woman. We had an agreement, but to call the naughty shit we did a relationship was overstating it just a tad. I gave him the stink eye and saw the corner of his mouth twitch.

"Well, aren't you stunning, Izzy? Is that short for Isabella?"

I turned my attention to the genius and smiled the biggest bullshit smile I could muster. "Yes, it is." I swallowed the other words I wanted to say, still smiling like an idiot.

He wasn't a bad-looking man for someone his age. His long, gray hair was pulled back in a low-slung ponytail, making his emerald-green eyes stand out. A small patch of salt-and-pepper facial hair framed his thin lips. He looked a little like Santa Claus on crack. The vest covering his black T-shirt was the same cut as the one Flash was wearing, but it had more patches—including one that stated he was the VP.

"Why don't you sit down with us and have a drink?" He lightly patted the empty chair next to him, never taking his eyes off me.

Flash moved in front of me and started to sit, but the VP grabbed his arm.

"I meant her, you idiot. Not you."

Flash stopped dead, with his ass hovering just above the seat. "Oh, sorry, man."

What type of man would let another one talk to him that way? The way he'd said "idiot" hadn't been the same as when my brothers called each other "jackass" or "dumbfuck." His dislike for Flash was clearly evident in his tone, but Flash did as he was told, like a good soldier.

I slid into the wooden chair as Flash gripped my shoulder. "Thanks," I whispered, folding my hands in my lap.

"My name's Rebel," he said as he brought my hand to his mouth, running his prickly lips across my skin. "These are the guys." He placed my hand on his leg, patting it, and then grabbed his beer.

Flash's grasp on my shoulder hardened, but I didn't dare look up at him.

Fuck. How had my dumb ass gotten into this situation? Flash was a stupid bastard. I should've listened to Joe and Mike, but then again, I never did.

"Hey," I said, slowly looking around the table. I tried not to linger on any one man too long.

They all said, "Hey" and smiled—except for one man. The long hair hid his face as he picked at the label on the bottle. His reaction to me wasn't friendly or welcoming like the others'. Nope, he was avoiding me.

"So, Isabella," Rebel said, pulling my attention back to him. "Can I call you that? You don't mind, do you?" He leaned into my personal space and squeezed my thigh. The stench of cigarettes and stale beer invaded my nostrils.

Flash gripped my shoulder and Rebel held my thigh. I knew Flash wouldn't do shit. He was the prospect, the one trying to get in the club, and Rebel knew it. I just needed to be agreeable and get the hell out of here for my sake and for Flash's pussy ass.

I bit the corner of my lip before responding. "Sure." The only people in my life who called me Isabella—who I allowed to call me by my full name—were my parents. I didn't think telling Rebel to go fuck himself would be good for anyone.

The tiny hairs on the back of my neck rose, and I felt like someone was watching me. Without looking, I noticed the unfriendly guy staring at me out of the corner of my eye as I kept my attention on Rebel. It bugged the fuck out of me. I wanted to get a glimpse of him, just for a second, but Rebel wanted my total attention.

"Flash, go fetch me a beer, and get something for the beautiful girl too," Rebel demanded, staring at me, paying no attention to Flash or anyone else.

My eyes flickered to his face as he barked orders to Flash. "I'm fine. I don't need anything to drink." The last thing I wanted was to drink anything that wouldn't allow me to be in control or make it easier for someone to hurt me. Being around Flash was one thing, but I didn't trust the men sitting at the table.

Flash didn't move. He kept his hand on my shoulder, squeezing it lightly, and I could almost feel the tension radiating from his body.

"What the fuck are you waiting for? Get the fucking drinks, boy!" Rebel roared, slamming his fist on the table.

I jumped. The anger that oozed out of him put me on edge. My heart stuttered in my chest and I wanted to get out of here. Flash released my shoulder, leaving me alone with Rebel.

Rebel leaned over, twirling my hair with his fingers. "So, darlin' Isabella, tell me about yourself."

I looked down at my hands, trying to stop the urge to bat him away. "Not much to tell," I whispered.

He pushed the hair over my shoulder, running his fingertips down my skin, lingering on my collarbone. "I doubt that, Isabella." As he drew out my name, rolling the last bit off his tongue, his breath tickled my nose.

Small prickles slid down my neck, the hair still standing at attention. I leaned back in my chair, trying to escape his invasion of my personal space, pissed off that Flash had brought me here and then left me like a pansy ass.

"Tell me about you, Rebel." I was deflecting. A man like him had to be full of himself, drunk off power, and I prayed it would take the focus off me.

"Tsk, tsk," he said, shaking his head. "I know all about me. I want to know about you." His eyes bored into me as he started to slide his hand up my leg before settling on my thigh.

I swear to shit I wanted to rip Flash's dick off and shove it down his throat. I didn't care if I ever fucked him again. His cock was not worth this bullshit.

"I'm a tattoo artist," I said with a sigh while looking into his eyes, knowing that I wasn't going to get out of the situation without being cordial. It wasn't one of my better traits, but I knew how to play the game. "It's my life." I plastered a fake smile on my face, trying to maintain eye contact with him. I wouldn't show weakness. I was a Gallo girl, not a shrinking violet.

"I love a girl who does ink. Maybe I should come to you next time I need some work done. I wouldn't mind dropping my drawers for you, beautiful."

I wanted to heave. The mere thought of seeing any of this man's junk or ass made me gag. "I'm between gigs right now," I lied, biting the inside of my cheek.

"The MC has a shop. Job's yours if you want it." Rebel squeezed my thigh, running his hand farther up my legs, stopping mere centimeters from my pussy.

"Just like that, huh?" I couldn't keep my mouth shut. I didn't want to seem too eager to please, or too easy. "Maybe my skills are shitty. Then what?"

He inched his chair closer, squeezing my thigh again. "If your ink skills are shitty, I'm sure we can find *other* ways for you to earn."

"Listen," I said, about to lay into him and give him the nicest "fuck off" he'd ever had, but the sound of Flash slamming the drinks on the table stopped me from finishing the statement.

"Flash, you fucker," Rebel said, releasing my leg and leaning back in his chair. "You spilled my beer," he growled, wiping the glass with his finger. He turned to me, drawing his fingers into his mouth and sucking them as he stared.

Sam, a.k.a. Flash, didn't speak. Cool biker nicknames were reserved for badasses, and Sam had lost that right when he'd pussied out on me. He hadn't stood up for me, and he'd left me high and dry in the hands of Rebel.

As Rebel grabbed the bottle to bring it to his lips, I turned and gave my "I hate you" scowl to Sam. He shrugged, grimacing before giving me a halfhearted smile. I closed my eyes, trying to calm the fuck down because, at this point, I wanted to tell Sam exactly how I felt and get the fuck out of the shitty-ass bar. I counted to five like they'd taught in a college psychology course I'd taken on a whim. I slowly opened my eyes to find Rebel staring at me *again*.

Sam leaned down, resting his hand on my shoulder, and whispered in my ear, "Want to get out of here?"

What a clusterfuck. Would he have balls big enough?

"I'm getting tired," I complained, standing to say goodbye. Before my ass was five inches off the chair, Rebel had his hand on my wrist, pulling me back down.

"I wasn't done talking to you." He smiled, licking his lips.

My eyes flickered to Sam, who now had wide eyes and an "Oh fuck" face. I narrowed my eyes at him, wishing he'd man the fuck up, but nope. He must've checked his cock at the door. I turned back to Rebel, looking down at his hand, which was still wrapped around my wrist. *Be diplomatic, Izzy. Do not piss off the MC vice president.*

I turned my wrist, breaking the hold he had on me. "I-I," I stuttered, trying to figure out something other than, "Keep your fucking hands off me."

Just as I opened my mouth, a voice called out to Rebel. "Leave the fucking girl alone, you horny ol' bastard."

I turned to look in the direction of the gravelly voice, where Rebel's attention was now focused. My breath vanished and a dull ache settled in my chest as I sat there wide-eyed and in shock. The blue eyes shooting daggers across the table at me I'd seen before—I knew them. They were mine looking back at me.

The smile I loved so much and the handsome, boyish looks were gone. His features were hard. Small lines had formed around his eyes since the last time I'd seen him. He didn't look like the man who had pushed me on my swing set and taught me how to throw a punch to defend myself. The man's lips were set in a firm line as his glare focused entirely on me. He didn't look anything like the brother I remembered, like the Tommy I loved.

"You want a piece of this ass?" Rebel asked, looking from me to Thomas. "I wouldn't blame you, Blue. It's mighty fine," he said as he turned back toward me, running his finger down my jaw.

I snarled, moving my face away from his fingers. Rebel gripped my hair, yanking my head back and holding me in place.

"Where do you think you're going, Isabella?" He stared into my eyes, a smirk on his face.

My heart started pounding, growing louder by the second as it beat out of control. This was bad, a real fucking nightmare.

"I want her," Tommy said, slamming his hand down on the table. "You got the last piece of ass, and this one's mine."

Rebel laughed. "I'm going to take a spin at the ol' gal myself. You can have her after if you want."

"I don't want your filthy hands on her. She looks too innocent and pure. I want to take that from her," Tommy replied, laughing with the rest of the guys, his eyes only on me.

"Oh, I plan to do all of her, and she's going to like it," Rebel replied.

Sam released my shoulder. The fucker still hadn't said a word. He'd stood there like a fucking idiot and stayed silent.

"Don't I get a say?" I whispered, grinding my teeth. "I'm not a piece of property."

"Flash brought you here, darlin', and you came out of your

own free will," Rebel said, laughing like a hyena. "You can thank Flash later."

I turned to Sam as his eyes dropped to the floor. "Don't you have anything to say?" I hissed, the venom dripping from my voice.

He shook his head as he kicked an imaginary piece of dirt on the floor.

"Fucking pussy," I muttered before turning back to look at Thomas. He was fuming. Tonight wasn't going to end in a pretty way. I had to have faith that Flash and Thomas would find a way to make it stop before Rebel tried to have sex with me.

A small smirk played on my brother's lips; he knew I could never hold my tongue.

Rebel slapped Sam, his laughter filling the air and mingling with the other guys'. "Even the girl can see you're a pussy, Flash," he teased, wiping his mouth with the back of his hand.

8

As I followed Rebel out of the bar, I tried to make an escape plan. I couldn't let him get me alone in a hotel room. It would put Thomas and Flash at risk to have to rescue me, and Thomas would have to divulge his double life in the process. Someone would end up dying, and even though I was okay with that being Rebel, I didn't want to take a chance.

The parking lot was filled with bikers, holding their women and sipping beers. I had to run for it. What other choice did I have but to try to escape here before he got me alone?

"Get on," he barked as he threw one leg over the bike.

I shook my head and began to back up. "No!" I yelled as I turned my back to him and started to run.

"Fuck," he spat. "Get her!"

Before I made it another five steps, a giant fist filled my line of sight and collided with my face. Searing pain radiated across my cheeks and nose as my body fell to the cement. Once again, everything started to fade to black as the sounds around me dulled.

My eye fluttered open as I took in my surroundings. I wasn't in Rebel's room, but once again, in a hospital. Surrounded by equipment, hooked up to an IV, and with Thomas by my side.

"Am I okay?" I asked as I looked over at him.

His eyes came to mine, but there was no smile. "Yeah, you're okay."

"Why am I here?" I couldn't for the life of me figure out why I was in a hospital. It was a simple punch to the face. I'd take one or two in my lifetime.

"We wanted to make sure you didn't fracture a bone in your face and that you didn't have a concussion," he explained as he moved his chair closer.

"But everything is all right?"

"Izzy," he started as he touched my hand. "When you started to come to, you started yelling something repeatedly."

I swallowed hard, knowing my big mouth wouldn't stay sealed for long. "What did I say?" I whispered.

"You kept repeating 'Is the baby okay?' as they wheeled you into the hospital."

"Fuck," I whispered and glanced at my hands. "I must be delirious, Thomas. I don't know why I'd say that."

"Stop the bullshit, Izzy. The doctors checked you after you

wouldn't stop about the baby. Lo and behold, you're going to be a mother."

"Damn," I mumbled.

He stood from his chair and began to pace. "Why haven't you told anyone? Why in the fuck would you come to Bike Week with Flash when you knew you were expecting, Izzy? That's just plain stupid."

My stomach turned as guilt overwhelmed me. "I don't know." I shrugged and rested my hand against my stomach. "I wanted one last fun weekend before I told everyone. I figured I'd go out with a bang. Does Flash know?"

God, I hoped he didn't hear me blabbering about the baby. It was bad enough I had to deal with Thomas; I didn't want to hear Flash barking in my ear on top of it.

"No, he's dealing with Rebel."

I chewed on my lip. "How?" I asked, wondering if I really wanted to know.

"Turns out Flash isn't who he says he is."

"He isn't?" I adjusted my pillow, trying to get more comfortable.

"No. We're not changing subjects, Izzy. Is Flash the father of that baby inside of you?"

"I think so," I replied.

"Have you been with anyone else?" he asked as his eyes narrowed into slits like he was weighing the honesty of my answer.

"One other person," I answered truthfully.

"Who?"

"It's not of your damn business, Thomas." I was defensive, and I had every right to be. James and Thomas were best friends.

Thomas's phone began to ring. I'd been saved.

"What's up?" he said as he glared at me.

I fumbled with the edge of the sheets, feeling like I was ready to throw up. I don't know if it was from the punch or the entire house of cards that was about to collapse before me.

"Got it. I'll be here." He set the phone on the bed when he ended the call.

"Everything okay?"

"Shit is over with the club. It's too risky for me to stay. The DEA has started an extraction plan and is about to raid the compound."

"I fucked up your entire operation, Thomas?"

"You ended it early, but we have enough to nail them all for a lifetime."

"Damn it," I mumbled and sniffled, feeling tears begin to tickle my nose.

"It would be too dangerous for me to go back now, Izzy."

"Can I leave yet?"

"The doctor needs to check you out. They were waiting for you to wake up fully before assessing you."

"Go get him, please. I just want to go home."

"Fine," he said as he left the room.

I'd managed to make a clusterfuck out of everything. Not only had I gotten knocked up, I'd ended Thomas's investigation earlier than he wanted. I hoped that someday he'd forgive me for it.

When he returned with the doctor, I answered his questions

in detail. I'd been given the green light to leave since there was no concussion. My face was just badly bruised and swollen but would heal over time.

"Everything will heal, Ms. Gallo. The baby seems to be fine also."

"Baby?" a deep voice asked from the doorway.

"I'll go finish your paperwork so you can leave, Ms. Gallo," the doctor said before leaving.

As my eyes drifted to the voice, the only thing I could think was…fuck. James stood there with folded arms and one eyebrow higher than the other.

"Come in, James," Thomas answered before I could tell him to get the fuck out. "I just found out I'm going to be an uncle."

I gritted my teeth but said nothing.

"How exciting. Hey, Izzy."

"Hey," I bit out. I didn't have anything else to say. I wanted to crawl under the covers and disappear. The last time I saw him, I'd snuck out of his hotel room without a goodbye or a thanks.

"When are you due?" James asked as he sauntered toward my bedside.

Just as I was about to open my mouth and lie, Thomas said, "August sometime."

James's face changed, and I could see him doing the calculations in his head. "November, huh?" he asked with pursed lips.

"Seems so," I answered with a smile.

"Who's the father?" he asked.

Thomas turned toward James and crossed his arms. "What's it matter to you?"

James glanced at me and I shook my head. I did not want

Thomas to know I'd slept with James. "I have to be honest with you, Thomas," James said.

"No!" I yelled, wanting to be anywhere but here.

Thomas held his hand up and shushed me. "Go on."

"It was a shitty thing to do, man, but when you sent me to your brother's wedding, I ended up sleeping with Izzy."

I hung my head, feeling heat creep up my neck and shame permeate my ever fiber. I didn't want that to come out, especially not this way.

"You slept with my sister?" Thomas asked as he cocked his head.

"Yeah. I'm sorry."

"My sister. The girl over there?" he asked as he pointed at me.

I swallowed hard as I tried to get rid of the lump that had formed in my throat. Not only had I ruined his investigation, I'd fucked his best friend and never mentioned it. Based on the conversation, I'd say James never mentioned it either.

"Yes."

Thomas took two giant steps forward to stand toe-to-toe with James. "I asked you to deliver a card because I trusted you, and this is how you repay me?"

James stared at Thomas but didn't back away. "I did as you asked, but I couldn't resist her, Thomas."

Thomas pushed James backward and threw a right hook. As it smashed into James's face, his head snapped back but he didn't wobble. "I deserved that," he said as he wiped the blood from his mouth.

"Stop!" I yelled, holding my forehead. The last thing I

wanted was for these two men to beat the shit out of each other in my hospital room.

"Is that my baby, Izzy?" James asked as he moved toward my bed and pointed at my stomach.

I shrugged 'cause fuck if I knew. "I don't think so, James. We had sex once."

"Once? You must not remember that night very well," he said with a slow, lazy grin on his face.

"James," Thomas warned and closed his eyes.

James didn't take his eyes off me. "Thomas, why don't you give your sister and me a few minutes to talk?"

My stomach fluttered as he spoke. He looked better than I'd remembered. I'd had so much to drink that night and much of it was a blur, but I couldn't forget James—at least not entirely. The details came in bits and pieces in the weeks following our night together.

"I'm giving you five minutes and that's it." Thomas stormed out of the room, stomping his feet as he left.

"Before you say anything..." I held up my hands, closed my eyes, and took a deep breath.

"Do you remember that night?" he asked as he sat down on the end of the bed.

"Somewhat. It's still a bit fuzzy," I said with one eye open.

"We fucked a lot. Not just a couple times, Izzy. The condom broke."

My heart began to race and my pulse quickened. It broke. The fucking rubber broke. "I don't remember that." I rubbed my forehead slowly, stretching the skin under my fingertips.

"The last thing you said to me was 'But I'm sure it'll be fine.'" He sighed, blowing out a breath.

"Damn it."

"I know you've been with Flash. Did you always use protection with him?"

"That's kind of personal, James."

"Izzy, I've licked every inch of your body. I don't think a question is too personal at this point. Now answer me. Did you always use protection with him?" He rested his hand on my leg, the warmth searing my skin.

"Always," I replied as I bit the inside of my mouth and thought back on my sexual "relationship" with Sam.

"That baby is mine, Izzy." His fingers wrapped around my shin, gripping my calf firmly with his fingers.

"Seems like it," I whispered as I dropped my head and closed my eyes.

God, what was worse? The fact that this was James's baby or that it could've been Sam's. He was at least a friend and I could deal with him. James was...James. He scared the crap out of me. He was too intense and bossy as hell. He reminded me too much of my brothers and their "do as I say" bullshit for my liking. I couldn't deny my attraction to him, and the sex, from what I could remember, was off the charts.

Like it or not, I was now tied to this man in some way for the rest of my life.

"James, I don't want you to feel obligated to be part of the baby's life." I wanted to give him an out because, in the end, it would be easier for both of us.

"Are you serious?" He grimaced and squeezed my calf.

331

"Yes. Just because we had sex one night doesn't mean you have to be a father. We can think of you more like a sperm donor."

"That's not happening."

"Seriously. You're so busy with work. We barely know each other. There's no reason this should change anything in your life."

"That," he snarled and pointed at my stomach, "is my baby growing inside you, and I'm not going anywhere."

"Great," I said sarcastically as I ran my fingers through my hair.

"We have time to figure everything out. My work with Thomas and the MC is over. I can ask for a transfer to Tampa to be closer to you and the baby."

"Hold up," I said, giving him the hand. "If you want to move to be closer to the baby, then fine, but don't do it to be with me."

He scooted forward, dragging his hand up my leg before it settled on my thigh. His touch made me feel light-headed and drunk with lust. That's all it took to bring back all the memories of that night. The pleasure and yearning I experienced were more than I'd ever felt in my life.

"Izzy," he whispered as he brought his face close to mine. "Why did you leave without saying goodbye?"

"I don't know," I lied, swallowing the lump in my throat.

"Don't lie. I never pegged you as the type of girl who didn't face shit head on."

"You don't know me, James," I reminded him as I licked my lips and felt my heart pounding inside my chest.

His eyes dropped to my mouth as his breath skidded across

my face. "I know enough about you. Thomas has talked about you for years. I read body language, Izzy. I know exactly what you felt for me that night. I know you want me still."

"How?"

He rested his hand on my neck as he inched his face closer. "I can feel your heartbeat. You want me," he whispered and brushed his lips against mine.

I sucked in a breath and blinked. "James," I replied, closing my eyes. "Just because I want you doesn't mean we should be together."

"It means we should date and see what happens."

"I don't know."

Before I could respond, he crushed his lips to mine, pulling me to him by my neck. My toes curled and my insides fluttered from the tiny sparks that erupted across my skin. The way his breath quickened as he kissed me sent a shiver down my spine. I couldn't deny that my body wanted him, but my head told me to run for the hills. James Caldo would be a heap of trouble in my life, and I didn't know how to deal with him.

"Just say you'll give us a chance," he asked as he backed away from my mouth.

With my eyes still closed from his kiss lingering on my lips, I replied, "Okay."

I don't know where the hell that came from. Maybe it was the way he made me feel, or the electricity from his kiss short-circuited my brain.

"I have to get back to work. As soon as I can come to Tampa, I will. I'll take you on a proper date and we'll see what happens."

"Okay." God, I sounded like a moron. I'd never been at a loss for words, but with James this close and my pregnancy hormones raging, I suddenly sounded like an idiot.

"We owe it to our baby."

Our baby. I liked the sound of that.

"Uh-huh," I mumbled as he stroked my cheek.

"Get some rest and take care of that little one," he said as he dropped his hand to my belly and rested it on top. "I'll be there for you soon." His eyes shifted from my stomach to my face. "And for you."

My mouth instantly turned drier than the Mojave Desert. I didn't respond to him. When he stood from the bed, he leaned over and kissed me on the forehead, lingering against my skin as he inhaled.

"I'll call you tomorrow to make sure you got home safe."

I nodded, still at a loss for words, as I watched him stride out of the room with his head held high.

I sighed, banging my head into my pillow. "Fuck," I muttered as I pushed out a breath and stared at the ceiling.

"Hey," Thomas said as he stood in the doorway. "What happened?"

I hid my face in my hands. "It looks like he's the father."

"I can't believe you did this. Jesus Christ, Izzy."

"What the hell did I do? I'm a grown woman. I had too much to drink and James was there. One thing led to another, Thomas. I'm not a child. It's not like I've ruined my life or anything. It's just a baby."

"Just a baby?" he seethed as grabbed the chair and pulled it next to my bed. "You still act like a fucking child sometimes. How are you supposed to be a mother?"

"Don't start your shit with me, brother. You haven't been around for a long time. I've grown up. Shit happens. I'm not the first person to get knocked up. I have a job, a home, and I can survive on my own. I'm sure I'll be fine raising a baby. Don't doubt that I'll give this baby more love than even I was given as a child." I rested my hands on my stomach, wishing I could feel it move inside of me.

"I didn't mean you won't be a good mother," he replied in a softened tone. "I didn't mean that. I'm just so pissed you slept with James. I'm angry at him for taking advantage of you." His nostrils flared when he spoke.

I snorted. "He didn't take advantage of me. Drunk or not, I wanted to sleep with him."

He threw his body back into the chair and ran his fingers through his hair. "There's nothing I can do about it now. It's happened and we need to deal with it."

"I need to deal with it," I corrected him as I scooted into a sitting position.

"We can help."

"I got this, and James said he wants to be part of the baby's life. Hey, it could be worse," I teased, cocking my head.

"Yeah. How's that?" He rolled his eyes. "How could it be worse than my best friend knocking up my sister?"

"It could be Sam's baby instead." I threw my head back and broke into laughter.

He held his face and shook his head. "You're going to make my head explode. Let's get you checked out and I'll take you home."

"But don't you have to work?" I asked, not really liking the idea of a three-hour car ride with my pissed off brother.

"I'll come back and do it. It's just paperwork."

"Thomas, let me tell Mom and Dad."

"Fine, but you're telling them this weekend."

I suddenly felt nauseous. "Fine," I snapped. "Bossy fucker."

"There's no reason to wait any longer."

I crossed my arms over my chest and pouted like a child. I hated being bossed around, and I feared this was only the beginning.

EPILOGUE

One month after I found out I was going to be a father, I moved to Tampa to be closer to Izzy and the baby. Getting Izzy to admit her feelings for me had been a challenge. It took the first month after I inserted myself into her life before she finally admitted she liked me. The girl was the most pigheaded human being I'd ever met.

She finally said I could go to her doctor's appointment for the six-month checkup. I wanted to hear the baby's heartbeat and experience seeing it for the first time. I'd seen a photo, but it wasn't the same thing. That day brought us together and changed our relationship forever.

Izzy's belly was larger, looking like a basketball when exposed. I took every chance I had to hold her stomach and talk with the baby. I knew the baby couldn't hear me, but it made me feel better about the situation. Izzy would run her fingers through my hair while I rambled on about how beautiful its mother was and how excited I was to meet him or her someday soon.

"Stop fidgeting," she chastised me as I stopped moving.

"I didn't realize I was," I replied as I leaned forward and rested my hands on the exam table.

The doctor looked at me and smiled as she squeezed the blue gel over Izzy's abdomen. "This is just a simple ultrasound, Mr. Caldo. There's nothing to worry about."

"I'm excited, Doctor. Not nervous at all." I stared at Izzy, feeling the familiar jitter in my chest from the way she made my heart beat just a little faster when she was around.

"Let's see if we can get you a good view today," she said as she started to glide the wand over Izzy's skin.

Izzy gave me a lopsided smile before we both looked at the screen. "Is that it?" I asked as a fuzzy shape came into view.

"Yes, let me get a better view," she replied as she pushed it down on Izzy's side. "Now that's interesting." She leaned toward the screen and stared at it.

"What?" Izzy asked.

I glanced at Izzy and her eyes were as wide as saucers.

"Nothing bad, let me just…" the doctor trailed off.

"You're killing us, Doc," I said through gritted teeth. My heart was hammering, about ready to burst from anxiety that something was wrong with our baby.

"Huh, that's funny," she said as she looked at us with a giant smile.

"Oh God, what?" Izzy muttered as she peered at the screen with her head raised.

"I didn't see it before now. There's definitely another baby in there. You're going to have twins."

"Fuck!" Izzy yelled, throwing her head back into the paper-covered pillow.

"Twins, as in two?" I asked as I started to break out in a sweat.

"That's what it means, Mr. Caldo."

"Jesus," I mumbled, wiping my forehead.

"I can't handle two. Oh my God. I just can't," Izzy whined as she closed her eyes.

"Izzy," I said as I rested my hand on her arm, stroking her skin with my thumb. "You won't be alone. We can do this." I gulped down the bile that had risen in my throat. I thought about double the diapers, two crying babies... Oh shit, two sixteen-year-olds wanting to drive. Double the trouble was about to enter our lives.

"Doc, can you tell us the sex?"

"Please say they're girls. Please," Izzy said, opening one eye and turning toward the screen.

The doctor pressed a few buttons on the screen. "Are you sure you want to know?" The wand moved across Izzy's belly feverishly as she stared at the screen.

"Yes!" Izzy cried out. "This is all too much. Twins. James, what are we doing to do?"

"Shhh, baby. We'll be fine."

"I can't tell the sex of the one fetus. It's hidden behind its brother."

"Brother?" Izzy croaked. "Another penis."

"A son. I'm having a son!" I exclaimed as a giant smile spread across my face.

"I can't give you anything on the second, but maybe by the next visit, they'll shift positions and make it easier."

"I can't breathe," Izzy complained as she rested her hand on her chest.

"You're fine," I said, patting her hand.

"I can't handle another man in my life." She threw her arm across her face and hid.

"Don't listen to her, Doc. She has four brothers and me to deal with every day. She just needs some time to digest it."

"God hates me."

"Stop being a baby. Think of how much he's going to love you. He's going to be a total mama's boy."

"Yeah?" she asked as she moved her arms enough to look at me.

"Totally. Boys are always closer with their mothers, and you're going to steal his heart. You'll be his first love. Maybe the other baby is a girl. We can split the difference, and I can have a daddy's girl."

"She's so going to hate you when she's a teenager." Izzy put her arm down and smiled.

"Why?"

"Girls don't like controlling fathers, and I know you're going to be a total pain in the ass."

"If she's anything like her mother, then I have to keep my eye on her and make sure that no guy even thinks about coming near her." The bile that had returned to my stomach started to creep back up. I couldn't think of my little baby dating. I wanted to get through the birth and a good fifteen years before I even thought about such things.

"Total pain in the ass." Izzy laughed.

That was it. We were going to be parents to twins. Not only would we have to figure out who we were as a couple with one baby, we'd have to do it with two.

Izzy didn't have a choice but to let me in.

No longer could she deny that she wanted to be with me. No matter how much lip she gave me, I knew where her heart lay. She loved me as much as I loved and wanted her. I didn't want to be an absentee father who was there for his weekly visitation. I'd be a permanent fixture in their lives along with Izzy's. She was mine and would forever be the mother of my children.

INKED FANTASIES

1

CITY

"Sugar, stop talking." I settled between her legs, staring up her beautiful, soft body.

Suzy curled her fingers into my hair as I leaned forward. "I wonder what..." she started to say, but she grew quiet as I ran my tongue across her clit.

She didn't listen, but she never does. The girl was quiet as a church mouse when I met her, but somehow, I turned her into a chatterbox. Even in bed, she wants to yammer on about the kids and shit.

The only thing I cared about was the sweetness and slice of heaven between my wife's legs. I could give two fucks right now if the kids are sleeping, how they feel, or what was on their schedule for tomorrow.

It was our first night without the kids in weeks. The twins had a sleepover birthday party, and Gigi was on a school trip that probably involved zero learning. Freedom. I loved my kids, but damn, I missed my wife and the days we used to have without interruptions and clothing.

"Maybe we can…"

I propped myself on my elbows and glared at her. "Let's try something new."

I can't do this all night, babbling on about the kids when we may not have another weekend alone for God knows how long. So, it was time to pivot and do it big because I didn't want to spend the entire weekend with her thinking only of the kids.

"Okay," she whispered with her eyebrows drawn together.

I slid off the bed and grabbed my jeans off the floor. I was about to stage an intervention with my wife, and it had to be sexy as fuck to keep her in the right headspace. "Get dressed." I hadn't thought this out because my cock wasn't too cooperative as I tried to jam it back into my pants. "Put on the sexiest dress you have in that closet. We're going out."

"What?" She didn't move, just gawked at me like I was speaking a foreign language.

"You have thirty minutes," I told her as I stalked out of the room, leaving her naked and spread-eagled.

I heard her feet land on the floor before she scurried across the carpeting to her closet.

"Whore it up," I yelled from the stairway as I headed downstairs to set my plan into motion.

Suzy had shared her fantasies with me. Many of them we'd lived out, but lately, motherhood had become her main focus. It was time to center her again and remind her of who we are…what we used to be.

Within minutes, I had reservations at a hotel downtown with

a swanky bar in the lobby for tonight's fantasy. I changed quickly in the downstairs spare bathroom and had plenty of time to spare before Suzy started to walk down the grand staircase with her tits spilling out of the top of a very tight and small black dress. To top it off, she had on sky-high red heels that screamed sex and, again, made my dick hard.

It didn't matter that we'd been married for fifteen years; the woman did wicked shit to me. There wasn't a day that went by that I didn't want to stake my claim and leave my mark on her. She could still steal my breath with a single glance and captivate me with her smile. Her innocence hadn't been lost, even being married to an asshole like me. Suzy was and always would be Suzy. Sweet, innocent, and loving to a fault, but she was mine forever.

She'd swept her hair to the side in a partial updo reminiscent of Julia Roberts in *Pretty Woman*, a movie Suzy'd made me watch more times than I could count. She loved a good fairy tale and bragged to everyone she met that she was living one after I found her on the side of the road and rescued her.

"You look..." I swallowed, unsure of the words I wanted to use next. There were so many that fit her as she descended the stairs with a gentle sway to her hips, somehow walking gracefully in the heels. "Fuckable."

It wasn't the classiest word, but it was the first thing that came to mind. Leaving the house wasn't going to be easy. I wanted to grab her hand and march her right back upstairs and rip the dress from her skin, but I needed to stay on course.

Don't be an asshole.

She blushed and tossed her hair over her shoulder before

coming to stand in front of me. "Thank you very much." She placed her hands on my chest and pushed her marvelous tits against me. "So do you."

"Ready to go?" I asked, and my voice cracked on the last word. My resistance was on the edge of breaking, and she knew it.

The corner of her lips turned up as she grazed my cock with her stomach. "Are you sure you want to go out?" Her smirk grew more sinister.

I didn't answer in words. Hooking my arm around her waist, I hoisted her over my shoulder and carried her out the door.

2

CITY

"You want me to what?"

"Just do it, and don't give me lip." I pointed toward the bar behind her before I turned her around and gave her ass a little pat, pushing her toward the entrance.

She glared at me over her shoulder. Her theatrics were strong tonight, but I knew she was secretly loving every minute of this. I knew my wife better than anyone, and I could almost bet my entire fortune on the fact that her panties were already wet.

I watched from the lobby as she slid onto a stool and placed an order. I told her absolutely no virgin anything. Tonight was a night to let go, and that included alcohol. She wasn't Suzy Gallo. Nope. She'd decided her name was Vivian Ward, and I was Edward Lewis, giving props to *Pretty Woman* after I told her about my plan as I drove way too fast to get to our final destination.

A few men in the bar were staring at her, but I resisted the urge to run inside and turn their heads the other direction. My wife was beautiful and deserved the stares. A woman wanted to feel beautiful, and getting the attention of men, even if they're not me, had to be flattering.

I'd grown as a person. Years together will do that. Old me, the one who met her on the side of the road, would've already had at least two men on the floor, begging for mercy, but I'm not him... or at least that was the lie I told myself.

Unable to take another moment of their not-so-casual eye-fucking of my girl, I stalked inside and slid onto the empty stool at her side. I didn't speak to her and barely glanced in her direction. She stirred her drink, a daiquiri of some sort, but remained silent.

I ordered a drink, whiskey neat, and let the tension build. I could practically feel her excitement as we sat in silence. It was probably killing her inside not to say something to me. I told her under no circumstance was she to speak to me until I broke the ice first.

Once the bartender set the drink down in front of me and left us in peace, I lifted my glass and turned to my side. I stared at her profile over the rim as I let the first taste of whiskey slide down my throat.

Her skin glistened in the overhead lighting, and her eyes danced around nervously as I stared at her. She twirled the little straw against her lips. Man, this was harder than I thought. Sitting here, not talking as I tried to take it slow was pure torture.

I remembered the night we met. I'd wanted to fuck her so badly. She sat next to me at the Neon Cowboy, looking and talking innocent. I thought it was an act, a cute one, but still an

act. Little did I know, Li'l Suzy Sunshine was even more innocent than she let on.

"Can I get you another?" I asked, motioning toward her glass
with mine as I set it on the bar top.

Not my smoothest line ever. I hadn't picked up a woman in a
bar for so many years I almost forgot how it was done. I had
always been suave and had never had a problem, but tonight I
felt rusty.

"I'm fine." She didn't look in my direction, but she placed
her glass next to mine. "I'm not much of a drinker."

"I'm Edward, and you are..." I let my voice trail off and
waited for her to say the name I knew was coming next.

"Vivian," she said and turned toward me, holding out her
hand. "Vivian Ward."

She said the name with a slight twang, playing every bit of
the part.

"Vivian, it's my pleasure." I lifted her hand to my lips and
kissed it gently, maintaining eye contact the entire time.

She blushed and tipped her head back. "What do you do,
Edward?"

Fuck. I scrambled, running through the movie in my head
and trying to recall exactly what he did with the little fuckhead
that eventually attacked Julia. Something with companies. Jesus.
Only my wife would put me on the spot. "I take over
companies."

Her eyes brightened, and I knew I was close enough to
satisfy her with my answer. "That sounds exciting."

"Not really," I grumbled because I'd slit my wrists if I had to
sit in an office every day wearing a suit with a tie wrapped

around my neck like a noose. "But it can be at times. Are you sure you wouldn't like another drink?"

I wanted her a little buzzed and relaxed because I knew she was way out of her comfort zone.

"Sure." She smiled and pushed her almost empty glass forward. "But my company requires more than a drink, Edward."

I almost swallowed my tongue. She wasn't just using the name; she planned to play the entire part. Whorey Vivian was all right by me. "How much?" I turned my head and cocked an eyebrow.

"I'm not cheap." She smirked and placed her hand on my knee before giving it a tight squeeze. "But I'm worth every penny."

"Money is no object, Vivian."

"A thousand an hour."

"You must be good."

"Oh, honey." She leaned forward, her breasts almost toppling out of her dress. "You have no idea."

But I did. My woman was the best. I'd been with a lot of girls before her, sowing my wild oats and shit, but none of them compared to my l'l wildcat in the sack. No one had ever brought me to my knees and had me on the verge of begging like my wife.

I placed my hand on her leg, letting my fingers slide up her inner thigh. "How much for all night?" I felt good about this. I'd played along and came as close as I could to the movie dialogue without actually remembering a single spoken line.

"Ten thousand." She opened her legs and granted me more access, giving me a taste of what was to come.

"Sold. Baby, I would've paid a million to lie with you tonight," I tell her.

"I'm going to bring you so much pleasure, you won't want to get rid of me."

The words kind of made my stomach hurt. I couldn't imagine a day without Suzy in my life. Nothing and no one would ever make me want to get rid of her. I never understood the assholes who stepped out on their wives and fucked everything up.

"Shall we?" I motioned toward the lobby with my head as I continued to stroke her thigh.

"But what about my drink?"

"For ten thousand dollars, I'll have it delivered to the room because I'm not wasting another moment with you."

I already had the room set with strawberries and champagne waiting for us, along with an entire assortment of things that would be messy and divine to eat off each other. I had everything covered and had somehow been able to do it on short notice. It was amazing what a guy could accomplish when pussy was involved.

"I have limits, Edward," she said as she slid off the stool and her red heels touched the marble tile floor. "I don't do..."

"For ten thousand dollars, there are no restrictions."

"I don't do threesomes."

"Agreed. Everything else is on the table."

"Everything?"

"Everything."

I threw a fifty on the bar and ushered Vivian toward the bank of elevators. We walked in silence with her arm hooked in mine and bowed our head to passersby. If they only knew the dirty shit

I was about to do to this woman, they'd… Hell, they'd be jealous as fuck because let's face it, their sex lives were probably more boring than watching paint dry.

She stayed at my side as we walked out of the elevator and made our way down the hallway. When I grabbed the key from my pocket, she leaned against the wall and stared at me. "Why me?" she asked, tipping her head to the side. "You can have any girl. Why me?"

I took a step to the side and placed my hands on the wall, caging her in. "Because you're the most beautiful girl in the world. I acquire pretty things, and tonight you're my sole possession."

She blinked and was at a loss for words. I leaned forward, sweeping my lips across hers. She gasped, no doubt feeling the same electric spark I felt just like the first night we met so long ago.

"Last chance to change your mind."

"Never," she breathed against my mouth. "I want you."

"I own you tonight," I told her. "I've never wanted anything more than I want you right now."

"I'm yours." She smirked, jutting those tits closer to my face.

3

CITY

I backed away and pushed the door open, waiting for her to step inside before I followed her inside the suite. She squealed quietly when she saw the champagne and food. It was typical Suzy, but also a little Vivian too, and I couldn't hide my happiness.

I sat down and stared at my wife, watching her fidget and not knowing what to do next. "I want to see your natural beauty. Strip for me." She started to pull down the strap of her dress, but I stopped her. "In front of me," I told her and pointed at the floor near my feet.

Leaning back, I didn't take my eyes off her as she pulled down the straps of her dress. Slowly she removed the dress, swaying slightly, trying to be sexy with her stripper moves. They were pretty damn impressive for Suzy.

When her dress hit the ground, I crooked my finger, needing to touch her. She gave me an innocent smile as she stepped away from her dress wearing nothing but delicate black lace panties and a matching bra.

"Closer."

She shuffled her feet across the carpeting, moving with more grace than usual. "You like this?" she asked, running her hand across her stomach. "You want a piece of this, big boy?"

I couldn't stop the corner of my mouth from twitching. Even though Suzy had lost much of her innocence, her attempt at being a sexy, high-class prostitute didn't fit, but I wasn't going to tell her that. I loved the frisky side of my wife. She was stepping outside of the box and her comfort level, which wasn't easy for her even if it was her fantasy.

I reached forward, tucking my fingers inside the waistband of her skimpy underwear and pulled her toward me. She crashed against me, and her breasts practically fell into my face as she stumbled forward. In one quick movement, the lace dissolved in my fingers and fell away from her body.

"I want all of you," I growled softly in her ear.

She shivered and let out a small, deep moan. "Whatever pleases you."

I grabbed her around the waist and easily lifted her into the air. Her lips smashed down on mine as I carried her toward the bed, and she slid her tongue against mine. I dug my fingertips into her skin, wanting more than I could get in this position and swallowing her needy groans as our tongues worked together feverishly.

Leaning forward, I placed her gently on the bed and tried to pull my lips away from hers. Her arms slid across my shoulders, locking behind my head and holding me to her.

"Baby, I wanna taste you," I murmured against her lips.

"I need your mouth," she replied, tightening her hold.

"My mouth needs your sweet, greedy pussy."

With those words, she released her grip and spread her legs, relaxing into the mattress. Starting at the swell of her breasts, I kissed a path down to her stomach and paused just long enough to savor her scent and softness before I settled between her legs to feast.

"Dad."

Damn kids. Even when they were away, they found a way to creep back into my mind.

"Dad!" The voice grew louder.

I squeezed my eyes tighter, trying to clear my head of the little monsters.

"Dad!"

A slap to my face by tiny little hands woke me in a hurry. I blinked, confused for a moment. I was just at a hotel with Suzy, or Vivian, and now I was in my bedroom with Gigi standing above me, her hands on her hips just like her aunt Izzy.

"Are you drunk or something?" she asked and rolled her eyes.

"What time is it?" I pulled the covers over my head and groaned, trying to adjust the wood I knew I was sporting.

"It's seven."

"Gigi, it's so early. Come on, kid."

She peeled the covers away from my face and scowled. "I have to be at the school for my class trip in ten minutes and mom's still making breakfast."

My ass flew out of the bed like the police were coming. I had dreamed the entire thing. Gigi hadn't even left for her trip yet, but I knew exactly where I was taking Suzy tonight.

"I'll meet you in the car in three."

She turned on her heel and marched toward the bedroom door. "Okay, old man. If you can move that fast."

I took a deep breath, trying not to shoot off my mouth at the kid. She was exactly like Izzy. It would be a miracle if I didn't age prematurely or end up in prison within the next few years. The boys were already calling, and one of them was bound to do something, like try to kiss her, and I'd be taking a ride in the back of a police cruiser.

I saw it as vividly as the dream. Gigi Gallo wasn't going to make my life easy, and someone was going to have hell to pay.

Made in the USA
Middletown, DE
22 June 2023